THE BIG ONE

ALAN PARKIN

FIRELIGHT PRESS LLC

Contents

THE BIG ONE

How to Prepare Before an Earthquake

Earthquakes can strike suddenly and without warning, causing significant damage and disruption to daily life. It is crucial to be prepared for such an event to ensure the safety and wellbeing of yourself and your loved ones. This book outlines the essential steps you can take to prepare for an earthquake:

1. Create an Emergency Plan:

- Develop a comprehensive plan that includes evacuation routes, designated meeting places, and communication strategies for your household.

- Practice the plan regularly with all family members, including children and pets.

- Identify safe spots within your home, such as under sturdy furniture or away from windows and heavy objects.

2. Prepare an Emergency Kit:

- Assemble a kit with essential supplies, including water, non-perishable food, first aid supplies, a flashlight, a battery-powered radio, and necessary medications.

- Store the kit in an easily accessible location.

- Consider additional items such as a whistle, dust masks, and sanitation supplies.

3. Secure Your Home:

- Anchor heavy furniture and appliances to the walls or floor to prevent them from toppling over.

- Secure items on shelves and cabinets to prevent them from falling.

- Install latches on cabinets and drawers to keep contents from spilling.

- Consider reinforcing your home's structure if necessary.

4. Stay Informed:

- Learn about the earthquake risks in your area.

- Sign up for earthquake alerts and warnings.

- Stay updated on the latest safety recommendations and guidelines.

5. During an Earthquake:

- If indoors, drop to the ground, take cover under sturdy furniture, and hold on until the shaking stops.

- If outdoors, move to a clear area away from buildings, trees, and power lines.

- If driving, pull over to a safe location and stay inside your vehicle.

6. After an Earthquake:
- Check for injuries and provide first aid if necessary.

- Be aware of aftershocks and potential hazards, such as damaged buildings and downed power lines.

- Follow the guidance of local authorities and emergency responders.

Being prepared can significantly improve your ability to cope with and recover from an earthquake. Take the time to develop a plan, assemble a kit, and secure your home to ensure your safety and peace of mind.

"We imagine 'the end' as a world-devastating event, but every time there's a terrible earthquake, a tsunami, an outbreak of disease - that's apocalyptic, on a micro-scale."

Marjorie Liu

"Whether it is a tsunami, or whether it is a hurricane, whether it's an earthquake - when we see these great fatal and natural acts, men and women of every ethnic persuasion come together and they just want to help."

Martin Luther King

"Why did the earthquake and tsunami occur in Japan? Was it the act of an angry God? No, it was the result of the movement and collision of the earth's tectonic plates - a process driven by the earth's need to regulate its own internal temperature. Without the process that creates earthquake, our planet could not sustain life."

Adam Hamilton

"It has been said, by engineers themselves, that given enough money, they can accomplish virtually anything: send men to the moon, dig a tunnel under the English Channel. There's no reason they couldn't likewise devise ways to protect infrastructure from the worst hurricanes, earthquakes and other calamities, natural and manmade."

Henry Petroski

"Although earthquakes cannot be prevented, current science and engineering provide tools that can be used to reduce their damage. Science can now identify, with considerable accuracy, where earthquakes are likely to occur and what forces they will generate. Engineering provides design and construction techniques so that buildings and other structures can survive the tremendous forces of earthquakes."

The **Cascadia subduction zone** is a 960 km (600 mi) fault at, about 110–160 km (70–100 mi) off the Pacific coast, and it stretches from northern California to Vancouver Island, British Columbia. It can produce 9.0+ magnitude earthquakes reaching 30 m (98 ft). The Oregon Department of Emergency Management estimates that shaking would last 5 to 7 minutes along the coast, with strength and intensity decreasing further from the epicenter. It is a long, sloping where the plates move to the east and slide below the much larger, mostly continental. The zone varies in width and lies offshore.

A 1996 study published by seismologists supplemented the research by Atwater et al. with tsunami evidence across the Pacific. Japanese annals, which have recorded natural disasters since approximately 600 CE, had reports of a sixteen-foot tsunami that struck the coast. Since no earthquake had been observed to produce it, scholars dubbed it an "orphan wave."

Translating the Satake, the incident occurred in 1700, around midnight on January 27–28, ten hours after the earthquake. The original magnitude 9.0 earthquake in the Pacific Northwest had thus occurred around 9 pm Pacific Standard Time on 26 January 1700. Before the 1980s, scientists thought that the subduction zone did not generate earthquakes like other subduction zones around the world, research tied together evidence of a large tsunami on the Washington coast with documentation of an orphan tsunami in Japan (a tsunami without an associated earthquake). The two pieces of the puzzle were linked, and they then realized that the subduction zone was more hazardous than they previously thought.

In 2009, some geologists predicted a 10% to 14% probability that the Cascadia Subduction Zone will produce an event of magnitude 9.0 or higher in the next 50 years. In 2010, studies suggested that the risk could be as high as 37% for earthquakes of magnitude 8.0 or higher.

Geologists and civil engineers have broadly determined that the Pacific Northwest region isn't prepared for such a colossal earthquake because they expect the rupture to be as long as the earthquake. The resulting tsunami might reach heights of approximately 30 meters (100 ft). It may leave some 13,000 fatalities, with another 27,000 injured, which would make it the deadliest natural disaster in American and North American history. FEMA predicts that a million people will become displaced, with another 2.5 million needing food and water. About 1/3 of public safety workers will not respond to the disaster because of a collapse in infrastructure and a desire to ensure the safety of themselves and their loved ones. Other analyses predict that even a magnitude 6.7 earthquake in Seattle would cause 7,700 dead and injured, $33 billion in damage, 39,000 buildings severely damaged or destroyed, and 130 simultaneous fires.

Prologue

September 7th, 2027

At the sound of her alarm at 8:20, Sarah's eyes opened. A sleepy grin slowly spread across her face. This was no ordinary Tuesday. It was her final year at the prestigious University of Washington. After endless research nights fueled by energy drinks, she was finally on the brink of achieving her dream—a Master's degree in communication.

Stretching, she prepared for the day ahead as excitement bubbled within her. This was her time to shine!

Sarah had always been an avid explorer, her insatiable curiosity leading her to find hidden truths and unravel complex puzzles. As she pushed back the warm cocoon of her duvet and sank her toes into the plush carpet, she reflected on the journey that brought her to that moment. Each decision and experience shaped who she was and as she stepped forward with gratitude, she knew she was exactly where she needed to be.

Freshly brewed coffee filled Sarah's nostrils, coaxing her further into wakefulness. She walked to the bathroom, relishing the feeling of cool ceramic tiles against her bare feet.

She set her phone on the windowsill that bore traces of overnight dew. She reached for the shower knob. A frisson of anticipation tingled under her skin as she waited for droplets to reach a perfect balance between scorching heat and an icy chill.

As she shed her nightclothes one by one, thoughts whirled around like a carousel inside her head. The impending graduation was more than just an academic achievement. It was a gateway to dreams that had laid dormant and were now becoming tangible realities. Journalism was no longer just an idea but an attainable career path; she could contribute financially to their shared life.

Sarah's thoughts wandered toward Ethan, as her phone trembled. It lay on the windowsill, his name pulsing brightly on the screen. She answered, setting him on speakerphone as she gathered her shower essentials.

"Hey there, handsome," she greeted. "What's new in the world of Ethan?"

His voice was clear and gentle, a soothing balm against her nerves.

"I won't keep you long. I just wanted to know how my favorite journalist is?"

Sarah laughed. "I'm buzzing! I feel like I've been waiting forever for this."

Ethan chuckled at her enthusiasm. "Can I score your first interview then?" he asked.

"Of course! You always get the exclusive scoop," she teased. "And what about you? How's your day shaping up?"

"Just another day in paradise," he responded dryly. The familiar sounds of city life echoed behind him - street traffic and people chattering – and it painted a vivid picture of him amidst the concrete jungle. An idea sparked in Ethan's mind. "How about we escape to the beach today? We could use some sun and sand after your class."

A gentle breeze wafted through the open window, causing the curtains to sway and it cast playful shadows on the tiled bathroom floor. Sarah closed her eyes and envisioned herself on a tropical beach with warm sand beneath her feet and the soothing sound of waves crashing against the shore.

"I know just the spot," she said, picturing a secluded cove. "Our little piece of heaven..."

Ethan chuckled. "Sounds like a plan. Can't wait to see you later, babe."

"Me too," she replied before hanging up and setting her phone back on its perch.

Stepping into the steamy shower, Sarah let the hot water wash over her body like liquid silk. She let her mind wander as she relaxed under the cascading stream. Today was going to be a good day, she thought with a smile. Scratch that - it was going to be an amazing day.

Sarah twisted the shower knob and was met with a sudden jolt that shook the ground beneath her feet. The bathroom tiles rattled and groaned under the force, sending shivers down her spine. She tried to dismiss it as an old plumbing quirk, but then the intensity increased, as if the earth was writhing in agony.

The wail of car alarms echoed through the air like a symphony of terror, drowning out all the other sounds and amplifying the sense of impending doom. Her instincts screamed "earthquake," and she grasped onto the sink for dear life as the world around her continued to convulse with violent energy. But even as she braced herself, a terrifying thought crept into her mind: how bad could this earthquake really be?

"Get out. Now," she thought, her mind racing with panic. The ground beneath her feet trembled as if about to crumble at any moment. Without hesitation, she grabbed her towel and flung open the window, ignoring the shards of glass that dug into her skin. With fierce determination, she hoisted herself onto the windowsill and leaped toward the unknown ground below. As she fell, she glimpsed her pale towel still clinging to the ledge above, but there was no time to retrieve it or her phone. Her home was crumbling behind her, threatening to swallow her whole.

As she sprinted down the sidewalk, each footfall jolting through her body, the smell of gas filled her nostrils. "This can't be happening," she said in disbelief, her fingers digging into her arm as she tried to wake herself from the nightmare that unfolding before her eyes. "Please," she said. "Please, Ethan, be safe!"

"Sarah, watch out!" a neighbor shrieked, wrenching her from her thoughts as a power pole careened down onto the street, sending lethal sparks dancing.

Trees groaned and toppled around them, their limbs crashing down in a symphony of destruction. Screams tore through the air as another house collapsed, reduced to a pile of rubble and heartache.

"God, Ethan," she murmured. "Please be safe."

The quake continued its assault, and Sarah knew she had to act. With steely resolve, she took one step, and then another, into the unknown.

"This can't be happening. This can't be happening." As she ran down the street unclothed, she knew it was undeniably real and far more devastating than anything she'd ever imagined.

Minute after minute, the quake raged on, thrashing the world around her with a fury that seemed to defy all reason. Sarah's thoughts remained focused on one goal: reaching the shopping center just a block away. The vast parking lot would provide some measure of safety, she told herself, at least for the time being.

Sarah's feet scrambled on the uneven asphalt as she ran across the busy street. Cars swerved past her, desperate to escape the eerie scene. Suddenly, a car disappeared into a sinkhole, mere feet away. The unforgiving earth swallowed it whole.

"Oh God, save us," she murmured, her pulse drumming against her ribcage as she stared with terror at the colossal fissures ripping the road. They were too wide for any vehicle to cross and too treacherous for any human to venture near.

"DIVE!" The shout reverberated as Sarah approached the parking lot that was now teeming with scores of bewildered souls.

The explosion reverberated in her eardrums and it caused her to whirl around. She saw the neighborhood's beloved grocery store erupt into an infernal pyre, belching out shards of its former self, transforming into a sky-high spectacle. Adrenaline pumped through her, propelling her toward the ground. She curled up to shield her head with arms that trembled with shock as lethal fragments of glass rained down around her.

"Is everyone okay?" Sarah's voice was barely audible over the chaos. Her gaze swept over the grim sight before her—people pinned under twisted metal and rubble, their bodies frozen in unnatural poses that spoke volumes about the violence they had endured. Smoke spiraled upwards from the wreckage, casting an eerie luminescence over what was once familiar but now resembled an apocalyptic wasteland.

The woman's voice trembled, her sobs etching rivulets through the sooty mask on her face. "What on earth? Why won't it stop shaking?" She latched onto any nearby soul, craving solace amid pandemonium. But all she could discern was the cruel dance of devastation enveloping them. "We will not escape this nightmare, will we?"

"Deep breaths," Sarah urged. They were all caught in this maelstrom of ruin together, clutching at straws of hope.

Surveying the destruction, Sarah felt despair wash over her. The remnants of lives were scattered like shards of glass, and the once-familiar landscape was unrecognizable. She prayed Ethan was safe, but the distant sirens and cries only amplified her fears. She tried to calm herself by thinking of his athleticism and strength, but the darkness that now enveloped the city seemed all consuming.

"Keep him safe," she pleaded, her voice strained with desperation as she clutched her own body for comfort. The future that once gleamed with hope and dreams now lay obscured by a thick fog of dread and unpredictability.

After seven minutes the earth finally relented, leaving an eerie stillness.

A woman with a kind face approached Sarah, offering a thin blanket to shield her from prying eyes. She wrapped herself in it. Amidst the tense atmosphere, an officer's voice boomed through the crowd, sending shivers down Sarah's spine.

"Remain calm," he said.

"What good will that do?" a man in the crowd cried out.

Sarah battled back tears while processing his words; knowing that fractures could be the least severe injuries Ethan might have sustained. Shrieks echoed from the fragmented remnants of what used to be a store—now reduced to smoky ruins resembling an eerie graveyard.

Sarah squared her shoulders and marched through the ruins of Seattle, her eyes fixed on the crumbling skyline ahead. She navigated skillfully through the debris. The air was thick with smoke and the acrid stench of burning buildings, but Sarah pressed on, ignoring the searing pain shooting up her injured leg.

"He has to be okay," she repeated like a mantra. "He works in a modern building designed to withstand earthquakes."

"With each step forward, Sarah's resolve hardened into unbreakable steel. This was no longer just a journey; it was a battle against fate itself. She could feel an unshakable belief coursing through her veins, driving her forward with fierce determination. Nothing could stop her from reaching Ethan. Their love was stronger than any disaster."

With a yawn, Sarah's eyes were open to the gentle morning light. She rubbed the sleep from her eyes and tried to shake off the lingering memories of her dreams. Today marked a new start. After months of careful planning, she was returning to Seattle, three years after surviving the most devastating natural disaster she had ever experienced.

Sarah felt a flutter of anticipation in her stomach as she envisioned the city that had once lain in ruins. The memories were vivid, yet they no longer held the same terror. Instead, they were transformed into a testament of resilience and survival. The seismic tremors that once shattered buildings now shook her resolve to understand and heal from the past. The choking smoke had cleared away, replaced by an air of resolution and fortitude. And those screams? They echoed with bravery as people chose life amidst chaos.

She had once promised herself never to tread back on those grounds—the pain seemed unbearable then. But now, an irresistible pull tugged at her heartstrings, a quest for closure, for understanding. If she could just witness the city's rebirth and hear stories from fellow survivors, perhaps it would help her make sense of everything.

While Sarah was lost in thought, a bright and cheerful ringtone suddenly lit up her phone. It was Tim, her partner in crime for her journey back home. Aspiring filmmaker and self-proclaimed documentary expert, he was determined to capture every single moment of their road trip.

"It's go time! We have twenty minutes to hit the road," Tim declared through the speaker.

Sarah couldn't help but laugh at his infectious enthusiasm. "Copy that, Captain. I'll be ready in five."

She tapped the red icon on her cell phone screen, ending the call. Her gaze lingered on a framed photo that sat on her desk—a jubilant duo perched atop the Space Needle, captured in their joyous ignorance just days before calamity ensued. A smile tinged with melancholy played on her lips as she traced their grinning faces.

"I'm coming home," she murmured to herself, a spark of resolve igniting within her.

She drew in a deep, steadying breath and allowed her eyes to sweep over their assembled supplies one last time. Rows of water bottles, stacks of canned food, an emergency first aid kit, even water filters. She had meticulously gathered enough provisions to sustain them for an entire month. For lighter moments, she had tucked in a pack of playing cards.

The distant hum of an engine gradually morphed into a pronounced roar until a white van came to a halt right outside her house. Tim hopped out with the vivacity of a child unwrapping presents on Christmas morning, and his face glowed with unrestrained enthusiasm.

"Ready for our monumental journey?" he queried, enthusiastically swinging open the van doors to disclose an array of cameras and tech equipment worthy of any Hollywood film set.

Sarah arched an eyebrow and let out an amused chuckle at his extravagant arrangements. "Are we going as ourselves, or should I be expecting a full-blown movie production?"

Tim flashed his signature grin. That was radiant enough for any toothpaste commercial. "I don't want us to miss capturing even one moment of this adventure!"

They did a last sweep, packing and double-checking their bags before locking up the house. Tim hopped into the driver's seat with an air of excitement while Sarah gave her cozy little home one last glance. It had been her sanctuary for the last three years, her own private retreat.

With a quiet sigh, she locked the door behind her and jumped into the van.

A quick nod to Tim, and they were off, hitting the open road with miles ahead of them. She didn't know what awaited them at her old home's ruins, but she was ready.

Sarah settled into her seat as Tim navigated their large van through the quiet suburban streets toward an unfamiliar destination: Leavenworth, Washington.

"I've never heard of this place," he admitted. Tim relied on Google Maps for directions, claiming his sense of direction was "worse than a blindfolded mole." "Looks like we have 30 hours of driving ahead of us," he commented, glancing at the GPS. "Hope you have some good Spotify playlists ready."

A smile flickered across Sarah's face before anxiety gnawed at her stomach again as rolling plains zipped past them—a sight so alien compared to her rugged hometown nestled among mountains.

Catching sight of Sarah's furrowed brow reflected in his side mirror, Tim asked, "You okay?"

Sarah nodded and took a deep breath that felt like inhaling tranquility. "It's just weird leaving behind everything so familiar," she confessed. "But it's time."

"I can only imagine how tough this is for you," Tim offered. "Heading back to your home..."

"It was a nightmare," she admitted. "But it was also where I had some of the best times of my life and met people who became family." She looked at him. "That's why I need to go back—to honor them."

As the morning sun blazed, Tim extended his arm. His fingers found hers, intertwining in a quiet gesture of solidarity that needed no words.

Sarah's hand trembled as she reached for the radio dial, her eyes stinging from unshed tears. She scrolled through the stations, searching for a distraction from the painful memories that flooded her mind. But then, a familiar melody filled the car—the haunting tune that had become synonymous with 'The Big One.' Sarah's throat tightened as she listened to the lyrics, each word like a punch to the gut.

Her mind drifted back to those dark days, huddled in makeshift shelters with only scraps of memories to cling onto. She thought of the faces of friends, neighbors, and loved ones, who were now just shadows from her past. Tim noticed Sarah's quiet tears and reached out to lower the volume.

"I'm sorry," he said. "I didn't realize..."

Sarah wiped away her tears with shaking hands. "It's fine. I just didn't expect that song to affect me so much."

"It's like reliving an old Snapchat story that still hurts, isn't it?" Tim murmured, sympathy etched on his face.

Sarah nodded, unable to find words to express the pain and loss that still lingered within her.

Tim suggested switching stations, but Sarah shook her head.

"No," she decided after a moment. "Let it play." She closed her eyes and let the moving lyrics wash over her. "It keeps their spirit alive, the ones we lost," she explained. "They deserve this tribute."

The morning light streamed through the car windows as they drove, and Sarah allowed herself to feel the weight of her past ordeal. The song playing on the radio was a mix of bitter and sweet memories, but it also offered a glimmer of hope for their future. Their journey was far from finished, but having Tim by her side—a loyal and understanding friend—made it all seem a little less overwhelming. And for that, Sarah was deeply thankful.

CHAPTER 2

U nder the starless shroud, Sarah and Tim stood at the precipice of the notorious Washington zone. Silence clung to the night. An almost palpable dread permeated, mirroring Tim's mounting terror.

The oppressive darkness weighed heavily upon them, pierced only by the feeble glow of their van's headlights. As they approached the boundary of the Washington zone, a chilling sight unfurled before them. Monstrous cyclone fences loomed ahead, standing at least twenty feet high with barbed wire crowning its peak like some twisted crown. Signs screamed warnings of electrification and impending death for unauthorized intruders.

Tim swallowed hard, a knot of dread forming in his throat as he took in the sight of the gun-toting sentinel guarding this nightmarish portal. He'd heard stories about these fortified borders stretching from Cali to Canada, but seeing it up close was like stepping into a dystopian novel.

Their van jerked to a stop as a figure, straight out of an action movie with an AR-15 slung casually over his shoulder, stalked toward them.

His eyes were like flint - hard and unyielding; his voice was an arctic blast as he barked, "What's your purpose?"

Sarah handed over their press passes. She had to keep her cool. Their documentary was crucial. They needed to broadcast the survival tales from the quake and its aftermath. Fear was not an option.

"Keys," the guard demanded, his palm open and waiting.

With reluctance, Tim surrendered them. The guard attached a wheel lock to their van. Tim's hands clutched the steering wheel tighter.

The guard retreated to an office structure, leaving them in silence. Each minute felt like an hour as they waited.

"Are we going to make it?" Tim asked.

"We have to," Sarah said, her gaze locked onto the shadowy office where the guard had vanished.

Sarah's fingers danced over her phone screen, sifting through her contacts for anyone who could help them navigate this nightmare. Anxiety clung to every surface as Tim's breaths became clipped and frantic. His eyes skittered from one military guard to another.

Before she could dial out, five uniformed figures materialized at their window. Their shadows stretched toward them like spectral hands reaching out from beyond. "We're going to need to search your vehicle," boomed a voice. The man's face hid in the darkness. "Both of you need to follow that officer there."

"Sure thing," Sarah responded, injecting false bravado into her tone as she tried to mask her fear. She shot a look at Tim, whose skin had turned an alarming shade of white. "C'mon Tim."

One guard took point while two others brought up the rear, their boots crunching on gravel.

"Are we getting arrested?" Tim asked.

"Chill," Sarah murmured back. "We have done nothing sketchy."

Even as she tried to soothe him, her mind spun with terrifying possibilities. What if their press passes didn't cut it? What if they were seen as threats? Stories they'd heard about journalists disappearing echoed ominously in her head.

She forced herself to remember the faces of the survivors they were there to represent.

"We're here to make their voices heard, put them back in history where they belong," she thought. Each step toward that office felt like moving deeper into a creepy forest, but Sarah knew they couldn't let fear hold them back. Not when stories were waiting to be shared and harsh truths needed exposure.

The dim light from the flickering fluorescent bulb above cast shadows across the locked office, where Sarah and Tim huddled together. Their breaths mixed in the stagnant air while outside, and the unsettling sound of their van being searched sent chills down their backs.

"Remember that story about the dude who got shot at the border?" Sarah said, her eyes darting nervously. "It's batshit crazy. We're dealing with this stuff right in our backyard."

"You think it happened?" Tim asked.

"I don't know," Sarah said, her eyes glued to the window. "But it wouldn't surprise me," her eyes fixed on the window.

The grating sound of a door cut their conversation short. The top cop strutted in.

"Follow me," he ordered, leading them down a tight hallway.

Tim's voice trembled as he spoke up. "What is happening? Where are you taking us?"

"Interrogation rooms," came the emotionless response.

As they were herded into separate rooms, Sarah shot Tim a look that screamed volumes. "Keep your cool."

Sarah stood her ground, facing her interrogator with a steely gaze. This wasn't how things were supposed to go down in the land of the free, being questioned and scrutinized for simply exercising her rights. Despite trembling hands, she summoned all her inner strength and spoke with unwavering conviction and determination. Every word fell from her lips like daggers, piercing the silence and making her interrogator flinch.

His eyes drilled into her. "You got any ties with any terrorist organizations?" He spat out the question like a bitter pill.

Sarah's blood sizzled in her veins at the audacity of his question. "Not on your life."

"What is the purpose of your visit?"

"We're reporters," Sarah shot back. "We're here for the voices that were buried under rubble and swept away by waves." She paused before adding, "Survivor stories from the earthquake and tsunami disaster."

"Spill it. Every detail!" he commanded. His tone was icy.

Sarah wove their tale with precision and care. Every pit stop they made, every face they were supposed to interview, became etched into her memory like lines on a map. The reason behind this mission—she laid it all bare before him. Even as he tried to find cracks in her narrative, she stood firm.

"Any other dirt you want to dig up?" She challenged.

The officer scrutinized her for an agonizing moment before abruptly rising and exiting without uttering another syllable. Sarah knew this ordeal was far from over, but she allowed herself a moment of triumph. She refused to be bullied or silenced.

Tim found himself in a stark interrogation room lit by dim light; his hands cold and shaky on the table. The sound of approaching footsteps echoed in the room as another officer walked in, shooting him a disdainful look before taking a seat across from him.

"You look like shit, Rezner," he said sharply, his voice low and menacing. "Got something to hide?"

Tim swallowed hard, trying to get his nerves under control.

"No, sir. It's just... this is so damn intense."

"Intense or not, we need to know why you're coming into the Washington zone," he pressed, leaning in closer. "If you're lying to us, there will be hell to pay."

"Like what?" Tim asked.

"Jail time," he said, tapping his fingers on the table. "Now tell me why you're here."

"We're journalists," Tim said, forcing himself to meet the man's gaze. "We're making a documentary about survivors of the earthquake and tsunami."

"Really?" the officer sneered skeptically. "Why would anyone want to go into Zone 1? It's suicide."

"That's exactly why," Tim asserted. "Their stories need telling."

The officer gave Tim a long, hard look before rapping on the wall to summon another uniform into the claustrophobic space.

"There's one more checkpoint before you even hit Seattle," the second officer stated, his voice as inflexible as iron. "And I need to stress this—any illicit activities could lead to death. This isn't some video game."

With that statement, the officers vacated the room, leaving Tim alone. He reflected on the many survivors they would encounter on their perilous journey.

After an agonizing half-hour, the door groaned open and the officer reappeared.

"You're good to leave," he said in a clipped tone. "But don't forget what we told you."

Tim felt a wave of relief crash over him. This was merely the kick-off and he felt an odd sense of liberation.

The van's inner light stuttered to life, bathing their faces in an eerie yellow hue as they clambered in. Their hearts were still echoing the adrenaline rush from the recent confrontation. A mutual glance passed between them, eyes wide like saucers reflecting shared terror before they clicked their seatbelts into place.

"Can you even process what just happened?" Tim asked. "What if we hadn't slipped through?"

"Let's not go down that rabbit hole," Sarah countered, her fingers white-knuckled around the steering wheel. She drew in a deep breath. "We're here on a mission–to give voice to their stories. We can't let fear deter us."

The engine growled to life. The gates groaned open, unveiling the dimly lit path stretching out before them. Sarah nudged the van into motion, and Tim's eyes focused on the electrified fence towering over them.

He couldn't stop thinking about Randy M., who pulled seven colleagues from a fiery hell despite burning most of his body, and Tania C., who saved two strangers from a flaming car during the quake. They were here because of people like Randy and Tania.

"Check it out," Sarah murmured, tilting her head toward a distant guard tower. A lone silhouette stood vigil. "We're being watched."

"Stay calm" Tim said. "Just keep driving." They slowly passed the ominous building. "Two more checkpoints like this one," Tim muttered, his mind spinning with thoughts of the other survivors they hadn't yet connected with. "How are we supposed to get their stories out there if we're getting hassled at every turn?"

"We'll figure it out. Their experiences need a spotlight, no matter the hoops we need to jump through."

With a low hum, the van trudged past the last stretch of buzzing electric fence, leaving behind the intimidating border check. The night air was heavy, but as they delved deeper into Washington territory, they braced for whatever was coming.

"Keep going," Tim's gaze was fixed on the road ahead. "Don't give that rearview mirror any attention."

United in their mission, they plunged into the all-consuming darkness.

CHAPTER 3

The growl of the engine pierced the stillness of the freeway. Sarah had been at the wheel for what felt like an eternity, her gaze sweeping over the ghostly expanse of Zone 3 that sprawled out ahead. The once teeming interstate, now devoid of life, sent shivers down her spine.

"Peep this," Tim said, pointing toward a weather-beaten billboard looming in the distance. They were used to vibrant hues and snappy taglines, but they had vanished.

"Better than nada," Sarah retorted. "Let's scope it out."

A mutual understanding passed between them, their hunger gnawing at their insides demanding attention. As they veered off the main road and rolled into the truck stop, unease seeped into them like icy water. Only a handful of trucks huddled together in the vast parking lot under a neon sign promising round-the-clock service.

Military vehicles stood imposingly like dark guardians, casting elongated shadows on the fractured asphalt below.

"Guess this is America 2.0," Tim mused.

They both disembarked from their vehicle, feeling like they were carrying an extra weight from their new reality. Keeping low profiles and their hands hidden from view, they shuffled into the cafe.

Inside was an eclectic mix of people. One man looked straight out of a trucker movie while six others, were in uniform.

"Feels like we've stumbled upon some dystopian fever dream," Sarah said to Tim, her gaze darting nervously between fellow customers and military rigs outside.

Tim nodded, his thoughts mirroring hers, but he kept his anxieties hidden behind a mask of stoicism. "Let's just get something to eat and go.".

Stale coffee and grease hung heavily as Tim and Sarah slid into a booth far from the other occupants. The worn vinyl seat squeaked beneath them. Military personnel didn't glance at the newcomers, their stoic expressions revealing little.

A voice, young and vibrant, declared, "Here are your menus." It pulled Tim and Sarah's attention to the server that was standing next to their table. She looked almost too young for the job, her features painting a picture of innocence that felt misplaced amidst the oppressive ambiance of the truck stop diner. Tim wondered how she had landed in such a forsaken place.

"Cheers," he muttered, taking the menu with an unconvincing smile.

"Rudy's Restaurant—where it's always sunny," Sarah read from the front of the menu.

Flipping through it, they found most items crossed out, leaving only pancakes, sausage, bacon, and eggs on offer. Coffee and water were their only beverage choices.

"So we're rationing grub now?" Tim asked incredulously.

Sarah nodded solemnly. "If Zone 3 is this bad... I don't want to think about Zone 1."

The young server returned. Her name tag introduced her as Anna. She offered them a strained smile as she asked for their orders. But Sarah was more interested in getting some answers than deciding on breakfast.

"You local?" she asked Anna.

"Seattle," Anna confessed. "When the quake rocked our world, Uncle Sam packed me off to this place." She swallowed hard. "A military truck rolled up one day and just yanked me away." Her eyes shimmered with unshed tears as she admitted, "I haven't seen my parents in person since..."

Sarah took a sharp breath. She couldn't wrap her head around the idea of being yanked from your family and chucked into a life you didn't sign up for. She rummaged in her bag and shoved a business card at Anna. "Take this," she said, pushing it into Anna's hand. "We might have some sway, help you get back to your family."

Anna's eyes sparked. "Seriously?"

Sarah bobbed her head. "One hundred percent."

Anna dashed off to rustle up their orders while Tim squirmed in his seat. Even though unease was practically their new perfume, there was no hitting reverse now.

Sarah eyed her untouched food; the aroma of bacon and eggs making her stomach flip. Her hunger had done a runner after hearing Anna's gut-punching story and she felt sick to her stomach over the government's cutthroat moves. Tim asked for their food to be boxed up.

"Ready to bounce?" he asked.

She gave him a silent nod, and they peeled themselves from their seats under the watchful eyes of the military guys hanging around.

Anna handed them their breakfast with a grin on her face. "Keep your eyes peeled," she said.

"Doesn't this feel like a scene from one of those eerie futuristic films?" Sarah asked.

The first light of morning pierced the horizon, creating strange shadows across the empty parking lot. The sight of military trucks scattered around made her heart race with anxiety. Tim shook his head, taking in the disturbing scene before them.

"I don't think anyone can ignore this reality now," he conceded.

An ominous feeling seemed to hang over them despite the dawn breaking. The deserted roads, scarce food supplies, and overwhelming military presence indicated something was wrong. As they traveled further, it became obvious the land had transformed into a twisted version of what it once was. Their route led them toward Zone 1. Fate had forced them onto this path, and there was no turning back.

CHAPTER 4

Tim's fingers wrapped tight around the steering wheel as the sun blasted through the hazy windshield. The highway before him sprawled into an infinity of nothingness, not a single vehicle in sight. The silence was deafening.

Beside him, Sarah shifted uncomfortably in her seat. "It's eerily silent out here," she said. "Feels like we've stepped into another world."

"Yeah," Tim agreed, his eyes narrowing against the glare of the sun. "It's so barren and deserted..."

Sarah peered out at the desolate gas stations they passed by. Their shutters were down and the pumps were lifeless. "Do you think we'll find any gas station open before hitting Leavenworth?" She asked.

"We better," Tim responded. "The fuel gauge is flirting with 'E.'" His heart pounded at the thought of them getting stuck in this forsaken landscape. What if they ended up stranded there? Would anyone even be available to help?

A road sign loomed ahead, marking their entrance into Zone 2. But there was no gate, no electrified fence, just a short tunnel carved into a mountainside.

As they passed through at a crawl, Tim said, "I bet that's a scanner searching for contraband."

"Contraband?"

"There's talk of smugglers bringing guns into Zone 1 and hauling out loot."

Sarah looked over her shoulder, the ominous tunnel fading into the rearview mirror. The tales of Zone 1 had her nerves jangling like wind chimes in a storm. Out here, they were exposed, cut off from all familiarity. She reached out, fingers curling around Tim's arm in a silent plea for comfort.

"Hey," she said, "how about I take over? You could use some shut-eye."

Tim managed a weary smile and nodded, his face relaxing as he pulled the car to the side of the road. They switched places, and Sarah took up their journey into the unknown badlands. Their future was hazy at best, but at least they weren't alone.

Sarah kept her eyes on the road stretching before them while Tim found solace against the cool glass window, sleep claiming him despite his anxiety.

After what felt like an eternity of driving, an isolated structure came into view, an old-fashioned fuel station that seemed to double as a truck stop. As they drew closer, Sarah noticed signage showing it was an FBI outpost. Weird. Several nondescript cars were parked around.

"At least there's gas," Tim said as he woke up.

As they pulled up to the pumps, a man in military attire approached them with brisk strides. "What can I do for you?" His voice held no warmth.

"Just need to top off," Tim responded casually.

"Six-gallon limit," he informed them. "Should get you to Leaven-worth and back."

Tim nodded before asking tentatively, "How's life out here?"

"It's been calm for half a year now," he admitted grudgingly. "Before then... chaos reigned supreme." He sighed. "Looters smuggling contraband into Zone 1, returning with stolen goods. We do our best to catch them."

"That's rough," Sarah chimed in sympathetically. "Stay safe out here."

With a curt nod, the man turned and walked toward the outpost.

The silence that followed was heavy as Tim pumped gas into their car. The soldier's words had only served to amplify Sarah's unease about venturing deeper into this lawless land. She could only wonder what they would face next.

Angela was their only shot at sorting this out. They couldn't afford to back down now. Sarah, taking over the driving again, noticed the fuel gauge hovering just above a quarter tank. Tim slouched in his seat, pretending to sleep, but she knew better. His mind was likely churning with thoughts as they ate up miles toward Leavenworth, a place holding all their answers.

The closer they got to Leavenworth, the more the surroundings morphed. The wasteland they had been traversing gradually gave way to signs of recovery and reconstruction.

Tim blinked awake and sat up straighter, eyes wide at the sight. "No way," he breathed out.

New buildings were being erected throughout the town, now serving as the state capital. Cranes dotted the skyline while the rhythmic symphony of saws and hammers filled their ears. The heart of downtown buzzed with activity as construction crews worked tirelessly on governmental structures.

"It's crazy how much it has changed," Sarah mused. "Leavenworth used to be such a sleepy town."

They cruised past, a temporary camp filled with FEMA trailers and tents. "It sucks that so many people are still without homes," he said.

Sarah reached across and gave his hand a comforting squeeze. "They're bouncing back, you know," she said. "It might take time, but they will."

A few blocks later, they rolled into an enchanting Bavarian-themed village that seemed plucked straight out of a German fairy-tale book. Quaint boutiques and eateries lined cobblestone streets, brimming with flower boxes, adding splashes of color against rustic architecture. For one fleeting moment, Sarah imagined things were back to normal.

She whipped out her phone, but of course, no bars. "Let's grab some grub while I try to email Angela."

They ducked into this cute café, and the aroma of fresh bread and sizzling meat hit them like a warm hug. A violin was playing in the background. They snagged a table right by the front window.

Once they ordered, Sarah flipped open her laptop. "Gotta let Angela know we made it to Leavenworth early," she said as she typed away.

As she hit send, a server walked up with two pints of dark beer. "These are from the couple over there," he said, pointing.

Sarah glanced over and saw a man and woman grinning like they'd just won the lottery. They raised their glasses in a toast. Sarah and Tim did the same.

"Let's go thank them," Tim suggested, halfway out of his chair.

The couple is from New York and helping to build new government buildings. They all chatted about the town's rebirth until their food arrived.

Back at their table, Tim attacked his bratwurst with gusto. "Hard to believe we're less than two hours from Zone 1. Feels like we're on another planet."

Sarah nodded, but couldn't shake off her anxiety. "Yeah, it's surreal. I'm waiting for Angela's email. Hope she comes through."

Tim looked thoughtful for a moment before smirking. "If not, we can always become professional beer tasters in this cozy little village."

Sarah laughed, feeling lighter. "Don't tempt me."

They finished their meal in comfortable silence. Stepping outside, the late afternoon sun bathed the alpine village in a golden glow.

"Alright," Tim said, stretching his arms above his head. "What's next? More exploring, or should we check in on that email again?"

Sarah pulled out her phone, squinting at the screen. "Exploring sounds great, but let's keep an eye out for Wi-Fi hotspots."

"Sure thing," Tim responded with a wink as they walked along the charming streets. "This place is stunning."

Sarah nodded. "It's hard to believe there's so much chaos just a short drive from here."

As they wandered down the street, Sarah felt her phone buzz. She took it out and saw a new encrypted email from Angela. After entering the provided code, she connected their phones.

"Hello?" Angela's voice came through.

"Hi, it's Sarah. We've arrived in Leavenworth."

"Great. Can you meet at 6 pm?" Angela asked. "I'll send the location right before."

"We'll be there," Sarah confirmed.

After finalizing the details, Sarah ended the call, feeling a mix of nerves and hope. If anyone had the answers they needed, it was Angela.

"All set?" Tim asked.

"She'll send the location at six. I hope she has the intel we need."

Tim squeezed her hand tightly.

CHAPTER 5

Tucked away in the innards of their unremarkable van, Tim and Sarah engaged in a tense game of 'watch and wait' for Angela's cue. Sarah, her fingers tapping out a beat on her jeans-clad thigh, was a whirlwind of anxiety cloaked in a threadbare façade of tranquility. The oppressive silence between them extended indefinitely, interrupted only by the relentless ticking of the dashboard clock.

"Ever experienced an earthquake?" Sarah asked.

Tim's gaze remained fixed on the world beyond their metallic refuge. "Can't say I have. But I danced with a twister once when I was eight." His hands fluttered over the steering wheel, sketching images as if they could summon visions of demolished houses and overturned cars from his past. "I remember gazing at what used to be my block, thinking nothing could surpass this nightmare." He forced out a laugh that resembled more of a stifled choke. "Turns out, Mother Nature can be quite the prankster."

Catching the tension in Tim's posture, Sarah switched gears. "Hey, spill some tea about your future wife. The big day is in May, right?"

Tim's body language shifted. His shoulders dropped and a half-smile curved his lips. "Yeah," he admitted with a light laugh, "she's not exactly stoked about me jetting off on this adventure."

Sarah raised an eyebrow. "Oh? And why's that?"

"Well," Tim started, his gaze wandering off as if he could see his fiancée standing there. "She worries I guess... But she gets it - the gig requires sacrifices." Determination replaced the far-off look in his eyes as he continued. "I want to make waves, you know? Leave my mark on the world with this documentary."

The van clock blinked to 6:01 pm, yet their message remained elusive. Tim rapped his fingers on the wheel. "Will this Angela even show?"

Sarah shook her head. "It's part of the business, I guess. We should get going."

Tim twisted the key in the van's ignition. The engine roared to life, filling the air with its deep rumble. But suddenly, three blinding flashes erupted from behind them, causing him to yank the wheel to the side. "What in the world...?"

Sarah shot a glance at the side mirror. A powder blue vehicle was behind them. "Looks like we've got company from the boys in blue," she noted.

A heavy feeling of dread anchored itself in Tim's stomach. What had they screwed up? The other vehicle sidled up next to them at an agonizingly slow pace before rolling to a halt.

Sarah's leg twitched rapidly as she watched the driver's side window glide down smoothly. A woman sporting cropped blonde hair and piercing eyes leaned out toward them. "Tim? Sarah?" she announced.

Relief flooded over Sarah as she realized it was Angela. She glanced sideways at Tim and noticed his tense shoulders relax at their un-expected ally. "Angela, thank God," Sarah breathed out, unable to contain her gratitude. "We were freaking out for a moment there." She took a moment to observe Angela's sharp suit and shiny car that reflected the sun's rays like diamonds. "How did you track us down?"

Angela's expression turned serious as she explained, "Remember when you crossed into Zone 3? That's when they slapped trackers on you." Her tone was casual but Sarah could sense the underlying danger in her words. They were lucky that Angela had found them before anyone else could trace their whereabouts through those trackers.

Tim's grip tightened around the steering wheel like a vice. "They bugged us?" He choked out.

Angela nodded. "It's pretty much standard practice these days," she explained. "Please hop into my car. We're on the clock here."

Sarah bit her lower lip apprehensively. Something about Angela's explanation didn't quite add up. Her eyes darted around the van, taking in their high-end camera gear. "What about our van?" she asked. "We can't just abandon all this stuff."

"I've got it covered," Angela assured them, a hint of steel in her voice. "Thieves aren't exactly popular around these parts."

A chill went down Sarah's spine at Angela's words. Thieves? She exchanged an uneasy glance with Tim. The equipment was worth thousands. Leaving it seemed unwise.

He cleared his throat. "At least let me take the cameras."

Angela fixed him with a stern look. "No cameras allowed. Your things will be secure, I assure you."

Sarah bobbed her head. Who was Angela? A dark secret was hiding behind that flawless façade. But they had few options. She hopped out of the van, the door groaning loudly as it swung wide open. Her shoes crunched on the gravel path as she made her way to the shiny blue Volvo. Angela revved up the engine while Tim clambered in beside her.

"Strap in," Angela commanded with a clipped tone. The car hummed to life, its headlights carving through the twilight haze. Sarah let out a breath she didn't know she'd been holding and slumped back against the plush leather seat. As they rolled on, daylight retreated below the horizon, painting shadows across their surroundings. An unsettling quietness swallowed them whole, and the streets were deserted.

"Where's everybody at?" Sarah asked.

"Seven o'clock curfew. Nobody wants to be caught outside when it gets dark."

"Curfew?" Tim echoed incredulously. "Why so early?"

Angela glanced at his puzzled expression in the rearview mirror before answering coolly, "Gangs from the west side causing trouble with cops. No one's signing up for that drama."

Sarah's mind filled with images of bullets flying around them. She studied Angela's demeanor with awe; nothing seemed to rattle this woman. Sarah couldn't decide if that made her feel more secure or terrified.

As they drove on, the cityscape morphed into desolate farmlands outside her window, and a gnawing anxiety twisted her stomach into knots. She desperately needed more information – about Angela and this place. "So, what's the deal with Zone 1?" she asked, shattering the uncomfortable silence.

Angela's hands tightened around the steering wheel like it was a lifeline. "Well," she said after a beat, "it's under new management now."

Tim jerked upright in his seat. "New management? Here in the US? What is this, some dystopian HOA?"

Angela snorted. "Close enough. A rogue military faction took over a few months back."

"Wait, hold up," Tim said, eyes bugging out. "A rogue government? Seriously?!"

"They've got a fancy name for it—Cascadia. Stretches from the Canadian border to California."

Sarah felt her pulse spike. A secret government? This wasn't just off the grid. It was off the map entirely. "Why doesn't the government roll in with tanks and take it back?"

Angela let out a hollow laugh, devoid of any joy.

"The U.S. government doesn't need this to become public. I don't think it would be well-received if they were to enter there to kill Americans they deemed as terrorists."

Sarah's mind spun with disbelief and dread as she processed the situation. It was like a cruel joke, a twisted punch line to their journey. Welcome to America: where even an apocalypse came with bureaucratic red tape. She could feel Tim's anxious gaze, mirroring her overwhelming confusion and helplessness. They had risked everything to reach this point, only to be met with seemingly insurmountable obstacles. "We have to find a way inside Zone 1."

Angela nodded slowly. "There are channels," she said cryptically.

Sarah's heart sank, realizing they would have to rely on shady means to reach their goal. And what about documenting their findings? Would it all be for nothing? They had journeyed too far to retreat now.

"Any chance you can get us a camera?" Sarah inquired.

Angela's eyes flicked to the rearview mirror before responding. "I can snag you a government-issued one. It won't be top-notch, but it'll do."

Sarah's face brightened. "So we can film inside Cascadia?"

"Only within their strict limits," Angela cautioned, her tone grave.

Tim leaned forward, curiosity piqued. "How do you even have access to that? You're with the US government."

Angela chuckled dryly. "Let's just say my job has its... perks. I shuttle things back and forth when necessary."

Tim and Sarah exchanged impressed looks.

"But aren't you worried about getting caught?" Tim probed further.

Angela's eyes sparkled mischievously as she smirked. "Isn't life all about taking risks?" She shook her head slightly. "My expertise grants me entry where others can't go. Cascadia wants my insights on seismic activity. The US figures will reclaim control eventually, so I roam freely for now."

She turned down a side street, and a familiar van came into view. Tim's van. Angela pulled up beside it.

"Here," she said briskly, handing them a phone. "It's untraceable. I'll call at 06:00 with further instructions." Her eyes drilled into them. "Don't be late."

With that, she disappeared into the darkness. Tim and Sarah slumped with exhaustion. It had been a long day full of shocks and revelations. Wordlessly, they spent the night in Tim's van. The next day, the dangerous passage into Cascadia awaited.

Sarah lay curled in her sleeping bag, unable to sleep despite her exhaustion. Tim's steady breathing filled the van's interior. Outside, the night pressed close and heavy. Her mind raced as she replayed the day's events. The mysterious government agents tracking their every move, the revelation of Cascadia's independence, Angela's dangerous double-dealing.

What were they getting themselves into? This was a simple documentary recording the aftermath of a tragedy. Now, here they were, sneaking illegally across a border into a rebel territory with a woman of dubious motives. Fear gnawed at Sarah. Were they risking their lives for nothing? What if things went wrong?

Tim stirred, sensing her distress. He reached out and squeezed her shoulder.

Sarah turned to meet his calm gaze. "It'll be okay. We're in this together."

They would plunge into the unknown.

Sarah rolled over and stared out the window into the void of night, drawing comfort from Tim's presence. Together, they would document this new world unfolding before them. Come what may, their journey was only beginning.

CHAPTER 6

The night was dark and foreboding, with only slivers of moonlight peeking through the poorly covered windows of the van. Sarah lay awake on the hard floor, her flimsy sleeping bag offering little protection against the frigid metal beneath her. She listened for any signs of danger outside, a passing car, approaching footsteps, anything that might suggest their safety was compromised. This was their new reality. But despite it all, they had to trust Angela and her promise of a better life.

Sarah questioned if this was all worth it. Leaving behind their old lives, with their comforts and familiarity, for a wild and uncertain journey ahead. But then she looked at Tim, who was peacefully asleep beside her.

Sarah felt a twinge of nostalgia for the life she left behind. The constant buzz of notifications from her phone, the comforting distraction of social media - all replaced now by a cold GPS phone that connected them to the world but offered no solace from it. Despite it all, Sarah knew deep down that this adventure was what she needed, an escape from a world that had become too suffocating.

"Maybe I could shoot off a quick text... just to let the family know we haven't become road pizza," she pondered, her fingers twitching with the urge to text someone. The gentle hum of her GPS phone morphed into an impromptu concert, its vibrations making her vertebrae do the twist. "What's this about?" she exclaimed. The phone came alive in her hand, its screen pulsating.

Hesitantly, she accepted the call. The line was as silent as a mime convention, except for an irritating hum that reverberated in her ears like an obstinate housefly.

"Sarah," hissed an unfamiliar and eerie voice.

"Yes?"

A pause followed, punctuated only by what sounded like Morse code in the background. Then Angela's voice cut through. "I've sent you the coordinates. You have fifteen minutes. Your countdown starts now." And then silence.

Sarah's heart raced as she surveyed the situation. This was no longer just a game, but a potentially deadly mission. Every second counted, and danger lurked around every corner.

"Tim!" She shook him awake. She could see the panic in his eyes as he struggled to comprehend the gravity of the situation.

"What's going on?" Tim looked around.

"Angela called. We have to get to this location," Sarah showed him the location on her phone. The flashing red dot seemed to taunt them, daring them to reach it in time.

"No Wi-Fi? Are you serious?" Tim's voice rose.

"It's a GPS phone, not a toy," Sarah retorted, her fingers frantically tracing the route on the screen. "We have less than fifteen minutes. Scratch that; we have less than thirteen." Time was ticking away.

"Let's hit it!" Tim declared, clambering into the van's driver seat in his PJs and bare-chested. As Sarah tossed him a shirt, her gaze lingered briefly on his sculpted physique before mentally snapping herself back to the task.

The engine roared to life, cutting through the silence as Tim steered the van out of the parking lot. The streets were awakening, a stark contrast to the ghostly emptiness they had experienced the night before. People wandered about, some wearing hard hats and tool belts, while others clutched steaming cups of coffee, their breath visible in the crisp air.

"God, I hope we can trust her," Sarah thought, her hands tightening around the GPS phone. "There's no turning back now."

"Trust" had never weighed so heavily on their minds, as the clock ticked down and the van sped toward its enigmatic destination.

"Looks like this place is waking up," Tim muttered.

Sarah glanced around, taking in the pickup trucks marked by paint stains and the signs announcing new construction projects. Despite the budding sense of renewal, an undercurrent of unease still ran through her veins. It would be quite some time before this town truly represented the bustling new capital of Washington.

"Turn left here," Sarah instructed, her voice wavering as she clutched the GPS phone. The van rolled onto a ranch road, flanked by open pastureland dotted with cows and sheep. An apple orchard stretched along the other side, branches laden with ripening fruit. In this strange moment of tranquility, Sarah felt a fleeting sense of comfort, the gentle sway of the trees soothing her frayed nerves.

"Feels like a different world out here," Tim mused. "I can't help but wonder what Angela's got in that garage."

"Let's hope it's something that'll help us." Sarah's grip on the phone tightened as the rolling doors of an enormous garage came into view. It loomed at least twenty feet tall and spanned one hundred feet across, its steel exterior gleaming beneath the rising sun.

"Trust." Angela stood just inside, beckoning them to park in a specific spot. Their eyes locked for a moment before Tim guided the van into place, the tension in the air palpable.

"Here we are," Tim said, his voice barely concealing the trepidation they both felt. The garage doors closed, sealing them inside this unknown world, placing their trust in someone they had just met.

The acrid scent of oil and machinery filled the air as Angela gestured to the van, her voice steady and confident. "Your van will be safe here," she assured them.

"Safe?" Tim raised a skeptical eyebrow, his voice strained with concern. "What about the trackers on the van? We can't afford to be found."

"Relax, I'll take care of it. No one but us will know where the van is."

"Take enough clothes," Angela instructed, her focus shifting to the task at hand. "Washing machines are a rare find in Zone 1."

They moved quickly, their hands rifling through duffle bags as they gathered as many clothes as they could. They knew they would most likely be away for several days, and the thought of leaving behind Tim's equipment left a bitter taste in their mouths. But they had no choice; they needed to travel light and fast.

With a click, Sarah opened the trunk of another vehicle—a Rivian, sleek and rugged. Boxes of candy and hygiene products were nestled inside, their bright colors contrasting the shadows clinging to the garage walls.

"It's for the kids on the other side," Angela explained. "They don't see many sweets."

The garage door rolled open, revealing a world of bright sunlight beyond. For a brief second, Sarah shielded her eyes from the glare, the sudden burst of light feeling almost like an intrusion.

"Move," Angela's voice was steel-edged, slicing through the tension as they hauled themselves into the Rivian. The interior was silent but for their shallow breaths, each one trapped in a whirlwind of thoughts.

The vehicle's headlights cut through the dark garage, illuminating the path ahead as it trundled toward the open garage door. Its sleek design and rugged exterior contrasted to the shadows that clung to the garage walls.

The sleek, black Rivian came to life with a gentle hum, its clean lines and rugged exterior giving off an air of adventure and capability. The garage melted away as the vehicle emerged into the bright sunlight.

The vehicle was a sleek black, its paint reflecting the harsh sunlight as it rolled out of the dark garage. The wheels, thick and sturdy, left behind tracks in the dusty ground as they moved forward.

The early light from the sun cast long shadows on the gravel drive-way, reminding Sarah of the limited time they had left. She couldn't look away as she watched the swirling dust around the tires of their Rivian, a heavy feeling settling in her chest at the sight of their abandoned van. The world outside was a vast unknown, and she felt like they were standing on a tightrope with no safety net, just one misstep away from disaster.

"You scared?"

"Petrified," Sarah confessed. Doubts whirled in her mind like frenzied moths around a flame - were they courting disaster by leaving everything familiar behind? "And you?"

"The same." he squeezed out a tight-lipped grin. "But we're not alone."

Sarah nodded, forcing down the knot in her throat. The scenery morphed into an endless quilt of verdant fields and undulating hills.

"Trust me, we'll navigate through this," Angela said. Her eyes flicked back and forth between the anxious faces reflected in the rearview mirror and the winding road that lay treacherously ahead. "Just remember why we're doing this."

"Right," Sarah echoed weakly.

As they crossed into uncharted territory, Sarah risked one final look back. "Tim?" Her words were barely audible as the wind that surged through the gaping window snatched them. "Assure me we'll return."

He extended his arm over the console, interlacing his fingers with hers. His touch was a comforting contrast to the icy fear gripping her, radiating warmth and certainty.

"I give you my word," he declared. "We'll come back home safe and sound."

Chapter 7

As Angela's Rivian darted down the sun-baked highway, the eerie silhouettes of charred trees whizzing past entranced Sarah. The stark landscape was a silent testament to the devastation, and Sarah couldn't quite wrap her mind around it.

"Hey guys, what's your jam?" Angela asked, her eyes twinkling.

Sarah blinked in surprise at the abrupt change in topic. She turned to see Angela eyeing Tim expectantly.

Tim's face broke into an excited grin that rivaled Angela's own. "Well," he started, his voice brimming with excitement, "I've been a fan of EDM since I was a little kid. Kygo and Calvin Harris are like gods to me."

Without missing a beat, he launched into an animated monologue about his lifelong adoration for electronic dance music. He spoke so fast that his words seemed to tumble over each other in their rush to be heard.

Before Tim could finish his enthusiastic tirade about his favorite DJ's latest album, Angela cut him off with a wave of her hand and a command directed at Lexi, the car's AI system.

"Lexi," she said with an air of authority that contrasted with her playful demeanor from moments ago. "Blast some Kygo tunes!"

The car instantly filled with rhythmic bass beats as Kygo's song came alive through the speakers. Angela drummed her brightly painted nails against the steering wheel with the beat.

After letting them enjoy the music for a while, she reached over and dialed back the volume once again. She turned toward Sarah and Tim with a serious expression this time. "Just so you know," she said over the now faint strains of music, "We're less than two hours away from the Cascadia border."

Tim's eyes widened with disbelief as he took in the haunting sight of the charred tree skeletons that seemed to stretch forever. "I knew the wildfires were bad, but this is beyond anything I could have imagined," he muttered, his voice filled with astonishment.

Sarah's lips pressed into a thin line. "When it all started after the earthquake, it was like some sort of apocalyptic movie scene." She shook her head. "And as if Mother Nature hadn't thrown us a big enough curveball with that quake, thousands succumbed to respiratory issues because of the toxic air quality. Many survivors are now living with permanent lung scars. We had the worst air anyone could breathe on Earth for quite some time."

Angela's palm slammed against the worn leather of the steering wheel with a raw intensity.

"And our so-called leaders? What did those pencil pushers in their fancy suits do? Jack shit! They just sat on their high chairs and watched us suffocate." Her words were a potent cocktail of bitterness and accusation.

Tim asked. "Where were you, Angela, when The Big One hit?"

Angela's shoulders drooped as she released a heavy, uneven breath. "I was sitting at my desk, in my cubicle, on the first floor of my office building in downtown Seattle," she recalled. "We got an earthquake warning from near the subduction zone. We knew it was going to be catastrophic. But some people believed hiding underground would save them. They didn't realize the building was no match for a quake this big." Her gaze flicked to the rearview mirror. "I sprinted toward an empty stretch of street and crouched there, watching my workplace crumble like a deck of cards. So many lives were lost because they didn't escape when they had the chance."

An almost tangible silence followed Angela's chilling account; Tim and Sarah absorbed her story in silent agreement within the confines of their vehicle. The mood darkened even further as they navigated an infinite wasteland carved by nature's fury.

"Shocked, completely unprepared," Angela's voice echoed, each syllable carrying a bitter tang. "The quake warning system we'd put our faith in barely had time to emit its shrill cry before the earth started shaking beneath us. It was as if time had contracted, leaving us with a handful of precious seconds to scramble for safety."

Her gaze grew distant. "We were teetering on the precipice of comprehension, standing at the threshold of truly understanding and predicting such calamities. We had blueprints for an extensive study of the Cascadia Subduction Zone - plans that held so much promise." A sigh escaped her lips, heavy with regret. "But fate played its cruel hand, and we simply ran out of time."

A hollow laugh slipped from her throat, devoid of any humor. "They airlifted me with a few other seismologists to this makeshift office set up in Leavenworth." Her words hung heavy in the air as she recalled their arrival. "The media was swarming like bees around a hive when we arrived–cameras flashing, questions hurled at us from every direction." She paused. "Some even dared to point fingers at us for causing the earthquake." The absurdity seemed to hang over them like a dark cloud.

Sarah's eyes widened at a sign in front of her. "Sultan End of High-way'. How are we getting into Zone 1 if the road ends here?" she asked.

Angela let out an amused chuckle. "It ends for most folks. Not for us."

As they approached, flashing warning signs marked the highway's abrupt conclusion. An imposing concrete wall loomed, signifying the border.

Angela brought the car to a stop about fifty yards from the barri-cade. "This is it," she announced. "We're about to leave the good ol' U.S. of A. and enter the lawless neutral zone."

Sarah stared uneasily at the wall. "Okay, but how do we get past that thing? It's huge."

Angela gunned the engine and swerved sharply to the right, bump-ing over bushes and branches as if they were minor inconveniences. "Bulletproof exterior, run-flat tires, this baby can handle more than some shrubbery."

Approaching a ravine, Tim gripped his seat nervously. "Uh, where exactly are we going?"

Angela hit a button, increasing its ground clearance. It bounced roughly into the ravine as Sarah and Tim held on tightly.

At the bottom, they faced another barrier, a heavy gate barring entry to a dim sewer tunnel. As they slowed to a crawl, the car's AI announced, "Vehicle authorized for passage." The gate creaked open.

They drove into the tunnel and emerged on the other side as a second gate opened automatically for them.

"The neutral zone is like the Wild West. No rules at all," Angela said as they crossed into the no-man's-land. "The U.S. government created this neutral zone when they found out about Cascadia's plans for independence. They want to make sure no one from Cascadia can get through. And if they do, their fate will probably be death or a federal prison."

The Rivian clawed out of the gulch, jostling over underbrush and fallen limbs before it hauled itself back onto the neglected highway. Wild plants had burst through the pavement, staking their claim on what had once been a testament to human achievement.

"Nobody gives a damn about this place anymore," Angela remarked, her hand sweeping over the encroaching greenery and decaying structures. She told them of a close shave with marauders in no-man's-land.

In his mind's eye, Tim was navigating the labyrinth of Seattle's abandoned streets, his adrenaline-fueled heartbeat providing the soundtrack to an imagined high-speed chase. His heart pounded a wild rhythm against his chest as he reveled in this fantasy, only to have it abruptly replaced by a gnawing unease at the sight of looming guard towers dotting the next barrier wall.

Angela, however, remained unfazed. As they approached, the formidable wall revealed a fortified compound.

A guard's voice echoed from above, "Good to see you again, Angela!"

Another chimed in, "We missed you around here!"

Sarah blinked in surprise. "You're quite the celebrity among these guys," she said.

"Just know how to keep them happy. A little beer and weed go a long way."

She steered their vehicle toward a building emblazoned with 'Cascadia Border Patrol.' Sarah looked perplexed. "I thought this place was supposed to be lawless? Like post-apocalyptic wasteland lawless?"

Shaking her head, Angela retorted, "Don't believe everything you're told." She brought their Rivian to a halt and hopped out energetically. Gesturing toward Tim and Sarah, she urged them on. "Let's get moving! Aren't we here for your documentary? Let's hear some genuine stories."

Hesitant but intrigued by Angela's confidence, Tim, and Sarah clambered out of the car.

"Tim," Angela called back as she headed toward the border patrol building. "Grab that bag labeled 'Border Buddies' from the trunk."

Tim complied and rummaged through an endless pile of bags crammed into the trunk until he found one with 'Border Buddies' written on it. The bag felt heavy; its contents a mystery that piqued his curiosity. Beer and weed, perhaps, but the weight suggested more.

With a surge of effort, he wrestled the weighty bag onto his shoulder, each muscle straining against the hefty challenge. Angela's silhouette was moving ahead, her figure cutting through the dim light. Sarah matched his pace beside him. Every step she took echoed caution and unease. There was a steeliness in her eyes that spoke volumes about her resolve. She drew in a deep, determined breath, as if drawing strength from the air around them, and pushed forward. Retreat was no longer an option.

As they edged closer to the imposing edifice of the border patrol building, a symphony of hushed conversations and fluttering papers swelled around them.

CHAPTER 8

The door groaned on its hinges and revealed the towering figure of a guard. His smile was warm and inviting, contrasting his formidable presence in the tower.

"Angela!" he boomed, his voice bouncing off the cold stone walls of the empty corridor.

Angela chuckled lightly at his enthusiasm. "Juan," she corrected playfully, "I'm not alone." She gestured toward two figures beside her. "Meet Sarah and Tim."

Juan swiveled around, surprise lighting up his face as he took in the unexpected guests. A sense of anticipation hung thickly in the air; after all, the anniversary of The Big One was only three days away.

"Cody!" Juan's voice rang out again, beckoning another man into the room. Cody emerged from a second door, his physique mirroring Juan's intimidating stature.

Cody's face lit up with genuine delight upon seeing their guests. "What a treat! Two bona fide journalists here for our humble tale." He looked around expectantly before furrowing his brow in confusion. "But where's your gear?"

"We've got two phones and a government-issued video camera. We couldn't bring all the high-tech stuff we'd hoped to."

Juan sighed before breaking into a comforting grin. "Ah well," he said with an exaggerated shrug, "the cost of freedom is often surprising." He glanced over his shoulder conspiratorially and lowered his voice. "You know, they've got navy and coast guard vessels lurking offshore? They're trying to squeeze us dry... intimidate us... reclaim 'their' land." There was an unmistakable twinkle of defiance.

Angela touched his arm. "Stop talking and save it for the documentary," she said.

Cody's passionate words hung in the air as the office door swung open, revealing another guard, who was just as big and burly as Juan.

"Juan, I'm back from rounds," he said.

Sarah couldn't help but notice the dichotomy of their towering frames and tender demeanor. Juan, with a wave of his hand, motioned for Asher to join them. "These two are on a mission to capture post-split life in Cascadia through the camera lens," he said.

"Really? That's incredible!" Asher's eyes lit up as he pumped their hands with infectious enthusiasm. His excitement dipped noticeably when he realized they were devoid of professional filming gear. He stroked his chin thoughtfully before breaking the silence. "I might know someone who can bail you out. They're holed up on Whidbey Island."

"Whidbey?" Sarah parroted back. "Who would choose to remain there after the tsunami?"

Asher's laughter rang through the room. "Unlike our eastern neighbors, bureaucratic nonsense doesn't shackle us."

Sarah shook her head in disbelief, her eyebrows knitting together in confusion. "It all seems so...ruined."

"Well, you'll just have to witness it for yourself."

He reached for a red phone on the wall and conversed with someone on the other end about Sarah and Tim's predicament.

"Good news," he announced as he replaced the receiver. "My friend will lend you guys some gear. I bet this isn't quite how you envisioned your trip going?"

Sarah and Tim traded wide-eyed glances. If help was waiting on Whidbey Island, Zone 1 was far more intriguing than they'd ever expected.

Asher scribbled an address on a piece of paper and laughed. "Little good this will do without the internet or GPS to guide you."

Sarah marveled at the primitive nature of getting directions this way. No voice from a phone to tell you where to go.

Asher rattled off some coordinates that Angela quickly plugged into her phone.

Sarah's eyes widened in surprise.

"How can your phone work when no one else's does?"

Angela explained that the U.S. government had given her a special satellite phone, allowing direct access to their network.

Sarah raised her eyebrows in astonishment, realizing the extensive reach of the stealthy U.S. government.

Meanwhile, Tim spoke with Cody, learning about his life guarding the border. Juan explained they lived there indefinitely, alternating shifts every six hours. He took pride in protecting their fledgling country.

When he asked how long it had been since he'd been to Seattle, Juan shrugged and answered, "Weeks."

The only thing he missed was his boyfriend back in the city. Angela frequently ferried letters between them.

He asked whether Juan felt sad about being away from his boyfriend for a long time. Juan met his gaze steadily.

"If it's a choice between him or guarding the very land we stand on, I'll choose to protect him and the others. It's worth it."

He marveled at the young man's selflessness. He was barely twenty, yet resolutely guarding the border of Cascadia. Cody's commitment gave Tim hope for the future.

Sarah's mind raced with anticipation as they headed to their Rivian parked outside. This new destination would take them across Seattle to Whidbey Island, an area nearly destroyed by the tsunami three years prior.

Before leaving, Juan and Asher wished them luck.

"Please tell our stories," Asher implored. "Cascadia is too important to be swallowed back up by an indifferent government."

Sarah felt immense gratitude toward these kind men, so different from the aggressors she'd pictured initially. She hugged them, relieved by their humanity.

As Angela prepared to launch the Rivian into motion, she issued a cryptic caution. "We may encounter some sights that might rattle your cage on our way to Whidbey." Her fingers deftly danced over a button and the Rivian responded with a gentle hum, its electric motor awakening from slumber.

Tim flashed Sarah an encouraging grin as the vehicle moved. "This is nothing like I pictured," he confessed.

Sarah's laughter bubbled up in response. "Thank heavens for that! I was half-expecting we'd be thrown into some dystopian hellscape they told us about."

Her words seemed to carry away some invisible burden from her chest. Tim noticed the change in her demeanor and nodded, his heart echoing her newfound optimism. They were ready for whatever lay ahead as their Rivian devoured miles on the deserted highway, their minds still grappling with their surprising experience at Cascadia's border.

Tim mused aloud. "Juan, Cody, Asher, they were so unlike what we'd imagined."

"I know," Sarah chimed in. "Instead of getting pitchforks and torches, we got folks sharing heartwarming tales." She cast a sideways glance at Angela behind the wheel. "You hit the nail on the head about not judging them too soon."

Angela nodded, her gaze locked onto the dilapidated road unfurling before them. "Scratch beneath the surface and you'll find hidden treasures," she offered.

Peering out the window at the scarred landscape beyond, Tim shook his head again. The earthquake's aftermath was painfully clear. "It's mind-boggling that people are still clinging to life here after all this devastation."

"Desperate times breed desperate people," Angela murmured sagely. "Those who stayed have weathered much, but they hold on to the hope of a phoenix rising from the ashes."

Sarah's brows furrowed in thought. "Do you honestly believe Cascadia can pick itself up by its bootstraps with no external aid?"

"With unwavering resolve, we can move mountains. The fate of Cascadia is in their hands, not in those of defunct governments."

A fleeting look passed between Tim and Sarah. This was their chance to unearth the forgotten stories of courage and selflessness from the shadows of oblivion.

CHAPTER 9

The Rivian traced its path toward Seattle along the skeletal remains of the once-thriving Interstate 5. The highway was reduced to a single lane, but they, the sole travelers on this road, didn't mind.

Sarah squinted into the distance, her eyes catching an ominous structure blocking their way. "Angela, where exactly are we going?"

"Only southern route into Seattle. Looks like they've beefed up security since my last visit."

Tim's voice piped up from the backseat. "Another checkpoint? What's next? Strip searches and jumping jacks?"

Angela chuckled. "We're going to be okay," she assured them as she expertly eased off the accelerator, bringing their speed down to a crawl. "Take in the sights," she suggested.

Sarah's eyes darted; her breath hitching at the sight of vibrant flags dancing in the wind on either side of them. "Wait! Isn't that the Cascadia flag?" She couldn't mistake it. Striking blue stripes, sharp white lines, and rich green hues with a Douglas Fir at its core.

"You got it," Tim confirmed. "They're still waving that Doug flag, or whatever they call it. It represents something about this place being pretty or something."

Sarah turned to him incredulously. "Tim? Since when did you become Mr. Know-it-all?"

"Let's just say I did my homework before we hit the road."

To Sarah, though, seeing that flag stirred feelings from another time; memories of a simpler era when she had one hanging on her bedroom wall—not merely marking geographical boundaries, but symbolizing something deeper. Now it was morphing into the emblem of a new nation, a concept that seemed almost surreal.

"I wonder what Cascadia will be," she mused. "Will it reflect the untamed spirit of its wilderness? Raw and relentless?"

"I sure hope not," Tim chimed in, laughing.

As Angela deftly navigated her vehicle through the rust-streaked iron gates, she shared her vision for this emerging nation. "I picture something more refined... a society that's got its shit together."

Sarah's gaze lingered on the vibrant patchwork of greens and browns beyond them. "Who knows?" she said, mostly to herself. "Guess we'll just have to wait and see what time has in store."

The narrow lane loomed ahead, a chaotic mess of smashed cars stacked over twenty feet high. It was a formidable entry that would easily deter anyone with ill intentions.

Jumbled and haphazard, the pile of cars and debris seemed to be arranged in no particular order, creating an intimidating wall guarded by shadowy figures. Their weapons glinted menacingly under the bright sunlight, adding to the danger surrounding them.

Angela's grip on the steering wheel tightened as she eased her foot onto the brake, bringing their car to a stop with a crunching sound of tires rolling over gravel. The noise echoed around them, shattering any sense of peace or safety they may have had.

Tim and Sarah exchanged a worried look. "We're exposed, like sitting ducks!" Tim exclaimed.

"Don't worry," Angela retorted. "These checkpoints are nothing to worry about. They're trying to keep Cascadia safe from looters and agents from the United States government." She let out a sigh. "Who knew Cascadia could have such drama?"

From a makeshift office emerged a rugged man, his face set in a hard, unyielding expression. Clutched across his chest was a rifle, its weight bearing down on him as he scanned the area for any sign of danger. His eyes narrowed to slits as he peered through the open window.

"Angela?" he growled, his voice gravelly and menacing. "Is that you?"

A smile spread across Angela's face as she recognized the man, but it quickly faded as her nerves frayed. She hoped her facade of confidence was convincing enough. "Just passing through, Calvin."

Calvin's gaze shifted to Tim and Sarah, who were sitting behind Angela. His brows furrowed in suspicion.

"Friends of yours?" He asked, his tone dripping with skepticism.

"Documentary filmmakers," Angela explained. "They're here to share the stories of survivors."

"Well, why didn't you say so?" Calvin reached down and snatched the radio from his hip. "I've got a couple of VIPs here. We'll need the red-carpet treatment. Follow my patrol car." He ordered.

Tim leaned in closer to Angela. "What the hell is going on?" he said.

"Stay calm," Angela responded. "Everything should be fine."

But despite her words, Tim couldn't shake off the nagging fear that consumed him. Would they be forced to traverse the lawless zone again if they turned? The thought sent shivers down his spine. No, he refused to entertain such defeatist thoughts. They had come too far to give up now.

Angela's hands clung to the steering wheel with a vice-like grip. She locked her gaze onto the barricade that stood before her. She drew in a lungful of air, tasting the metallic tang of tension and adrenaline on her tongue.

In sync with the retreating barrier, Calvin's police cruiser surged forward, its bodywork gleaming under the sun. Its flank proudly displayed the Cascadia Flag.

Angela mirrored Calvin's every move, their coordinated movements like a well-practiced dance for two. As they passed the now-open barricade and ventured into uncharted territory, emotions flooded Angela. She felt determined and focused, her resolve hardening with each passing moment.

Together, they were forging ahead toward an unknown destination, a bold new country breaking free from its restraints, a fledgling nation reaching out for independence. And Angela couldn't resist the call, ready to carve out a future on this frontier of possibilities and uncertainties.

"So, where exactly are we headed?" Sarah asked.

"My guess is someone in power wants to meet with you two." Angela glanced at Sarah through the rearview mirror, meeting her questioning gaze. "Just stay quiet until I figure out what's going on."

Sarah bit her lip, her mind racing with questions and suspicions about Angela's true intentions. With her wealth and connections, who was she working for?

Tim squeezed Sarah's hand. "Don't worry," he said with a small smile. "We've made it this far."

But the flicker of doubt still lingered in Sarah's mind. They drove on in silence, taking in their surroundings. The once-great city lay in ruins, its towering buildings reduced to hollowed-out shells. Weeds sprouted defiantly through cracks in the pavement, reclaiming what was once their territory. It was a wasteland trying to rebuild itself, a bleak reminder of the world that was lost. And whatever lay on the other side of this journey, for better or worse, would never be the same.

Angela brought the Rivian to a halt in front of a massive sign that stood tall and proud ahead. Bold, imposing letters welcomed them to "New Seattle," daring anyone to challenge its authority.

"New Seattle?" Sarah said. "When did this take place?"

Angela's voice held a hint of pride as she explained, "It has been about three months since the residents changed things."

Calvin's voice crackled over the loudspeaker on the police cruiser, breaking the tense silence. "You guys get your photo op?"

Angela nodded, and they followed Calvin deeper into New Seattle.

Tim's gaze swept over the landscape before them. Once bustling streets were now barren and barricaded, giving off an eerie sense of desolation. The remaining houses looked like forgotten relics, their walls and yards devoured by wild foliage reclaiming its territory.

As they approached downtown, they caught sight of the skyline, or what remained of it. The once magnificent buildings, symbols of human ingenuity and achievement, stood as mere shells, their windows shattered and exposed interiors a tangled mess of steel and concrete.

Tim couldn't help but shudder at the thought of the brutal force it must have taken to bring such devastation upon these buildings. His mind reeled at the idea of an earthquake so powerful that it could reduce towering skyscrapers to rubble.

Sarah's eyes widened as she took in the scene before her. She had witnessed the early stages of the devastation, but she hadn't stayed long enough to see it turn into this post-apocalyptic wasteland. With each passing moment, her mind struggled to comprehend the magnitude of the earthquake that could topple buildings and leave a once-thriving metropolis in ruins.

"It was originally called a 9.3 on the Richter scale," Angela stated. "But after more research, they reevaluated it as a 9.5, followed by multiple aftershocks above 7.0 and several more above 8.0."

They drove through the rubble-strewn streets. The enormity of the situation sunk in with each passing block. This was no longer the Seattle that Sarah remembered and cherished; it was a nightmare come to life, a third-world country rising from the ashes of its former self.

Angela emphasized that a daunting task lay ahead of them, a task that would require the dedication and determination of thousands of people working countless hours. The cop car veered abruptly into an alleyway, and Angela tailed it at a careful distance. The destination remained a mystery.

They trailed the police vehicle down a sharply descending entrance into a basement parking complex. They plunged further into the poorly lit labyrinth. Tim shot Angela an anxious look, but her expression was an unreadable mask.

She pulled the Rivian up alongside the cruiser. Calvin and another officer, who seemed barely out of his teens, stepped out onto the cold concrete. A weather-worn "Seattle P.D." emblem hung dimly on the garage door behind them.

"Alright, keep up," the rookie ordered brusquely, motioning for them to follow.

Calvin bobbed his head and got back into the police car, departing as quickly as he came.

Sarah attempted to comfort Tim with a strained smile that didn't reach her fear-filled eyes. She clung to a shred of optimism, trying to convince herself they were being escorted toward fellow survivors who would greet them warmly.

Terror washed over Tim like a tidal wave. The burden of their unknown future bore down on him oppressively.

The rookie led them toward an unremarkable door at the far end of the garage; their footfalls reverberated ominously off the concrete walls.

Thoughts of potential outcomes and worst-case scenarios swirled in Tim's mind, but he forced himself to concentrate on each step he took. All they could do now was wait and see where this ominous journey would take them.

Chapter 10

The young officer pressed his back against the cool, damp hallway wall, silently motioning them toward their uncertain future. A blood-red door loomed ominously in their path. Sarah's eyes darted around the confined space, her heart pounding in sync with the deafening silence. The chilling realization hit her like a freight train; there was no turning back. With an eerie groan, the door creaked open to unveil a regal woman with hair cascading down like molten silver.

"Welcome to New Seattle, my dear guests," she greeted them, her voice a soothing balm of honey over the palpable tension. "I am Skye Flower, interim governor of Cascadia."

Sarah stood transfixed. The woman before her bore no resemblance to the tyrant depicted in hushed stories of despair and terror. Skye's smile shone like a beacon.

Shaking off the shock, Sarah was drawn forward, as if an unseen force was guiding her toward Skye's welcoming hand.

"Your leadership is awe-inspiring," she stammered. "A woman steering the ship of a fledgling nation, it's truly laudable." She took a moment to gather herself before adding, "I'm Sarah and this is Tim who documents our journey."

Skye's eyes sparkled as she clasped Sarah's hands tightly in hers. "Thank you," she responded, every word pulsating with humility. "We are all builders of this valiant new world."

"How long will you serve as Interim Governor?" Tim interjected.

"Until our first democratic elections in six months," she answered modestly. "The citizens will elect Cascadia's inaugural president."

Angela introduced herself as a seismologist studying earth tremors.

Skye nodded. "Yes! Your revolutionary research has been valuable. We're deeply grateful for your courage in smuggling resources to assist us." She turned back to Sarah with determination etched on her face. "I want you to broadcast our story—without censorship or embellishment. The truth holds power."

Sarah felt a rush at the thought of broadcasting such raw truth; it could place them all at risk, yet seemed bigger than their individual lives now. She locked eyes with Tim and saw mirrored resolve there—the story must be told, regardless of potential consequences. "We're committed for the long haul," Sarah pledged.

Skye's eyes welled up with emotion. She pulled them into a tight embrace. "Many reporters have faltered before," she murmured. "Thank you for your bravery."

Sarah motioned toward the sparse chairs arranged around a simple wooden table. As they settled down, she couldn't help but notice the austere surroundings—the fledgling government was subsisting on bare necessities.

Skye's smile was radiant, but her eyes betrayed traces of worry. "Will you tell our story?"

Tim shifted uncomfortably in his chair. "I'm dedicated to broadcasting the truth."

Sarah locked eyes with him. This story had the potential to shake the world to its core. Together, they would navigate this uncharted territory. She gave him an affirming nod, steeling herself for what lay ahead.

Skye leaned forward. "The Cascadian government will provide all necessary equipment and transportation for your journey."

Sarah and Tim exchanged stunned glances.

"But first," Skye added, "I'd be deeply honored if you interviewed me."

"Absolutely," Sarah said.

"Excellent! We have a studio downstairs." Skye glanced at her wristwatch. "Why don't we reconvene here in two hours? Until then, relax and refresh yourselves. My assistant will guide you to our cafeteria." Rising, she grasped each of their hands warmly. "It was so wonderful to meet you both. I look forward to our interview." She exited the office.

The familiar landscape of their existence underwent an irreversible reshaping, and she found herself between a thrill of adventure and a prickling unease. Her eyes darted toward Tim, his gaze reflecting an unshakeable determination.

They collected their bags from Angela's Rivian, each goodbye heavy with appreciation. Their arms entwined in a hug that silently narrated their shared journey.

"May fate bring us together again," Tim said sincerely, his words lingering in the air.

Angela responded with a kind smile that didn't quite light up her eyes. "I echo your sentiments. Travel safe, you courageous hearts."

They watched Angela's car disappear, leaving them alone. A woman stood in the distance, her hand waving in greeting.

"I'll show you to our cafeteria," she offered. Sarah's gaze shifted to Tim. "I apologize for pulling you into this chaotic situation," she confessed with a deep exhale. "I never could have predicted even half of what has unfolded."

Tim placed a hand on her shoulder. "No need for apologies," he reassured her. "We're on the brink of creating history - a revolution if Cascadia prevails." His smile shone like a beacon amidst the stormy waves of uncertainty. "This won't be easy, but remember, we're together."

CHAPTER 11

Tim squinted against the dazzling luminescence of the studio's high-powered spotlights as he stepped onto the stage. A trio of film cameras, perched atop towering monopods, loomed before him. A spotlight's halo illuminated a lone chair in the stage's epicenter, while the trio of film cameras, perched atop towering monopods, had their polished jet-black lenses fixed on it.

This new technology is the undiscovered country to Tim, and a sliver of uncertainty wove its way into his thoughts, prompting him to question if he truly had what it took for this Herculean task.

A tap on his shoulder jolted him from his thoughts, sending a shiver down his spine. With a quick turn, he came face to face with a young woman, her features illuminated by the bright studio lights. She wore a crown-like tangle of wires on her head, giving her a futuristic appearance that glinted in the light. The smile that spread across her face was infectious, filling Tim's veins with excitement and anticipation for what was coming.

"You can call me Sandra. I'm the one in charge here," she announced, her voice adding a bubbly touch to the otherwise serious atmosphere of the studio. "The camera crew should arrive any moment."

Tim bobbed his head, a weight lifting off his chest. They had pros coming. As Sandra busied herself with behind-the-scenes responsibilities, His eyes roamed over the stark studio setup. The conspicuous absence of the usual news desk struck him - this would be an up-close and personal grilling, no physical shield between Governor Flower and probing questions. The realization sent a prickling sensation across his palms.

In the dressing room, a lady with a serious countenance and razor-sharp efficiency led Sarah to an opulent chair upholstered in deep velvet. The assistant's voice echoed around them, sharp, guiding her toward a shower billowing with steam while she picked out an outfit that radiated sheer professionalism. A hint of amusement played on her lips at the assistant's almost amusingly extreme diligence.

The water cascaded down her body, transforming the once pristine glass walls into hazy murals. As she stood in the shower, her mind drifted into contemplation. She couldn't help but wonder where these people had honed their broadcasting skills. Had they learned their craft amidst the chaotic bustle of a newsroom, before nature unleashed its fury? Or was desperation driving them to master production and camera handling, wielding these talents like weapons to spread their crucial message? The steam from the shower enveloped her, adding to the feeling of being lost in thought as she pondered these questions.

The dressing room was a cramped space, filled with racks of neatly arranged clothing. Sarah emerged from the steam-filled shower, her hair wrapped in a towel. She ran her fingers over the options, trying to find the perfect outfit to convey professionalism and approachability.

This interview was the moment she had been waiting for, the pinnacle of her career. With millions of eyes watching, every detail mattered.

She settled on a crisp white blouse and a charcoal pencil skirt. As she dressed, her palms grew clammy. Despite conducting several interviews, none were as high stakes as this one.

A skilled makeup artist dabbed at Sarah's face, ensuring every contour and line was flawless. Meanwhile, an assistant carefully clipped a microphone to her collar, the small device almost blending into her outfit.

The assistant flashed a reassuring smile and guided Sarah toward the set. Bright lights flooded the stage with an intense radiance, causing Sarah to squint as she walked toward the center. The assistant arranged two armchairs strategically, facing a large screen displaying the words "Seattle's New Skyline."

The image behind the furniture made Sarah gasp. It showed a cityscape she could barely recognize. Jagged shards of buildings jutted at odd angles against a smoke-smudged sky. It looked like the aftermath of a nuclear blast. But what had hit Seattle was far more powerful than any warhead.

Sarah closed her eyes and took a deep breath, trying to hold back tears that threatened to spill down her cheeks. She sank into the armchair, her palms sweating as she anxiously smoothed her skirt. A smile spread across her face as she spotted the production team, their friendly waves and encouraging gestures filling her with excitement.

A young woman approached, holding index cards. "Here are some suggested questions," she said, handing them to Sarah. "You don't have to ask them verbatim."

Sarah sifted through the stack of cards. Each one held a carefully crafted question, typed out in bold font. As she read, relief washed over her. These were fair questions, not leading or manipulative. They truly wanted the truth to be told. This interview could be their best chance of clearing their names and avoiding the damning label of "terrorists."

She looked up to see Governor Skye looming over. "How are you feeling?"

"Nervous," Sarah admitted. "But I know how important this is."

The governor placed a hand on her shoulder. "You're brave for doing this. Thank you from all of us."

Sarah managed a smile. "It's an honor."

As the crew descended to wire their lapel mics, Sarah and the governor tilted their heads for the sound check. Their nerves were palpable, but they were determined to make this historic moment count.

"Ready when you are," came a voice behind the cameras.

Sarah and the governor exchanged looks and nodded. They were as ready as they could be for what was about to unfold.

Taking a deep breath, Sarah steadied her nerves. This was it, this is the moment. The producer, a woman who wielded her stern expression and piercing gaze, sauntered toward her, shattering the hush with her tone.

"Heads up everyone, we're live in ten." She raised both hands as though she were conducting a symphony. Gradually curling each finger into her palm as she retreated, a human countdown clock ticking away the remaining seconds.

In a fleeting second, the world around Sarah seemed to come to a standstill, as if even time held its breath in anticipation. The weight of this moment bore down on her. This wasn't just about her story. They were representing Cascadia, and all it stood for in front of a captivated audience.

CHAPTER 12

Sarah positioned herself before the lens, her heart pounding with the silent countdown of the camera. Drawing a steadying breath as the director yelled, "Action!"

"Greetings, I'm Sarah Bridges," she started, her eyes flickering to the teleprompter illuminating her opening script. "I stand before you today as a voice for the desperate pleas echoing from Cascadia's heart. Only three years ago, an unprecedented natural catastrophe shook the world to its core. The largest disaster in modern history hit the Pacific Northwest. Those who endured the storm are now on the cusp of independence.

She took a deep breath, scanning the room until she saw Tim. With a commanding presence, she spoke. "I've had countless dialogues with people from all walks of life. But none carry such weight as my upcoming conversation with Interim Governor Skye Flower."

Sarah continued. "Before stepping into this pivotal role, Skye dedicated her life to public service — first as Assistant District Attorney of Kings County for over ten grueling years and then enlightening young minds at the University of Washington School of Law for twenty-five commendable years."

"When disaster struck without warning, Skye found herself amidst helpless animals at a shelter where she volunteered–an act that ironically spared her life from being crushed under her apartment building's rubble."

Sarah's tone shifted. "Since that fateful day, Governor Flower has been ceaselessly rallying volunteers to lend helping hands and saving countless lives through tireless endeavors."

She sighed before adding: "This unwavering leadership has thrust her into such precarious circumstances today. Their actions are now considered acts of terrorism by the American Government, and several individuals have found themselves on the FBI's most wanted list." Sarah paused. "Today, my friends across the digital ether, you stand on the precipice of history. If Cascadia succeeds, the US will surrender land for the first time. I present to you all, our esteemed guest and champion of Cascadia's cause, Governor Skye Flower."

The governor turned toward the camera, her eyes shining for this rare opportunity to connect with the people. "Sarah, I'm grateful for your kind introduction."

Sarah met the governor's gaze. "Let's cut to the chase, Governor. Your reign is being met with a healthy dose of skepticism from various parts of the country. You're not perceived as a pillar of stability and order, but as the chief conductor of an environment that mirrors the tumultuous lawlessness akin to the Wild West, a stark contrast to the peaceful Seattle we remember before nature's fury ravaged it. There's an increasing belief that you might be in league with extremist factions intent on usurping control over our nation."

A muted chuckle slipped from the governor. "Our primary aim is to enhance and uplift our citizens' living standards, which they rightfully deserve," she retorted. "The last thing we want is for our people to live in constant fear because of federal government armored vehicles looming over their daily routines or obstructing their freedom to traverse city streets freely. That was never part of our plan."

"And why would the United States Government entertain your bid for independence?"

"We are not a fringe group of revolutionaries, as the United States media has tried to portray us. We are working Americans, trying to make a better life."

"So, governor, some people say your law and order approach makes Cascadia feel safe, while others say it feels like an authoritarian regime. What is your response?" Sarah asked.

"After the devastation, people were facing danger in their own homes. Murders were happening over petty things like jewelry. That's when we knew we needed change, and fast."

"I can't imagine. How bad did looting get in Seattle and Cascadia as a whole?"

"It was like an invasion of armed terrorists. They drove around in armored vehicles, breaking into houses and taking whatever they wanted. If anyone stood in their path, they shot them, killing many. Citizens should have the power to protect themselves and their loved ones."

"Speaking of using lethal force, leaked videos show people dressed in uniform shooting civilians on the street. Are these government officers?"

"I cannot comment on those specific videos. What I can say is that our officers often face tough decisions when it comes to using force. But thanks to a joint effort between citizen patrols and law enforcement, crime rates have dropped significantly."

"How does Cascadia handle looting?"

"Our laws state looters will face either death or life in prison. It may sound harsh, but it has resulted in a 93% decrease in reported crime. Of course, there have been shootouts between our Cascadia Patrol and these criminals, but as you can see, it's working." The governor paused before continuing. "The safety and well-being of our citizens is our top priority."

"Governor Flower, do you believe the American people will understand and support Cascadia's cause?"

The governor paused. "I hope they demand the truth. The government abandoned us after the earthquake. They closed off our borders under the guise of protection, but they did nothing while thousands died from starvation."

What's your response to those who label the Cascadia Government as terrorists?"

The Governor stared into the camera. "I'll share this with everyone worldwide, especially our eastern neighbors. The people of Cascadia are not terrorists. We stand for peace and justice. We will defend our land with non-violent means. Unlike The United States, which has a history of forcefully taking land from Native Americans."

"What's keeping Cascadia from making its mark on the global stage?"

The Governor's face hardened. "Our aspirations are being thwarted by America's naval blockade and their incessant meddling in our airspace," she revealed. "They're flexing their muscles like playground bullies, with no one to challenge them. We're not some fanatical cult or an insurgent communist group. We're American citizens who decided enough was enough - we were tired of bleeding ourselves dry through taxes, receiving no semblance of a safety net."

Sarah absorbed this information, nodding. She then asked, "Have you received international backing for your quest for independence?"

A spark ignited in the Governor's eyes. "There have been some encouraging discussions," she admitted. "However, nothing has materialized yet; it's an uphill battle when you have a juggernaut like America against you at every turn."

"And what about the United States? Is there a possibility they could reclaim this land peacefully?" Sarah pressed.

The Governor let out a chuckle. "I highly doubt it," she said. "They've had many opportunities and botched each one spectacularly. Besides, our newly formed government is better equipped to deal with cataclysmic disasters."

"And how does Cascadia plan on gaining independence?" Sarah probed.

"We've submitted our constitution and legal arguments for sovereignty to the United Nations. The responses have been promising. We want the freedom to govern ourselves responsibly."

Sarah inclined her head. "From what I've seen, it's clear that it would require an astronomical sum - possibly billions, even trillions - to restore this region to its former splendor. How do you plan on financing such a monumental endeavor for this emerging nation?"

"We'll be seeking the generosity of individuals from every corner of the globe. Our territories will remain untouched by seismic activity for generations, offering a sanctuary for those seeking safety and stability. We invite pioneers from all walks of life, encouraging them to join us in sculpting Cascadia into a vibrant tapestry of diverse cultures and traditions. We promise each citizen will receive a plot of land."

"What about those who owned property before the quake?"

"We will restore rightful ownership to those who held stakes here before the calamity hit, provided they pledge residence within Cascadia," Skye said.

Sarah kept a straight face. "A captivating vision indeed. I wholeheartedly hope you succeed."

"Thank you for the opportunity," Skye expressed, turning toward the camera. "To everyone watching this, we need your help to turn this vision into reality. You can join our cause by visiting the website addresses we've provided and learning more about Cascadia's plea for independence."

The director's voice boomed through the studio, "Cut! Fantastic job! Let's polish this for broadcast."

Sarah's forehead creased. "But how will you spread the message beyond Cascadia?"

A smile crossed the director's face. "We've got fearless couriers lined up for that, many of them are leaving their homes in Cascadia for good. They're not just citizens; they're revolutionaries."

Skye moved in, inching toward Sarah, and cushioned her hands. "Your bravery could be the ignition we've been waiting for. With allies beyond our boundaries, our message can reach the ears that need to hear it."

Tim appeared next to them. "The governor's aide is setting us up with everything we need for the trip, including a vehicle."

Skye turned toward Sarah. "Thank you for helping us."

Sarah enveloped her in a warm embrace. "My only wish is for Cascadia to flourish," she said.

They released each other just as Tim stepped forward and joined them in a group hug.

Tim flashed a grin at Sarah. "That was one hell of an interview," he said.

"This is just the beginning," Sarah responded.

Sarah couldn't help but hope he was right, despite her doubts.

CHAPTER 13

The 2027 Chevy Tahoe purred, navigating the fissured asphalt ribbon that snaked through the city. Sarah's fingers clenched around the armrest as her gaze roved over the remains of the once proud buildings. A bustling metropolis now reduced to a graveyard of rubble and debris.

Tim's eyes flickered, scanning their dystopian surroundings.

"It's eerily silent," Sarah murmured. "As if the entire city is holding its breath."

Tim nodded, his attention riveted on maneuvering around an upturned bus that lay sprawled across their path like a defeated metallic beast. "We need to reach Big Jim's," he muttered. "Being exposed like this sets my nerves on edge."

Sarah glanced at the scrawled directions on a crumpled piece of paper in her lap. "We're close," she assured him. "Just around the corner on our right."

The neon glow of Big Jim's Bar & Grill punctured through the gloom ahead. Tim guided their Tahoe into its fissure-riddled parking lot.

"I know we need a place to sleep, but this place gives me the creeps."

Tim checked his taser and pocketed a small canister of pepper spray. "I don't like it either, but we have little choice. Let's get inside and get our bearings. Stay close."

Sarah nodded, clutching her bag as she followed him to the entrance. He paused with his hand on the door handle, meeting her eyes. She took a deep breath and gave him a brave smile.

"Here goes nothing."

Tim pulled open the wooden door, the hinges creaking. He stepped inside, on high alert as he scanned the dim interior.

The bar was bustling, far more crowded than he expected—smoke and food, clinging to the walls and carpet like a permanent fixture. In the back, the click of pool balls colliding and the crack of breaking racks reverberated through the air. Sounds and smells enveloped him as soon as he stepped into the establishment.

Sarah trailed Tim, weaving through a labyrinth of occupied tables toward the bar crafted from seasoned oak. The ambient hum of conversation washed over, fragments of dialogue about abundant fishing trips, ambitious construction endeavors, and expected weekend escapades seeping into his ears.

Behind the bar, a towering figure with a beard as wild as an untamed forest polished a beer mug with practiced ease.

"What'll it be?" he inquired.

"We're looking for a room," Tim responded.

The bartender's welcoming grin evaporated like morning mist under the sun. His gaze darted between Tim and Sarah, eyes narrowing into suspicious slits. "We don't see many unfamiliar faces around these parts. Where are you two from?"

Tim faltered. The lively conversations around them were now fading whispers; patrons swiveling on their stools to cast glances their way.

His muscles coiled, every nerve in his body sounding an alarm that they were being encircled.

He flashed the bartender a smile. "We're just passers-by," he said while shifting his weight into a defensive position, as if preparing for potential conflict. He could feel the intensity of the bartender's scrutiny piercing through him like ice-cold needles. "We mean no harm. We're journalists documenting firsthand accounts post-earthquake."

At the bar's end, an elderly man broke his silence. "Journalists? I can't say we've seen any of those in a long while." He stroked his gray beard. "So, how'd you get past the border patrols?"

As Tim opened his mouth to respond, a massive figure emerged from the shadows of the crowd. Towering over six feet tall and built like a brick wall, the man's arms were thicker than tree trunks, and his presence alone seemed to fill the room. "So, how did you find your way here?" he growled.

Tim's throat tightened. "It's a long story, but we have authorization from Governor Flower herself." With painstaking care, he reached into his jacket, aware of dozens of pairs of eyes following his every move. He withdrew a folded document and presented it to the bartender, who scrutinized it with a piercing gaze.

The bartender nodded and returned the paper.

"Seems legit," he grunted. "Just remember to catch no one off guard around here. We have to stay vigilant at all times, you understand?"

Tim let out a breath he hadn't realized he'd been holding. The mood in the bar relaxed as patrons went back to their conversations. Out of the corner of his eye, he noticed Sarah sag against the bar in relief. That had been closer than he cared for. These people were wary of outsiders, but he hoped their story would open hearts and minds.

A woman in her 40s with kind eyes and long brown hair approached Sarah and took her hand. "Sorry for the gruff welcome. Life here in the zones ain't easy, but we look after our own. I'm Lara. This is my establishment."

Sarah smiled. "It's okay, I understand. I'm Sarah. Thank you for hearing us out." She paused, then asked, "Do you have family here?"

Lara's eyes clouded with sadness. "I lost my husband and daughter in the quake. It's just me now." Her voice cracked.

"I'm so sorry," Sarah said, squeezing her hand.

"It's alright, dear. Let me show you to your room." Lara led Sarah through a side door and up a creaking staircase. She unlocked a plain wooden door with an actual metal key.

"Real keys, wow. I'd forgotten what these were like!" Sarah said with a small laugh.

Lara smiled. "We do things a little old-fashioned around here. The desk phone connects to my place downstairs if you need anything."

After Lara left, Tim set their bags down. "I'm going to get the camera equipment from the Tahoe."

Sarah nodded, feeling the weight of the day. She sank onto the lumpy mattress, comforted by the familiar sounds of people living life drifting up through the floorboards.

Tim walked into the evening air, the setting sun casting an orange glow on the battered buildings. As he approached the armored Chevy Tahoe, Tim admired its structure. Though worn on the outside, the interior was immaculate, with bulletproof glass and armor plating. The electric motor provided stealth and speed when needed. Tim felt safer knowing they had a reliable escape vehicle.

The moment Tim's fingers touched the door handle, a sudden wave of coldness washed over him, as though an unseen figure was hovering nearby. Startled, he whirled around only to come face-to-face with a young woman whose choppy brown hair framed her curious gaze.

"Tim Rezner?" she asked. "I'm Tinsel Ivy. I know why you're here." He stammered as she pressed a walkie-talkie into his hand. "We have contacts and resources. The people need their stories told." She eyed him. "I hear you have a list?"

"Um, yes, but—" Tim started.

"Forget it. Government sympathizers for the U.S." she said. "They'll create stories of how oppressive Cascadia is."

Tim bristled at her dismissive tone.

"Use this if you want the actual story." She tapped the walkie-talkie. "And brush up on your Morse code. You'll need it."

With that, she blended into the shadows, leaving Tim clutching the device. He got into the vehicle and drove off to find a parking spot.

Tim pulled the Tahoe into an open lot a block from the bar. Glancing around, he tucked the walkie-talkie into his jacket before heading inside.

Taking the stairs two at a time, Tim entered the motel room. Sarah looked up from unpacking their bags with a puzzled expression. "What took you so long?"

"You won't believe this," Tim began. "Out of nowhere, this woman approached me, going by Tinsel Ivy. She said we can't trust anyone on our list."

"Tinsel Ivy?" Sarah grabbed her notebook, scribbling down the name. "Go on."

"She gave me a walkie-talkie to look for contacts," Tim said.

"Can we trust her?"

"I wasn't sure," Tim admitted. "But she seemed straightforward. I'm no investigator like you, but my gut says she was telling the truth."

Sarah's brows furrowed. There was no way to verify backgrounds as they cobbled together the interview list from vague sources. Only Angela's name came from an official. She walked to the window, pushing aside the faded drapes. Dusk was falling over the city, the sky fading from orange to purple. Below, dim street lights flickered on as people hurried home before darkness set in.

The sight before her was a harsh echo of the images she'd seen in conflict-ridden nations, yet it was far more startling to see it here.

Three years later, streets lay untouched. Buildings that once stood tall were now nothing more than piles of debris and twisted metal. A haunting stillness replaced the vibrant energy that pulsed through its veins. Recovery was a long road. Each step forward seemed minuscule against the backdrop of devastation. The earthquake left deep scars on the city's skin.

Sarah leaned her forehead on the cold windowpane, her eyes shut tight. The task ahead felt like trying to scale an insurmountable mountain. How could she possibly convey the magnitude of what had occurred here? Would people back home even want to face this stark reality?

She turned to find Tim beside her, his gaze filled with empathy. He didn't need to articulate his thoughts; their shared purpose hung in the silence between them. They needed to recharge.

CHAPTER 14

Sarah's nightmare ripped her body from its grip, causing convulsions. Her eyes snapped open, dilated and wild with terror as she gasped for air. The remnants of her torment clung to the edges of her consciousness, replaying the scene of her and Tim standing before a cold, unyielding tribunal, their fate hanging in the balance. She rocked her head back and forth, desperately trying to dispel the haunting image that threatens to consume her.

She slid out under the motel blanket and rummaged through her duffel bag with determined fingers. Her hand brushed against clean clothes, their familiar scent of laundry detergent offering a moment of comfort amid the chaos. She knew the musty smell of decay would soon take over as they continued their journey into unknown territory.

A voice shattered the quiet, husky from sleep. "Morning," Tim's voice echoed. "Everything alright?"

Her eyes traced the strands of his hair that had escaped the fortress of blankets. "I had a nightmare," she began. "It felt so real, as if I could reach out and touch it."

Tim let out a sharp breath. "Let's keep those Hollywood plots in your dreams. It's hard enough to imagine being locked up for expressing our free speech rights."

She nodded before adding, "Yeah, just a dream." After a brief pause, she spoke again. "I need some fresh air. I'm going to hit the streets."

Tim sat up. "Sure thing! Let me just get dressed," he said, throwing off the blanket and hopping out of bed with exaggerated speed.

But she shook her head. "No, I want to do this alone. Seattle and I didn't part on good terms."

Tim paused, propping himself up on one elbow, as he looked at her with concern. "Are you sure it's safe out there?"

She answered, "I reckon so." A moment of quiet lingered before she went on. "Cascadia's folks have put a lot into beefing up the safety of the streets."

"Just in case," he mumbled, bending over to dig through the mess on his bedside table. He fished out their little pepper spray can and lobbed it lightly toward her.

Sarah caught it and gave him a reassuring nod before tiptoeing down the creaky stairs and slipping through the side door into the deserted street outside.

The only noise that accompanied her was the scuffle of her shoes against the broken pavement, a sound eerily similar to those quiet moments after a snowstorm in Seattle when everything seemed still under a blanket of white fluffiness.

A light breeze drifted through the empty streets, carrying the burnt smell of a city that used to be alive and bustling. Sarah wrapped her arms around herself, trying to find comfort in her body heat. But the cold inside her wouldn't leave, despite the warm morning sun. She closed her eyes tightly, picturing what Seattle used to look like before it became a ghost town of ruins and forgotten memories.

As she walked further along the broken road, ruined buildings stood tall around her like sad reminders of what used to be. Her steps slowed as she turned a corner. There stood a glass building, untouched by destruction. It stuck out like a sore thumb among all the rubble. Seeing something so new after so much ruin shook her up. As she got closer, she read a plaque: "To remember those who are gone." Made with materials found nearby, built to withstand disaster. Together, let's rise from this ruin.

Sarah's throat tightened. Not a monument to power, but a tribute to the people. Perhaps there was hope here, after all.

The sun crested the Cascades, bathing the glass building in dawn's rosy glow. Sarah smiled. Even in the darkest hour, light finds a way through. The rubble no longer seemed so oppressive. Cascadia would rebuild, transformed like the phoenix from ash and fire. She was ready to share the stories of those who survived the flames.

She arrived at the motel, eager to share her hope with Tim. When she opened the door, she found him asleep, and the blanket kicked to the floor. She hated to wake him from such a peaceful rest.

"Rise and shine," she called.

Tim grunted, throwing an arm over his eyes to block the sunlight streaming through the curtains. After a few more prods, he sat up blearily. "Did you find anything interesting on your walk?" he mumbled.

Sarah's eyes lit up as she described the memorial building. "It was like finding an oasis in the desert. I think this place has potential."

Tim nodded, rubbing the sleep from his eyes. "Well, let's see if we can find some stories to share."

Sarah picked up the walkie-talkie, turning the dial through empty static. A woman's voice drifted out, chatting casually about coffee. Sarah waited for an opening, then pushed the talk button.

"Hello, my name is Sarah Bridges. I'm a documentarian looking to speak with earthquake survivors." She released the button and waited anxiously.

After a pause, the woman responded, "I know just the person. Let me give you his location."

Sarah scribbled the coordinates. With a tip of her head to Tim, she clicked off the walkie-talkie. The pieces were falling into place. She was ready to dive into the rubble and dig out the tales of those who had crawled from the wreckage and were building something new.

Sarah folded the paper with the coordinates and tucked it into her pocket. Tim had repacked their gear, his t-shirt clinging to his muscular frame.

Despite her best efforts, Sarah admired his physique. It had been ages since she had been this close to a man. Her heart fluttered despite her attempts to remain professional. She reminded herself Tim was engaged.

Dragging their bags, they arrived at the bar. The satellite phone blinked to life in the dimly lit room as they punched in the coordinates.

They walked to the lot where the Tahoe was the only thing there. Tim slipped into the comforting leather confines of the Tahoe's driver's seat, a sense of familiarity washing over him.

The engine purred as he reached out to Sarah, their fingers tangling together in an easy dance.

"You're putting a lot of faith in me," he admitted. "It feels like we're on the edge of digging up some seriously epic stories."

Sarah's cheeks flushed with color as she withdrew her hand. She knew she had to set boundaries. The focus was on uncovering the truth and exposing major secrets, rather than becoming overwhelmed by emotions.

"We'll see where this takes us and ride it out."

CHAPTER 15

With its crumbling walls and sagging roof, the dilapidated cottage stood precariously amidst the tangled thicket, as if it had emerged from the overgrown brush. A heavy sadness washed over Tim as he surveyed the structure, his eyes drawn to the boarded windows, the tattered tarps that barely shielded its brokenness, and the graffiti that mirrored the pain and despair of its surroundings. A sense of doubt washed over him, prompting him to steal a glance at Sarah, searching for any clues in her reaction.

"Are you sure about this?"

"As sure as I'll ever be," she said, stepping out of the Tahoe.

The crunch of glass under their shoes set Tim's nerves on edge as they approached the door. Muffled voices filtered through the cracked security door. Tim rapped his knuckles against the metal. The voices cut off abruptly. He knocked again, louder.

"We're here for a documentary," he called out. "Heard you might be someone to talk to."

Silence. Tim shifted his weight.

"Got press passes," he tried again. "From America."

A gruff voice finally responded. "America? This is Cascadia."

Sarah stepped forward. "We've also got a letter from Governor Skye Flower." She pulled a folded paper from her pocket and held it up to the narrow opening in the door.

Tim pictured the man behind the door scrutinizing the letter, searching for any sign of forgery.

"How do I know this is real?" the voice said. "Not even on official letterhead."

Tim suppressed an eye roll. The guy was paranoid as hell.

"I understand your doubts, sir," Sarah said evenly. "But we are who we say. My contact was…" Tim's mind went blank. Who had hooked them up again?

"Tinsel Ivy! That was her name."

A chuckle came from inside, followed by the screech of metal as the door swung open.

"That's all you needed to say."

Sarah and Tim stepped into the poorly lit shack. In the corner, a television emitted a soft glow, showing a paused scene from what seemed to be an old film. The room felt crowded, with a worn-out recliner only a few feet from the screen.

The man who let them in was rail thin, with only wisps of hair left on his mottled scalp. He introduced himself as Glenn, a lifelong Washingtonian.

"That must be a long time," Tim commented.

Glenn let out a husky laugh. "So, you wanna make me a movie star, huh?"

While Tim engaged Glenn in small talk, Sarah's gaze drifted over the walls. Photo frames hung haphazardly, some with cracked glass, others held up by yellowing tape.

"How long did you live in Seattle?" she interjected.

"Too long," Glenn grunted. "Going on forty years now. Bought this place over forty years ago." He shook his head, his expression turning grim. "Now it's worthless. Two years back, they slapped a yellow notice on it. 'Structurally Unsound,' it said. But she's still standing. Creakier, but still standing."

Sarah's eyes lingered on a photo of a smiling young family, a younger Glenn, alongside a woman and two young girls. Even now, his pain was palpable. She couldn't imagine his loss.

"This spot should work perfectly," she said briskly, redirecting her focus. She gestured for Tim to join her. "We can set up here for the interview."

Glenn shifted, looking uneasy. "Those pictures, they're personal."

"I understand," Sarah whispered. "Seattle was my home, too. I lost people in the quake as well."

She placed a reassuring hand on his shoulder. "We can position the camera so they aren't in the shot. And you can review the footage before we leave, we'll cut anything too private."

After a moment, Glenn nodded reluctantly.

Tim hefted the camera bag over his shoulder. "I'll grab the rest of the gear from the truck," he said, heading for the door.

As it swung shut behind him, Glenn turned to Sarah. "Don't know what good you think this will do," he muttered. "Doubt anyone will even see it. Folks out east don't want news of Cascadia getting out."

Sarah's lips quivered into a wry smile. "I interviewed your governor just yesterday. This may well see the light of day."

Glenn snorted. "Things don't change, I suppose."

The door creaked open again, and Tim lugged in several cases, each labeled "Property of Cascadia." He clicked one open to reveal pristine equipment.

"This stuff's nearly brand new," he remarked, impressed. "Must've made it through the quake untouched."

As Tim set up, Glenn regaled Sarah with tales of days gone by. She pointed to a photo of him as a young man, grinning, with his arm around a woman and two girls.

"Bet each of these pictures has a story," she said.

Glenn's expression dropped. "The youngest, she... she didn't survive the quake," he said with a shaky voice, eyes getting teary. "My other daughter, she's out east somewhere. Haven't heard from her since it hit."

Sarah squeezed his shoulder gently. "Tim and I will do everything we can to get a letter to her."

Glenn brightened. "You'd do that?"

"I've got contacts who can track her down," Tim assured him.

Glenn fervently shook their hands and blessed them both. "From the bottom of my heart."

Sarah took a deep breath as Tim announced they were ready to film. This was the moment she had worked so hard for, for months.

Glenn looked uneasy as he moved around in the old recliner. "Shouldn't I practice what I'm gonna say?"

"No need for that," Sarah whispered. "I want raw emotion. Just speak from the heart."

Though still hesitant, Glenn nodded. Sarah settled into a folding chair opposite him, gazing intently into his careworn face. Behind him hung the pictures, a visual chronicle of his decades in Cascadia.

Tim adjusted the camera angle, then stepped back. "Check, check - microphone levels sound good." He held up five fingers. "Rolling in five, four..."

As he silently mouthed "three, two, one," Sarah leaned forward. This was it. The shutters lifted on a life defined by both joy and sorrow. She would capture it all.

CHAPTER 16

Sarah stared at the lines on Glenn's face and at his eyes. Those eyes told a thousand stories and more.

"Glenn, I bet you've seen a lot."

Glenn's calloused hands rubbed together, his thick fingers knotted by arthritis. He let out a small chuckle as he thought back.

"I worked part-time at the local bowling alley in the afternoons and evenings. Got some free bowling with the job," he reminisced. "My days were nothing special, just the usual routine. I'd stop by the coffee shop in the morning to catch up with some old buddies."

Sarah leaned forward. "And your old buddies now?"

Glenn's hand shook as he fidgeted with the silver ring adorning his finger. He inhaled deeply, attempting to control the quiver in his voice, but it faltered. Recollections from that fateful morning at the bowling alley inundated him. "They were there too. But they never made it out," he said through a choked sob.

Sarah could see the pain etched on his face. She grabbed a tissue from her Kleenex box, offering it to him as if it were a lifeline.

Her voice trembled with compassion, resonating from the profound depths of her being.

"Glenn... I can't even comprehend your pain." She extended a tender hand to rest on his shoulder, aiming to provide some solace amidst his torment.

Glenn barely registered her words, dismissing them with a dismissive flick of his hand as though he could physically ward off the compassion she was extending toward him.

Sarah ventured further into his realm of torment. "What's your reality now? How do you navigate each day?"

The weight of Glenn's world seemed to pull his shoulders down further than ever, anchoring him to the harsh truth of his life.

"My day begins with the ritual of making coffee," he said, motioning toward an antiquated percolator on the counter. Its once radiant exterior was now marred and discolored by countless mornings spent in service. "Occasionally, Megan pays a visit. She never arrives unprepared - invariably bringing along some sweet temptation like a glistening donut or a croissant. Treats are scarce."

Sarah's gaze drifted to Glenn's coveralls. Layers of dirt and motor oil were encrusted around them, resembling a shell of hardened armor that revealed the countless hours he had spent in grueling labor. Each stain and tear told a story of hard work and determination, a testament to the man standing before her.

Her thoughts consumed her until Tim's snap of his fingers abruptly brought her back to the present moment. Her gaze lingered on Glenn's face, noting the years of exposure reflected in his weathered features, and the roughness of his hands caught her attention. Although he appeared tired and worn out, his eyes revealed a noticeable strength and resilience that contradicted his age. She wore a small smile as she directed another question toward him.

"Can you tell me more about Megan?"

Glenn's eyes misted over, lost in memories. "Megan's my grand-daughter. We visit at least twice a week to share stories. Her momma was my daughter." His voice cracked, and he reached for a tissue to wipe away tears.

"Megan and I, we've lost people dear to us." A wave of emotion washed over Glenn as he openly wept, his shoulders shaking with grief.

Undeterred, Tim kept filming, zooming in to capture the raw intensity of the old man's pain.

After a moment, Glenn took a shuddering breath and regained his composure. "Please, let's continue."

Sarah nodded. "Do you think New Seattle will ever look like its former self again?"

Glenn barked out a harsh laugh. "Who'd want to return to that crowded, expensive mess?" He shook his head wearily. "Sure, it was a beautiful city, but too overpriced. You can't imagine what this little shack was worth before the quake." The lines on his face deepened as he reminisced about a time long gone.

"Oh, I can imagine," Sarah said with a knowing smile.

Glenn looked exhausted, his eyelids drooping.

Sarah asked, "Are you up for more questions?"

Glenn laughed. "I didn't invite you in for a quick chat."

Sarah leaned forward intently. "What's your vision for this city in ten years?"

Glenn's eyes lit up. "A city with the sturdiest, most well-constructed buildings in the world. Make New Seattle the gateway to the future of engineering."

Sarah beamed. "What a wonderful vision."

Glenn stood abruptly. "Excuse me, gotta use the restroom." He hurried off.

Sarah turned to Tim. "Think we got enough?"

Tim nodded, looking satisfied. "That was a great interview. But we'll probably need at least ten more like it."

Sarah sighed deeply. This was going to be an extensive project.

Glenn returned with renewed energy. "I know someone else who may help you," he said to Sarah and Tim. "My granddaughter Megan. She sees the world through the eyes of young folk."

Sarah became intrigued. "How can we find her?"

Glenn walked over to a worn book on the counter, flipping through the pages until he found what he was looking for. He revealed a slip of paper with the words "Megan's Place" scrawled across it, accompanied by map coordinates below.

"How far away is it?" asked Tim, eager to continue their journey.

"Not too far," Glenn assured them.

As Tim gathered his equipment, Sarah hugged Glenn warmly. "It was lovely meeting you. We'll be in touch."

Glenn waved it off with a smile. "Y'all come back now."

With that, they set out on their quest once again. Tim turned to Sarah expectantly. "Shall we go meet Megan?"

She nodded. "Megan it is."

CHAPTER 17

The afternoon sun hung in the sky, casting a warm, golden hue that bathed everything in a radiant glow. The light illuminated the charred remains of what were once bustling streets and thriving businesses, creating a hauntingly beautiful scene.

Tim's fingers clenched the steering wheel tightly, his nails leaving indents on his palms as they cautiously maneuvered the treacherous roads.

They'd been driving for an hour, going through a never-ending scene of destruction until they finally reached what Sarah thought was Bellevue. Relief surged through her when she noticed some traffic amidst the desolate cityscape. Their headlights carved bright trails through the daylight.

"Take a right," Sarah directed, pointing down a tree-lined street. As they turned the corner, the once dim and desolate scene transformed into a vibrant oasis. Lush trees and plants lined the sidewalks, their branches reaching out toward each other in a friendly embrace. The sweet scent of flowers and freshly cut grass filled their nostrils.

The laughter of children playing basketball echoed through the street, bringing life to the previously quiet neighborhood. Adults gathered outside their homes, chatting and laughing with one another, their voices creating a symphony of community. Smoke rose gracefully from barbecues scattered throughout the area, inviting all who passed by to join the festivities. This was a place of resilience, where destruction had not won, but sparked a sense of unity and strength among its inhabitants.

A massive concrete barrier, towering over ten feet in height, dominated the end of the street. It was even more imposing because of the barbed wire that lined its top.

As they drove, a townhome with a small yard appeared before them, its untouched beauty serving as a painful reminder of the lives lost and the irreplaceable homes destroyed. After finding a suitable parking spot for the Tahoe, Tim and Sarah walked toward the front door. Summoning his courage, he inhaled deeply before knocking, his heart pounding as he wondered about the unknown that awaited him on the other side.

"Just a minute," a man's voice called out from inside.

Sarah glanced at Tim, her eyes searching his face for reassurance. "Do you feel safe?" she asked.

"Compared to the rest of our journey, this place is like a trip to Disneyland," Tim quipped.

Sarah's laughter bubbled up, breaking their tense silence.

The rhythmic thud-thud of approaching footsteps echoed beneath them, each thump making Sarah's heart skip a beat.

In a scene straight out of a suspenseful movie, the door ominously creaked open, and standing before them was a man whose size was as remarkable as his height. From behind a formidable metal screen, he watched them intently, his curiosity clear in his gaze.

"What do you need?" he grumbled.

Sarah's gaze flickered between Tim and the human mountain standing before them. She smiled and said, "We didn't come for food."

"ID?" the man asked, squinting at them through the crisscross pattern of the screen door. Tim sprang into action, whipping out their press passes.

The man took his time scrutinizing their IDs. After what felt like an eternity, he grunted and muttered, "Hang on." He then slammed the door shut.

Sarah could feel her heart as they stood waiting. She tried to focus on the vibrant street around them, the laughter of children playing, but the tension in the air was impossible to ignore.

After a few minutes, the door opened, and out came this young woman with wavy brown hair. The man was looming behind her with his arms crossed. Sarah wasted no time and started explaining. "We talked to your grandpa, Glenn, and—"

She gave them a once-over, eyeing their stuff.

Tim sprinted back to their Tahoe, snatched a video cam, and hustled back to the home.

"Look, here's part of the interview," Sarah said.

Tim pressed play, revealing their interview with Glenn.

"Come on in," she said, opening the security door. "Please sit at the round table in the kitchen."

As they stepped into the home, Sarah noticed the contrast between the world inside and the chaos just beyond the street. The warmth of the kitchen enveloped them.

The overhead lights illuminated the spotless walls and floors. Sarah admired their surroundings. Megan put a lot of effort into keeping the place immaculate, creating a sanctuary for those who entered it.

"The name's Antonio," the figure boomed, thrusting out a hand that could have wrestled a grizzly bear. He stood at an impressive six feet seven inches, his face chiseled like stone and topped with a wild mess of dark curls.

Megan chuckled lightly as she clung to his waist. "We met in this place they called Camp Myrtle after the quake," she added. "Some government genius came up with that name. We just called it Camp Apocalypse."

Tim gave them a look. "How many people did Camp Apocalypse accommodate?"

Antonio burst into laughter. "You wouldn't believe me if I told you! They never restored the internet. Three years without cat videos. It felt like we were stuck in some bizarre reality TV show, *Survivor: Caveman Edition*!"

Megan gently elbowed him. "Focus, Antonio! He asked about the headcount, not your social media deprivation."

"Oh, right," Antonio remembered. "At its most crowded? Over five thousand of us packed into tents and makeshift shelters. Picture the line for the portable toilets!"

Megan interjected, "Speaking of lines... anyone fancy some coffee and donuts?"

Tim patted his stomach and nodded at Megan. "That would be amazing."

Megan went into the kitchen while Antonio kicked back in a giant recliner. "Hey! You like football?"

"I played all four years in high school, never faced someone as big as you. It's been about a decade since then. The Chiefs have taken care of my football fix."

"Nice. I played tight end at Oregon State. Since we don't have any way to communicate with the outside, my football-watching days are over, unless some neighbors play."

"Antonio," Sarah interjected. "I think we should interview you and Megan together. Your story would resonate with so many people."

"Thank you. I'm honored." Antonio said, pulling Sarah into an unexpected embrace.

Megan walked in with a plate full of donuts. "An interview, you say? I would love to."

Tim slipped out, "Gotta grab something," before peeling away to retrieve the equipment from the Tahoe. He was hellbent on capturing every angle.

As he neared the SUV, a gangly teen with clothes that he swam in materialized at his side.

"Yo, what's all this?" The kid asked.

"We're shooting a documentary."

"No way! You gotta meet my family!" The boy's enthusiasm was contagious. He pointed toward a blue home tucked between two neighboring houses down the street.

Tim hesitated. "I'll chat with my partner. We might swing by later."

With that half-promised possibility lingering in the air, the boy bolted back toward his home, leaving Tim alone again. He mulled over potential issues of spending too much time in this neighborhood.

Inside, the shadows danced on the kitchen table, making Megan and Antonio's faces look all kinds of shades. The room buzzed with cameras as Sarah watched her subjects, knowing their story was super important.

As Tim entered the room, his "Okay" pierced the stillness, the sound bouncing off the walls.

I'll be ready in a minute," he snapped, his voice sharp. "We're good to go," his voice tinged with a hint of excitement. As the countdown reaches its last moments, the anticipation grows with each echoing number - "Three... two... One..." The word lingers in the air, filled with a palpable sense of excitement.

CHAPTER 18

The light from the overhead fixtures bathed Antonio and Megan in radiance as they perched on the worn-out kitchen chairs. They faced Sarah across the chipped table. Behind them, photographs clung to the white wall - snapshots of smiling faces, sunlit vacations, and cherished moments with loved ones.

"Antonio," Sarah began. "How long have you lived in the Seattle area?"

Antonio's eyes sparkled. Despite his tired expression, there was a flicker of adventure and liveliness in his eyes.

Sarah shifted her eyes to Megan. "And you, Megan?"

"Please, call me Megs!"

Sarah nodded. "So Megs, how long have you been here?"

"My entire life," she murmured. "And I don't plan on leaving."

Antonio's eyes snapped to Megan, his brows furrowed in concern. "Hey, let's drop the Grim Reaper talk, alright?" he interjected.

Megan nodded, her tousled, sun-kissed hair falling across her face. She swept it back with a graceful gesture. "Yeah, you're right," she agreed. "Let's rephrase that. I plan on sticking around for as long as I can see into the future."

A gentle breeze rustled through the air, bringing with it familiar scents of home - the smell of freshly cut grass, blooming flowers, and sizzling BBQs. For Megan, that place was more than just a physical location. It was a part of her identity, woven into her very being. Leaving it behind seemed unfathomable.

Leaning forward in anticipation, Sarah asked: "So you guys are planning to stay put?"

"Hell yeah!" they chimed in perfect harmony.

Antonio's fists balled up. "We've made up our minds," he declared. "We're going to rebuild this place brick by brick."

Sarah bobbed her head. She could practically taste the raw emotions swirling through the air—fragments of their shattered pasts coming together to form a mosaic of resolve and survival.

"So where did life kick-start for you, Antonio?" Sarah queried, while Tim silently held a cue card behind the camera.

"Torrance," Antonio answered casually. "It's close to L.A."

"Ah," Sarah said. "Did you experience one before?"

"No ma'am, this was my first quake," Antonio confessed. He fiddled with his fingers. "And hopefully, my last. They say it will be another 250 years or more before we get another one. I don't plan on living that long."

Sarah turned back to Megan, who sat with her head bowed, her hands clenched. "What about you, Megs?"

"Same here. This quake was my first rodeo, too."

Sarah leaned forward. Others' experiences validated her haunting dreams. "Can you share your experience on that fateful day?"

Megan's voice trembled. "It was like the start of senior year, right after summer break." Her eyes filled with tears. A choked cry stuck in her throat as she relived that devastating memory of her mom's last crushing hug before school. The memory was vivid, a burning agony that set her heart on fire.

"Hold up," Sarah cut in. "Give me a second." Tim nodded but let the camera keep rolling, capturing this raw display of emotion.

Sarah stood up from her chair and approached Megan. They wrapped each other in a tight embrace.

"I'm so sorry," Sarah said into Megan's ear. "You guys have been through a lot."

Still holding each other close, Megan and Antonio turned toward each other and shared a kiss charged with years of battles fought and victories won.

"This woman! She's my anchor," Antonio admitted. "She's the reason why I'm still here."

Sarah pulled back slightly and looked at them both, asking, "You guys good to continue?"

They nodded.

"Where were we?" Sarah asked, her voice gentle as she tried to ease back into their conversation.

"My day. I was at school. My first class was Spanish 3A. It was on the ground floor..." She shuddered. "I wouldn't have survived if I'd been there."

"Tell me about your next class," Sarah encouraged.

"It was creative writing," Megan continued. "I sat next to the windows, looking at the blue skies. It was comfortable, you know? Just a normal day." She paused. "Then it happened. There was this sudden jolt, like slamming on the brakes. All my classmates looked around, confused. Some were making nervous laughs... until the real shaking began."

Megan's face twisted. The echoes of that nightmare were still vivid in her mind. "It was like a freaking nuclear blast," she began. "The earth shook so hard it knocked people off their feet. Screams filled the air, and chaos broke loose. My heart was thumping like crazy. I could practically hear it as I bolted for the window." She paused, taking a second to gather herself. "Get out through the window! That's what I yelled at them. But some were too scared, choosing to risk it with the door instead."

"Once we made it outside," she continued, her voice breaking slightly, "we found ourselves scattered across this wide-open field. Trees toppled like sticks. The sound of our school crumbling to pieces still echoes in my mind. I was in shock. I didn't know what to do or where to go."

Tears streaking down her cheeks, Megan painted a chilling picture of how the ground beneath them seemed to ripple like some pissed-off ocean during a storm. As their haven crumbled into dust before her eyes, Megan could only remember the bone-chilling screams of classmates trapped within its falling walls.

"It's okay," Sarah chimed in. "Take your time."

Antonio reached out to Megan.

Sarah turned to Antonio. "Can you talk about what happened?" she asked.

He nodded. "I worked in construction," he began. "I was driving to my job site–a new skyscraper in downtown Seattle. The project I was working on was supposed to be one of the most advanced structurally, able to withstand the world's strongest earthquake, or so they claimed."

"I was on I-5, just a mile from my exit," Antonio continued. "The traffic was stop-and-go. I could see the skeleton of the building I was working on from the freeway. When the quake began, it was like the cars started dancing."

"It took me a few seconds to realize what was happening. I got out of my car to see sections of the freeway collapsing. The freeway swallowed some cars."

"Then… I saw my building swaying until it snapped like a stick." He exhaled.

Sarah asked if he was okay, and he nodded. "Please take your time," she said.

After taking a few deep breaths, Antonio continued. "The shaking didn't stop. Smoke was rising in the air, car alarms were going off, and the sound of the Earth moving; it sounded like a freight train."

Sarah couldn't shake the memories of that day, and she shuddered involuntarily. "Can we move ahead a bit?" she proposed. "Can you tell us how you two first met, as if it's just for the audience?"

They locked eyes and smiles broke through their somber expressions, the first glimmer of joy since they began the interview.

"Both of us ended up in the same camp," Antonio said

"Camp Myrtle." They echoed.

"Yeah, we were in a camp with thousands of others. It was a pretty depressing place. But one day at dinner, I ended up at the same table sitting across from her."

Megan sighed. "Dinner time was always so sad. Hundreds of others with kids screaming and babies crying. I remember asking for salt, and Antonio passed it to me."

Antonio smiled. "It was electric–something just clicked between us. We tried to start a conversation in the cafeteria, but eventually found a bench outside where we couldn't stop talking about our families and lives."

"We became besties real quick," Megan said. After a few months, we got work orders with housing choices. We thought it'd be better to stick together in this lonely world.

Sarah's curiosity piqued. "What type of work orders?"

"The U.S. government gave people a choice," Megan explained. "Either stay here and help rebuild or move to another region."

Sarah thought back on her camp ordeal, remembering how she had contacted a friend in Kansas who helped her find a job just two weeks after the quake. "Tell me about your jobs now."

"I'm a baker now. I've been making all those donuts and pastries."

"I've been helping rebuild homes that aren't very damaged. I've been working on this street, doing my part to turn it back into a neighborhood."

"Thank you both for your hard work and dedication," Turning to Tim, she gave him a nod. "I think we have enough."

With the cameras off, Sarah and Tim thanked them, and they all embraced, sharing a moment of solidarity amidst the lingering shadows of the past.

Tim packed the equipment into the car while Sarah stood nearby.

"Hey, Sarah," Tim called out. "I heard about a boy who lives in that blue home over there. His family adopted several orphans after the quake."

"We should try to interview them tomorrow."

Megan asked, "Do you guys have a place to stay tonight?"

Both hesitated before shaking their heads.

A warm smile spread across Megan's face. "You must be exhausted. You're more than welcome to rest your head on a comfortable bed. It may not be the luxurious Ritz, but it's home."

Sarah's tired eyes widened. "Really?"

Megan nodded. "Mi casa es su casa."

"Thank you so much," Sarah breathed.

Antonio joined in. "You can stay in the guest room if you'd like. It has two beds."

"Tomorrow is a new day," Tim remarked with a small smile.

They exchanged knowing glances, understanding the unspoken words that bound them together.

CHAPTER 19

Sarah's eyes opened to darkness. The only sound in the room was Tim's light snoring. She breathed a sigh of relief, grateful that horrifying nightmares had not plagued her during her sleep. Instead, her mind had drifted to hazy dreams of people coming together in their new community.

Careful not to disturb Tim, Sarah slipped from beneath the sheets and tiptoed across the cool wooden floor. She made her way to the top of the stairs, glancing at the clock on her way: 6:50 am. It was late enough for a quiet morning walk.

Stepping outside, the warm sun's gentle touch on her face only emphasized the emptiness within her as she longed for Ethan. Her hair rustled in the September breeze. Tomorrow was the third anniversary when The Big One completely transformed the world. Hoping for a fresh start, she prayed they could construct a new society, free from the errors that plagued their past.

The homes before her stood in stark contrast to the crumbling ruins, their vibrant colors and cheerful façades a painful reminder of the happiness she had lost. Fresh coats of paint gleamed under the morning sun. Gardens teeming with meticulously trimmed shrubs and colorful blooms lined the sidewalks, while some lots even boasted quaint miniature cottages that looked as if they'd leaped straight out of a fairy tale. The sight was far removed from the wreckage she remembered. Her mind whirled with questions. Was this resurrection a result of American or Cascadian intervention?

The hum of conversation wafted toward her from up ahead. She heard a conversation coming from two older men seated in lawn chairs, their faces marked with wisdom. Their hands cradled steaming mugs, steam dancing upwards to join the crisp morning air.

Sarah paused, feeling the warmth of the sun on her skin. Inhaling deeply, she gathered her resolve and plunged forward. With a spring in her step and an exaggerated smile, she confidently approached the men.

"Top of the morning!" she called out, ready to dive into conversation with these strangers and hopefully unearth some answers to the riddles bouncing around in her skull.

The man, with a beard as long and white as Santa Claus, gave her a look of disbelief. "You're here because...?" the stranger questioned, looking puzzled.

"I'm shooting a documentary," Sarah clarified. "I'm hunting for personal tales about life post-earthquake."

Santa Beard let out a belly laugh. "Well then! At the crack of dawn, I drag myself out of bed and stumble toward the kitchen to make some coffee. Meanwhile, Earl reluctantly drags himself over. He's not a morning person. We sit around jawing about this and that."

Earl grunted in agreement.

"So if you think our morning coffee klatch is worth filming, I'm game," Santa Beard finished.

Sarah chewed on her bottom lip thoughtfully. How could she coax them out of their shells? Then an idea popped into her head. "Are you two fans of sweets? I've got Snickers, Twix, Reese's..."

Santa Beard's eyes twinkled.

Earl scratched his grizzled chin. "What's the hook?"

"You grant me ten minutes of your time for an interview. You get your pick from my candy stash," Sarah offered temptingly. "I know sweets are harder to come by these days."

The duo shared a quick look before nodding in agreement. "Deal," they chorused.

"Does 10 am work?"

They nodded again. Sarah couldn't help but chuckle as she moved on. The smoky skies of Seattle felt like another lifetime. She respected those who stayed and rebuilt but knew this place would never feel like home. Or at least the home she remembered. Once they aired her documentary, could she return to America? No time for that now, she scolded herself. Concentrate on the present. She chanted it like a calming mantra, pushing away the encroaching shadows.

Today will be a good day.

Today will be a good day.

She spotted a young girl playing in her front yard, giggling as she chased a butterfly. The sight lifted Sarah's spirits, and she quickened her pace, determined to make the most of the sunny September morning. The little girl reminded Sarah of her niece back home and a pang of homesickness hit her.

Pushing away the cloud of troubling thoughts, Sarah drew closer to the tiny figure. "Hey there, little adventurer! Are you having a grand time trying to catch that fluttering butterfly?" she asked.

The child halted her pursuit, turning to peer at Sarah with a cautious gaze. A few seconds passed before she gave an affirmative nod, causing her two brunette pigtails to bounce animatedly.

"And what might your name be, brave butterfly chaser?" inquired Sarah tenderly.

"Emily," came the quiet response from the girl.

"What a beautiful name you have. I'm Sarah." She extended her hand for a tiny high-five. "It's lovely to meet you, Emily."

A modest grin tugged at Emily's lips. "Are you new here?"

Sarah responded with a nod. "I'm just here for a tiny vacation."

Emily tilted her head inquisitively. "Where do you live?"

"I used to live in Seattle, but now I live in Wichita, Kansas, I've been on quite an adventure around different places."

"Wow! Where is that?"

"Pretty far away. We drove many hours to get here."

"I'm here to film a documentary. My partner and I are talking to people who survived the earthquake."

Emily's eyes grew as round as saucers. "Wow! Were you in the earthquake?"

Sarah paused momentarily, contemplating how much truth she should reveal to this innocent soul. "Yes, I was."

Emily lowered her voice. "Was it scary?"

"Super scary," Sarah said. She pointed at the front yard, bursting with colorful flowers. "Your house is so pretty! And those flowers over there, they look as if someone sprinkled them with fairy dust!"

A smile spread across Emily's face. "Those are my favorites! My mom lets me water them every single day. Want to come smell them with me?"

Sarah followed Emily to the flower bed, which burst with vibrant blooms in all shapes and sizes. The sweet scent of the flowers filled her nostrils, and she couldn't help but feel a sense of joy. At that moment, surrounded by magical flowers and Emily's infectious happiness, Sarah forgot about her fears and worries. It was going to be a perfect day.

Chapter 20

Sarah strolled into the kitchen and a symphony of aromas, freshly baked bread and rich coffee, wrapped around her like a warm blanket. Antonio, Megan, and Tim huddled around the wooden table, their laughter bubbling up from steaming cups of coffee.

"No freaking way. Actual VHS tapes," Tim chuckled. "Those things are practically fossils."

"Right?" Antonio responded. "We were clearing out these abandoned houses when I stumbled on this treasure trove. Some football nut had left behind a box of vintage NFL films."

Megan playfully rolled her eyes. "Trust Antonio to turn a post-apocalyptic world into his football paradise. But hey, it's not all bad. Between his ancient sports collection, my hoard of cheesy romance novels, and his questionable collection of action figures, we're pretty much set for entertainment."

"This is my history class in action," he retorted.

Sarah slid into an empty chair that creaked under her weight, a comforting sound that took her back to lazy mornings at home. She reached for a bear claw pastry still warm from the oven and bit down;

flaky layers crumbled in her mouth, releasing buttery goodness that melted on her tongue.

"Mmm... Megan," she complimented. "Your baking skills are next level! Where'd you learn to cook like this?"

Megan beamed back. "I was lucky enough to work as sous chef at the Fairmont," she revealed. "But now, well, life's taken quite the detour."

Sarah marveled at how Megan and Antonio kept their spirits high despite the chaos. She sipped her coffee, letting the liquid soothe her nerves. She could almost forget about the crumbling world beyond their walls. For that fleeting moment, all her fears and worries seemed insignificant.

Clearing her throat, Sarah began, "So, I ran into these two old-timers today, Earl and some bearded dude. They've agreed to let me interview them at 10 am for our documentary."

Antonio chuckled. "Oh yeah, Earl and Waylon. Those two are like our local watchmen. They're out there rain or shine under their makeshift canopy so they don't miss any action."

"How'd you manage that? Those guys are as tight-lipped as they come," Megan inquired.

"Well... I might have bribed them with the promise of raiding our candy stash." Sarah said.

Megan and Antonio exchanged glances.

"Scoring a piece of candy is like hitting the jackpot these days," Megan mused. "I'd sell my grandma for a Reese's peanut butter cup right now."

Tim snorted. "Hold your grannies," he said, before vanishing.

Antonio shot her an amused grin, "Ah, you're getting the hang of our wild west here. Candy's the new bitcoin."

Like clockwork, Tim reappeared with two boxes of Reese's cups - their golden wrappers glinting. He handed them to Megan with an expression that screamed, 'Your wish is my command.'

Megan's eyes popped almost comically as she took one from the box and peeled off its wrapper with a reverence usually reserved for holy texts. "Tim, you're my hero."

Tim dipped his head before pivoting back to Antonio and Megan. "Post-interview, we can swing by the Blue home and see if any other brave souls are up for screen time. Our docu-drama is picking up steam."

Sarah felt a flicker of optimism ignite within her. They had food, a roof over their heads, and potential interviewees lined up.

Antonio flashed a toothy grin. "If you guys shoot outdoors, you'll have volunteers lining up."

Megan added, "And you can crash here for as long as you need."

"We appreciate everything," Sarah said. Things were looking up for their project.

Chapter 21

Tim zoomed in on Earl's worn face, the deep lines etched from years of living life to the fullest outdoors.

Earl's eyes lit up. The camera panned to him, revealing a wide grin on his face. "The seventies," he said, his voice loud and proud. "Music had soul."

Waylon's head jerked back, his messy hair flying around. "Are you serious?" he shot back. "The eighties punk scene was way better! The Clash and Black Flag were legendary - they made music that mattered." He leaned in closer. "And don't forget about Misfits or Dead Kennedys. Or Minor Threat." He pointed upwards for emphasis. "They were all part of this vast movement, their sound reflecting the rebellion against society!"

Tim smiled at their heated discussion. It was a pleasant change from days spent interviewing survivors who only had despair in their eyes. This conversation felt like a breath of fresh air.

Laughter broke out from the other side of the room. Tim turned his camera toward it. Earl laughed loudly at Waylon's passionate defense of punk rock.

Sarah was laughing so hard she could barely speak. "I'm sorry," she said. "But I just imagined you two dancing at a disco."

Even Tim couldn't help but laugh. They kept him and Sarah going amidst all the surrounding devastation. They knew they had to find humor wherever possible to keep their spirits high.

Shoes scuffling on the pavement caught Tim's attention.

"Are you filming?" the boy asked.

Tim met the boy's gaze and nodded. "We're gathering stories."

The boy nodded and ran off, his sneakers slapping against the broken asphalt.

Tim straightened up, steadying the camera on his shoulder once more. He knew that no matter how long it took, he and Sarah would continue to gather stories and shed light on the truth. It was the least they could do in the face of such tragedy.

Sarah took a deep breath as she turned back to Earl and Waylon. She had one last question that had been weighing on her mind this whole journey. "You two have seen a lot in your lives," she began. "Do you think New Seattle can rise from the ruins?"

Earl and Waylon exchanged a glance.

"I'd love to see this city get back on its feet, but I doubt I'll be around to witness the revival," Waylon said.

Earl nodded.

Sarah turned. "What about you, Earl? Do you think New Seattle can come back in your lifetime?"

Earl thought about the question. "If this place recovers while I'm still alive, it will require an enormous group of volunteers who will work hard and rebuild. But who knows, with so many vacant homes, we might all get free houses in Seattle!"

They shared a laugh at the absurdity of that notion. For a moment, the faint glimmer of hope lifted the gloom that had settled on their hearts.

Sarah's laughter abruptly died in her throat as she felt a cold shiver crawl down her spine, sensing the eyes of the growing crowd fixated on her.

A wide grin spread across Tim's face as he unclipped the camera from its tripod, his fingers eagerly pressing record to capture the vibrant assembly, the air filled with laughter and jubilation. Surrounded by a diverse group of people, their mismatched outfits reflecting a tapestry of unique experiences, their smiles and laughter filled the air with an infectious sense of joy and camaraderie.

Adding these unfiltered and genuine insights into how these individuals were managing amid destruction could be a valuable opportunity for their documentary. As he swept his lens across the crowd, it captured an array of expressions; some stared blankly, desensitized to their surroundings, while others watched him keenly, as if hoping that his camera signified incoming aid.

Tim focused on a boy's gaunt face and haunted eyes that held stories beyond his years. This child represented the city's potential future if there was one.

Sarah stepped up confidently to address the crowd, her voice echoing. "Who would like to contribute to our documentary?" she asked.

Almost half raised their hands enthusiastically. Sarah and Tim exchanged glances. How could they interview everyone?

Sarah leaned toward Tim. "Let's split them into age groups for individual interviews."

Tim nod.

Sarah took a deep breath and faced the crowd, her voice projecting as she asked, "Could you kindly organize yourselves by age?"

The crowd rearranged, creating separate groups of kids, teens, adults, and seniors. Optimism surged within Tim, seeing such unity amidst chaos.

Sarah approached her first subjects–about a dozen children–who looked up at her with wide-eyed anticipation. She crouched down to their level. "Will you help us tell your story?"

Tim kept the camera rolling as Sarah coaxed out their experiences. Some narrated chilling tales of loss, while others shared inspiring stories of bravery and compassion that brought tears to Sarah's eyes.

With each group she moved through–the anxious teenagers, the grief-stricken adults, and older adults with decades of memories–Sarah listened attentively, her voice filled with empathy as she encouraged them to share their experiences.

As the interviews ended, Sarah embraced Tim, tears streaming down her face. "Thank you," she said into his ear. In that moment of shared triumph, they kissed spontaneously.

Sarah pulled back, her cheeks flushed with embarrassment. "I'm so sorry..."

Tim's hand grasped hers. "There's no need to apologize." Their gazes met and held, acknowledging a spark ignited amidst desolation, something beautiful blossoming in ruins. The air seemed charged with electricity as they stood in the aftermath of their passionate embrace.

CHAPTER 22

The anniversary of The Big One was fast approaching, and memories of the tragedy that struck three years ago lingered in people's minds. Time felt stagnant. Sarah and Tim met up with their friends, Megan and Antonio, for a last dinner together. Afterward, they would gather under candlelight, reflecting on the loved ones they had lost too soon.

"Here it is!" Megan called out, presenting their dinner with a flourish. Meatloaf wafted invitingly from the table, flanked by mashed potatoes dotted with colorful vegetables and bread fresh from the oven.

"Good Lord," Tim exclaimed. "I haven't had home cooking in ages."

Megan's eyes twinkled. "We kept the ground beef in the freezer for this."

As they dug into their meal, laughter spilled like a soothing medicine for their troubled souls. Sarah couldn't help but join in.

"Imagine this. My last supper would be a crime spree just to get another bite of my mom's legendary fried chicken," Antonio declared. "I crave it like a zombie craves brains," he moaned.

Megan tried to interject, but Antonio playfully silenced her with a shush, wagging his finger like a schoolteacher.

"It's story time! First course: wings so hot they'd make a dragon consider a career in firefighting." His eyes sparked. "Next up is Doritos, hotter than a summer fling..." He paused for dramatic effect. "...crowned with pizza," he proclaimed.

"And for the pièce de résistance?" He reclined in his chair, arms folded behind his head with smug satisfaction radiating off him like heat from fresh asphalt. "Strawberry cheesecake and mint ice cream," he concluded.

Sarah's candle flickered ominously. Tomorrow, raw emotions would fill the air. But right now, amidst shared laughter and stories of times past, she felt a bond that only standing together through hardships could create.

She could feel the storm of anxiety gathering inside her, threatening to break loose. Gripping the windowsill tightly, she tried to steady her hands and blink back the tears in her eyes.

"Tim," she called. "Can you come up to the room?"

He appeared within moments. "What's wrong?" he asked, moving closer to her.

"I may need some help for tomorrow," she admitted. Her eyes brimmed with unshed tears, and Tim instinctively reached out to wrap her in his embrace.

"I'm here for you," he said.

Sarah took a deep breath. "I need to visit someone," she said.

"Who?" Tim asked.

"Ethan."

"I understand."

Sarah nodded. "I need to go to his grave. His job at the bank downtown. He had no chance. He would say his building could withstand an F-5 tornado and a 9.5 earthquake." She paused. "We were getting married on Halloween. It was our favorite day of the year."

Tim squeezed her hand, knowing that tomorrow would be a tough day. They gathered the camera equipment - one for the tripod with a steady shot and another to capture the raw emotions that would undoubtedly surface.

Descending the stairs, Megan and Antonio were waiting with candles in hand. Megan passed one to each of them. "We don't have a shortage of candles," she joked.

"Sarah told me there was no power for several weeks after the quake," Tim said.

Megan's nod was slow and weighted, her eyes glistening with unshed tears, a silent acknowledgment of her profound heartache. Through gritted teeth, she added, "It's infuriating! Not a single month goes by without a blasted power outage, disrupting our lives and leaving us boiling with frustration."

Tim's jaw clenched tightly, his head shaking in disbelief, bitterness filling his mouth like venom. "Unbelievable. I can't fathom living like that."

The moon cast a pale glow over the small crowd gathered in the park, their faces etched with grief and sorrow. Sarah clutched her candle tightly, the flame casting shadows on the ground as she walked beside Tim, Megan, and Antonio.

Silent tears and hushed voices permeated the atmosphere, with some standing still in reflection. Sarah noticed the younger children in attendance, wondering if they could recall the devastating earthquake that had changed their lives forever. She didn't like to think about it often.

A melody played, filling the air with its melancholy notes. Sarah recognized the tribute to those who had lost their lives after The Big

One. As the song continued, some mourners sang along while others wept, the music touching raw nerves and reopening old wounds.

"Does this ever get easier?" Sarah asked.

He hesitated. "I don't know, but we learn to live with it."

After an hour, one organizer stepped forward with a smile. "It's time for game night," she announced. Heads perked up and smiles replaced the sadness that had weighed heavily upon them all.

Sarah and Tim sat at a table, playing Trivial Pursuit Celebrity Edition. The game must have been at least thirty years old, its original box long gone and replaced by a tattered paper bag. Yet, as they played, Tim marveled at the passion of that community. He thought about how different things were when people were slaves to their phones, disconnected from each other.

The fading sound of a church bell snapped Sarah and Tim out of their daydream. Their eyes met; it was time to return to Megan and Antonio's home.

Out of nowhere, Ashley T.'s voice sliced through the silent night. She emerged from the crowd that had gathered behind them. Her eyes glistened with unshed tears.

"Thank you." They hung in the frosty air like an invisible banner. "You've brought us hope when we were at our lowest."

Sarah and Tim responded with modest smiles, expressing their gratitude for the warm welcome they'd received from everyone. Despite knowing what awaited them, they took comfort in this newly formed bond, which would linger long after they left.

Hand-in-hand, they began their journey back under a sky illuminated by the moon, casting a magical silver-blue hue on everything around them. The air was heavy with the fragrance of blooming flowers, intermingling with the earthy scent of dampness, a sharp contrast to the growing unease in Sarah's mind.

"Sarah," Tim announced. "Are you alright?"

She turned toward him slowly before nodding. "I'm just apprehensive about what lies ahead."

His grip on her hand tightened reassuringly as he confessed. "I feel it too."

As they ascended the porch steps leading to Megan and Antonio's home, an ominous creak sent chills down Sarah's spine.

"Sarah?" Tim squeezed her hand, his voice radiating comforting assurance. "Remember, we're facing this together."

His words touched her. "Thanks," she said. "That means everything to me."

His gaze locked with hers. "Always."

Megan and Antonio opened the door to their home. Cozy warmth enveloped Sarah, pushing back the darkness lurking outside.

Chapter 23

S arah jolted awake. Sweat coated her skin, chilling her in the cool morning air. The nightmare had been vivid, her fiancé waving desperately for help as the building crumbled around him. She shuddered, remembering the days after the quake that had torn apart their lives.

"Tim," she said. She reached over and tapped his shoulder, rousing him from sleep.

He grunted, shifting positions but not fully waking. "What?" he mumbled.

"Come on, Tim, we need to get moving. Today is a big day," Sarah insisted.

"Okay," Tim muttered.

"Let's pack up and go. I don't want to be driving around Portland after dark."

Sarah shuffled her feet across the carpet as she collected their meager belongings, her mind replaying the faces and names of those they had encountered on their journey: the warm smile of Angela, the quiet strength of Juan, the rough exterior but kind heart of Waylon, the wise words of Earl, the quick wit of Antonio, and the unwavering determination of Megan. And there was surely more to come, and more strangers turned companions with unique survivor experiences to share.

"Are you sure you want to do this?" Tim asked.

"I have to!"

With a nod, Tim shouldered his backpack.

Sarah's breath hitched at the sight of his chiseled muscles. She averted her gaze, feeling a strange mix of guilt and yearning.

"Hey," Tim said, tapping her shoulder. "I'll be with you every step of the way today."

Sarah turned to face him, a faint smile playing on her lips as she inhaled his earthy scent. They stood mere inches apart, their breaths mingling in the charged air between them. As Tim pulled her into a warm embrace, Sarah's resolve crumbled. She lifted her face to his, seeking solace. They kissed.

It quickly escalated, their mutual passion igniting like wildfire, threatening to consume them both. For a moment, they lost themselves in each other, forgetting the ruined world around them. Reality crashed down upon Sarah, and she pushed Tim away.

"What did I do?" Tim asked.

"You're engaged. I can't be the one who destroys your relationship." She drew herself up, trying to regain control. "I'm sorry. We need to remain professional."

Tim nodded. "Alright," He sighed. "I'm going to rinse off." As he headed for the kitchen to boil water for his makeshift shower. Showers were a rare luxury, with most people boiling water to clean themselves. The ever-present stench of body odor was a reminder of their reality.

Tim scowled at the thought of his smell, knowing that warm water and cloth could only do so much. The sound of boiling water fills the space. However, the water was only safe to drink after filtering.

Sarah listened to the steady hiss of the boiling pot. Her thoughts wandered back to the passionate moment they'd just shared. She couldn't shake the feeling that the fire within them, if left unchecked, could be their undoing.

After several minutes, Tim grabbed the pot and carefully walked to the bathroom. In the dimly lit bathroom, steam rose from the pot. The room filled with the comforting yet bittersweet warmth that momentarily banished the chill of the early morning air.

"Damn it," he muttered. Was their passionate embrace a fleeting moment of desire, or had they crossed a line they couldn't uncross? He was engaged, after all, and Sarah had been just a friend before this journey. Now, the possibility of something more loomed. "Focus, Tim," he scolded himself, splashing warm water on his face. He knew that if they were to survive the perils of Cascadia and complete their documentary, these desires needed to be kept at bay. Yet, the thought of being trapped somewhere together, with only each other for support, ignited a spark within him that refused to be extinguished.

"Sarah," Tim breathed out. Somehow, she had become more than just a colleague to him. She was the embodiment of their mission.

Sarah approached the bathroom door, giving a knock. "Tim. Is everything alright?"

"Just freshening up as much as possible. I'll be out soon."

"Take your time," she called back. "But not too much time. We've got work to do."

"I hear ya," Tim said, stifling an unexpected wave of affection as he patted his face dry with a damp towel. He had to keep reminding himself why they were there. It wasn't a love quest, but something more significant. He pushed open the bathroom door and found Sarah waiting.

"All set?" she asked with an arched eyebrow.

"Let's get this show on the road!"

Together, they made their way down to the kitchen, where a container of coffee sat on the counter like a beacon of hope in their early morning gloom.

Sarah grabbed it and started spooning grounds into the percolator. "Living like this every day," she mused aloud, "would definitely require a strong reliance on caffeine."

"That's exactly what I was thinking. This documentary is going to flip the world upside down."

"Yes, but that's our job, let people know what happened here."

The coffee machine beeped its last note and filled the kitchen with an inviting scent. Sarah poured herself a cup, took a careful sip, and found it tasted peculiar, nothing like her favorite boutique brews she remembered from her Seattle days.

"Here," Sarah said, pushing a mug toward him. "You look like you need a pick-me-up."

"Thanks," he responded as he sipped his drink.

"I grabbed some pastries," Sarah mentioned as she picked up a croissant from a box nearby. Even without butter, Sarah appreciated each bite of the flaky and tasty croissant from the nearby box, as if it might be her last meal, a coffee and croissant combo.

"Why are you chuckling?" Tim asked.

"No reason. Let's make today memorable, okay?"

"Sounds good to me."

Sarah looked at his face and then his cargo shorts' full pockets and laughed again. "What's with all the stuff?"

He grinned. "Just mace cans, a taser, and a Swiss Army knife, just in case."

Her thoughts wandered to the potential hazards they might face, "Better safe than sorry."

"We should get going." Tim grabbed pastries from the box and stuffed them into a paper bag. "These should hold us over until lunch."

As they were about to leave, Antonio's voice stopped them. "Wait! Don't leave!"

"Antonio, what's up?" Sarah asked, turning around to see him hurrying down the stairs with a flushed face.

"Megan's got something for you guys. Just a sec." Antonio and Tim joked around while they waited; their laughter was a welcome distraction for Sarah's jittery nerves. Megan arrived carrying two bags, which she handed over to Tim with a sly smile. "Here you go; this should keep you fueled for today," she said, nodding toward the bags.

Tim looked inside one bag. "Megan, this is crazy! Pastries, cookies, bread... This is incredible!"

"For sure," Megan assured them both with a glance at Tim and Sarah. "You'll need your energy out there."

"You do not know how much we appreciate this," Sarah said.

As they said their goodbyes and shared hugs, Sarah promised they would make it through this journey and return to share their story. It wasn't just about getting through anymore—this was about uncovering the truth buried beneath their world's wreckage.

With one last thank you, Tim and Sarah walked out into the unpredictable daylight beyond their haven's doorway. The door closed behind them with an unsettling sound, sealing their fate.

CHAPTER 24

As Tim and Sarah maneuvered their way through the streets of New Seattle, the car's windows framed a city still struggling to rise from the ashes. The sky above was an angry gray, casting shadows that seemed to swallow the surrounding buildings whole.

"Sarah," Tim glanced at her, his voice steady. "What do you remember from that day?"

Sarah closed her eyes, feeling the weight of memories she hadn't visited in months. "I was getting ready to go to school. My class started at 11," she began. "I was texting Ethan all morning. We were talking about wedding plans and invites. We were planning to get married on Halloween dressed in costumes. It was fast approaching, and I wasn't nearly ready."

"Wow, that sounds so cool," Tim said.

"It would have been. I had just gotten into the shower when I felt the first jolt that nearly knocked me down. I did not know what was coming. Then it started. I was trying to keep my balance and hoping it would end soon."

The car slowed to a crawl as they navigated around a pile of debris.

In the brief silence, the echoes of car alarms filled her ears once again, just as they had on that day. "The shaking gradually got worse, and it seemed to last forever," she continued, her voice trembling. "First, I heard car alarms, then the power went out, and then... screams from my apartment neighbors."

"God, that must have been terrifying," Tim murmured.

"I had to get out of there. The building was rocking and I panicked. The perks of living on the first floor, at that moment, felt like a death trap." She shuddered. "I squeezed through the small window in my bathroom, scraping my naked body against the rough edges. I fell and stumbled toward a nearby clearing. Trees were being uprooted and crashing down all around me. When I looked back, I saw my apartment building tremble before crumbling onto itself."

Tim glanced at her. "You don't need to continue," he said.

She shook her head. "I'm fine. It was completely unreal. I kept closing my eyes, hoping I would wake from this nightmare." Her voice wavered. "The streets were opening up with cracks, making them impassable. I lost my phone in the apartment. The quake continued for several more minutes."

As they continued driving, the shadows cast by the ruined buildings grew longer, their distorted forms stretching across the cracked pavement like fingers reaching out to capture them.

"I can hear the screams." Sarah's voice trembled. "They resonated off the crumbling apartment buildings, a haunting symphony." She paused. "And then the screams stopped. The buildings had given in to the attack, and it felt like I was drowning in my helplessness. People were losing their lives all around me. I couldn't do anything to stop it."

"Sarah," Tim's voice was gentle as he reached for her hand. "You don't have to continue if it's too painful."

Sarah shook her head. "The trees became matchsticks," she said. "A stray power line hissed and sparked against the bark of a tree, igniting into a raging inferno. The fire spread, consuming everything in its wake. I searched for a haven but did not find any."

Tim exhaled. "God, Sarah... You're so damn brave," he breathed.

Sarah shook her head dismissively. "No bravery involved there Timmy boy, just survival instincts kicking in." She glanced down at their entwined hands.

"Bullshit Sarah! It takes guts to search for Ethan with no idea what's coming next. And now you're on this journey? You're Wonder Woman!" He insisted.

"I pushed through. I reached the shopping center." She continued. "The parking lot was a madhouse, people panicking and screaming left and right." She paused. "And out of nowhere comes this booming voice. 'Get down!' I dropped face down, using my arms as a shield just as a massive explosion rocked the place."

Tim let out a low whistle. "Tell me you at least grabbed shoes?"

Her laughter rang out. "Oh no, Timmy. I was standing there completely naked until a compassionate soul came to my rescue and covered me with a blanket. After the tremors subsided, I gathered what I could find and trudged toward downtown."

Tim shook his head. "I can't even picture how terrifying that must've been."

"Downtown was like stepping into a war zone." She paused for effect: "The streets were littered with shards of glass and steel beams twisted into grotesque shapes. People started forming rescue teams."

"And Ethan?" Tim asked.

"His building was a mountain of rubble," Sarah said. "A piece of plywood was in front of what would have been the entrance bearing the address of his business tower. My heart plummeted. There remained this flicker of hope within me." She paused again." About fifty of us scoured through the ruins for survivors."

"Did you...?" Tim's question hung in mid-air.

Sarah shook her head. "No. I never found him."

She clung to that same glimmer of hope that had kept her going during those harrowing days, the belief that she could somehow piece together her shattered life from the rubble of her past.

"I can't help but wonder if things would have been different had I left just a little earlier," Sarah mused.

Tim cast a sidelong glance but remained silent.

"A day passed, and suddenly I heard a faint, mysterious noise emanating from the wreckage. And that's when it happened! I saw them: a survivor! A burst of elation filled my chest, my heart pounding with hope. Shrouded in a heap of debris, their faint outlines sent shivers down my spine. I raised my voice as loud as I could, my words echoing through the air, desperately seeking help from anyone within earshot. The Mexican search and rescue team, known as Los Topos, arrived with a sense of urgency, their eyes scanning the disaster scene for any signs of danger. The group brought their trained dogs, using their skills to aid in the search for additional survivors. After several days had passed, a heavy cloud of despair hung over most people, their faces etched with sorrow and tears staining their cheeks. Surrounded by the acrid stench of smoke and death, I fought to keep moving forward. The masks they provided did little to shield us from the overpowering stench. The government forced us to leave the area. We had no choice but to hike up the streets of Seattle until we arrived at another camp. The atmosphere at that camp was so oppressive that it felt like being in a jail. Fenced in with scheduled meals... didn't feel like freedom."

"It sounds like an awful movie," Tim says.

"Through clenched teeth, she spat the words, 'They grudgingly let us use a phone as if it was some favor they were doing for us. My friend from high school moved to Kansas with her family her junior year. Fortunately, I could locate her contact information online. Thanks to her, I was evacuated from Seattle and found myself in Kansas, a world away. When I arrived, all I had were the clothes on my back, which unfortunately reeked of body odor and a medley of unpleasant smells. No matter how much time passed, I never grew accustomed to the odor, not even after I departed.

"Tim," she said, "I never had a proper sendoff for my fiancé. I should have come back sooner."

As they approached the spot of Ethan's building, the air grew heavy with loss and despair. Massive piles of rubble littered the once-vibrant streets of downtown New Seattle, like silent sentinels guarding a graveyard of memories. Amongst the wreckage, Sarah noticed makeshift memorials adorned with flowers, photographs, and other mementos of loved ones swallowed by the disaster.

"Years will pass before they can sift through these piles," she thought. "And then, identifying people by bones and teeth... it'll be a grim task."

"We made it," Tim said, breaking into her thoughts. "This is the address, right?"

Sarah scanned the landscape, her eyes settling on a pile of debris. It looked untouched since her last days in the city, an unchanging monument to the tragedy that had shattered so many lives. She nodded, swallowing the lump in her throat. "This is it."

Tim parked the Tahoe across the street from where the building's entrance would have been. The haunting stillness of this abandoned town weighed heavily on them, suffocating any shred of optimism that may have lingered in this desolate place.

"Give me a minute, okay?" Sarah asked.

Tim nodded.

Stepping out of the vehicle, Sarah felt the ghosts of happier times swirling around her like leaves caught in a storm. She closed her eyes and drifted to the years she'd spent with her fiancé. His smiling face appeared before her as if he were free from the confines of the collapsed building. Taking a shaky breath, she began a one-sided conversation with him, her words a balm to soothe the wounds that had never truly healed.

As she stood amid the desolation, Sarah's voice trembled as she spoke. The eerie quiet of the devastated city seemed to amplify her words, making them echo and linger in the air.

"Hi... I'm sorry it took me so long to come back. I couldn't face it. But I'm here now, and I want you to know how much I still love you." She gazed at the surrounding ruins, a stark contrast to the love and life they had shared. With tears streaming down her face, Sarah could give her fiancé the sendoff he deserved, a tribute to their unbreakable bond that tragedy had torn apart.

Chapter 25

A putrid smell filled the air, assaulting Sarah's senses as she gazed at the massive pile of rubble. Her heart ached for the life she once knew, now destroyed by this disaster. She turned to look at the Tahoe parked nearby and waved to Tim, who sat patiently inside.

Tim's face paled as he stepped out of the vehicle, the smell assaulting his senses. The sight of the massive wreckage left him breathless, the sheer magnitude of it incomprehensible. He walked over to Sarah, his mind racing with images of terrified people running through the streets, seeking refuge in buildings that would eventually become their tombs.

Her watch beeped at 9:13 am, forever etched in Sarah's mind. It was when the world came crashing down on an otherwise ordinary morning. She shuddered at the memory, reliving the nightmare that had unfolded before her.

Tim approached her with a gentle embrace, his arms wrapping around her trembling body.

Grateful for his presence and understanding, she leaned into him.

"Thank you for listening," she whispered, her words filled with sincerity. "Thank you for being here," she whispered.

As Tim nodded, he took in the empty streets, once teeming with bustling crowds and the honking of cars.

"It's hard to imagine that just three years ago, these streets were bustling with the energy of people going about their day..."

Sarah's voice caught in her throat as she pointed to a distant corner. "That's where Ethan and I used to meet for lunch," she said. "At least once a week." She closed her eyes, trying to hold back the tears.

"I'm so sorry," Tim said, placing a comforting hand on her shoulder. They stood there in silence, united by the tragedy that had brought them together. "No one deserves this," he repeated, his words echoing hers as they held each other tightly.

"Let's go," Sarah said.

As they turned to leave, Tim gave her one last hug, feeling the warmth of her embrace and appreciating her resilience amidst indescribable anguish. Holding hands, they walked away from the ruins, their footsteps echoing with the memories of what once was and the determination to build something new.

The wind whistled through the shattered remains of the city, a haunting melody that echoed the desolation surrounding Sarah and Tim. They stood side by side, feeling the heavy weight of the harsh reality that had settled upon them.

"Will people ever feel safe here again? From earthquakes?" Tim asked.

Sarah's head shook slowly, her eyes fixed on the horizon where the sun was climbing higher, causing the ruins to cast long shadows. "How could they?" she said. "A thousand geologists can all agree that it won't happen again for centuries. But most people refuse to believe it. To them, if it happened once, it could happen again at any moment."

Tim sighed, his eyes tracing the path of destruction. He couldn't help but imagine how the destruction had irrevocably changed people's lives.

"Who can honestly tell people they don't need to worry about another earthquake in their lifetime or their children's children's lives?" Sarah continued. "It's not a bet I would make."

Tim reached out, briefly squeezing her shoulder in silent support. They stood there for a moment longer, enveloped by the weight of their shared grief and the impossibility of true recovery.

"Let's get going," Sarah said, her voice steady despite the turmoil within her. "As long as nothing blocks our route, we still have a few hours to reach Portland," Sarah said.

"Right," Tim agreed. As he opened the driver's side door, two identical Tahoes approached their vehicle. Tim looked at Sarah. "What's going on? Did we do something wrong?"

"Stay calm, Tim," Sarah said, eyes fixed on the approaching vehicles. The Tahoes blocked any chance of escape.

Tim's voice quivered as he turned to her. "Should we try to escape?" he asked.

"I'm sure everything's fine." But even as she spoke those words, a third Tahoe appeared behind them, boxing them in like prey awaiting the hunter's fateful strike.

A fourth Tahoe materialized and pulled up alongside their vehicle. The passenger window lowered with agonizing slowness, revealing a woman whose face was as cold and implacable as stone. "Sarah and Tim?" she asked.

They both nodded, unable to tear their gazes away from the woman's steely eyes.

"Governor Flower wants you," she continued. "We will escort you to her office."

"Are we in trouble?" Tim questioned.

The woman chuckled. "You're fine. But we need to go now."

Tim swallowed hard and started the electric motor, the vehicle lurching forward, desperate to escape this oppressive atmosphere. The two Tahoes in front of them eased off their brakes, their taillights glowing red. The convoy of menacing Tahoes slid through the desolate streets like a serpent, their dark windows reflecting the gloom that had settled over the city. Sarah could feel her heart constricting in her chest as she gripped the edge of her seat, trying to make sense of this sudden and enigmatic turn of events.

"Sarah. I don't trust this. Why would they send so many agents to retrieve us?"

"Do you think they want to question us?" she asked.

Tim hesitated. "Maybe we're in high demand," he suggested.

"I hope so," she murmured.

As they continued, the cars formed a tight formation around them, nearly blocking any chance of escape. She couldn't help but wonder why Governor Flower wanted them and what purpose they could serve in this broken world. And yet, despite the dread that gnawed at her, something within Sarah urged her to push forward, to confront whatever awaited them head-on.

"Tim," she said. "No matter what happens, we stay strong—together."

He nodded, his eyes meeting hers with a newfound determination shining in their depths. "Always."

Chapter 26

The dim light of the underground garage amplified the tension in the air. Sarah's heart raced as the metallic door groaned shut behind them, sealing off their only escape route. She wondered if she had done something wrong, inadvertently crossed a line, or offended someone important. She knew there were unspoken rules and customs she was yet to grasp, and the thought of frontier justice made her quiver.

"God, what have we gotten ourselves into?" she muttered, her eyes darting around the unfamiliar surroundings.

Tim sat anxiously by her side. He tried to conjure the image of his beloved, basking in the golden sun of their tropical honeymoon. But this thought shattered like glass as he weighed the consequences of being branded a traitor by his nation. The idea of being stranded, cut off from all he cherished, was a pain too great to bear.

"Are you okay?" Sarah asked.

"Uh, yeah. Just... thinking about stuff."

"Like what?"

"Like how things can change so quickly," he said. "One moment, we're just doing our jobs, and the next, we're accused of being terrorists by our government."

"Welcome to Cascadia, I guess," Sarah sighed. She recalled the news reports she'd seen before coming here, stories filled with chaos, riots, and lawlessness in Zone 1. But now that she was here, it was quite the opposite. The people they had encountered so far, Calvin, Angela, Antonio, and Ashley, were all remarkable individuals who showed courage and compassion in the face of adversity.

"Maybe it's not that bad," Tim suggested. "These people here… they've been through hell and back. If they can survive this, maybe we can, too."

"Or maybe we become another casualty in their fight for freedom."

The electric motors hummed as the cars rolled to a stop. Tim and Sarah's eyes met. The others exited their vehicles, leaving Tim and Sarah alone in the silence.

"Move it!" The woman's voice was a cold slap, her spine-rod straight posture and the curt snap in her tone making Sarah's skin prick. Her aura screamed danger and Sarah's mind went into overdrive, conjuring up many nightmarish scenarios. Was she facing some Cold War secret police? Could she even stand a chance if she tried to bolt?

Tim leaned closer. "Easy, Sarah. We've got this." His attempt at reassurance did little to quell the rising panic as they exited their vehicle, the looming figures of several uniformed officers behind them amplifying the tension.

Walking toward the building was like trudging through quicksand at every step. The silence was suffocating, broken only by their labored breathing as they desperately sought comfort in the face of fear.

They walked down a lengthy, slender corridor flanked by daunting portraits of stern-faced individuals. A mysterious red door marked the end, unremarkable in appearance.

"God," Sarah muttered under her breath, her fingers white-knuckled around Tim's hand as they neared the door, "I hope this isn't our swan song."

The door opened to a familiar smiling face, Governor Skye Flower grinning broadly. "I'm so happy you made it."

"It's not like we had a choice," Tim smirked.

Sarah gave him a slight jab in the ribs. The studio crackled with an electric energy, making the hairs on her arms stand on end. She glanced at Tim, his furrowed brow mirroring her confusion. "Is everything okay?" she asked.

"More than okay. You two may have saved Cascadia after all."

"How so?" Tim asked.

The governor leaned in. "The interview has crossed many borders, spreading its impact far and wide."

As Sarah's heart clenched, a chilling sensation spread through her stomach. When she agreed to conduct the interview, this outcome was not what she had in mind. Despite the unsettling nature of this truth, Governor Skye Flower forged ahead without dwelling on it for too long.

"With over a million views and more than half a million shares, the interview has garnered significant attention. The impact of your work is truly profound, surpassing our initial expectations by a considerable margin. However," the governor added, her voice trembling. "We need every frame you've captured, no matter how unsettling or disturbing. Our crew will edit the footage and send more runners. It's just a matter of time before the U.S. begins propagating its messages. Sarah, I need you to conduct a second interview. We have a carefully chosen panel waiting for you to engage in a discussion."

Sarah swallowed. "I'm honored that our efforts have been success-ful, but..." she trailed off.

"Governor Skye Flower," Tim interjected. "We'll do it. We'll con-duct the second interview."

Sarah looked at him, and he offered her a reassuring smile. Together, they had faced countless obstacles and challenges. Now, with the fate of Cascadia hanging in the balance, they would face this new trial head-on, emboldened by their shared resolve.

The governor extended a welcoming hand to Sarah and Tim. "You both must be exhausted. Please, enjoy a shower and something to eat before our next interview in two hours."

The production crew surrounding them seemed to inch away, re-pelled by their body odor. Tim and Sarah exchanged sheepish glances, fully aware of how unkempt they appeared after their journey.

"Follow me," said a short man, grabbing Tim by the arm. His voice was cheerful. "You look like you haven't seen a shower in weeks."

Tim chuckled. As he followed the man, he couldn't shake the feeling he was stepping into a surreal dreamland–where danger and hospitality coexisted.

"Once I'm done with you," the man promised, "you'll look like a model." He cast a critical eye over Tim's physique. "You have a nice body; we should find you some more form-fitting clothes."

As the man led Tim to the dressing room, he shared his past as a famous Broadway makeup artist stranded in Seattle when the earth-quake struck. "No matter what the disaster, people still need to look good," he mused with a grin, putting Tim at ease with his easy-going demeanor.

A woman took Sarah by the hand, leading her to another dressing room. Sarah noticed a paper bag adorned with a bow sitting atop the makeup table. She inquired about its contents, but the woman merely shrugged, claiming ignorance.

Curiosity piqued, Sarah approached the bag and found a hand-made card attached. Tears welled in her eyes as she read the heartfelt message, thanking her for her bravery and granting her honorary citizenship in Cascadia. The words twisted a knot of pride and fear in her chest–she had made a difference here, but at what cost?

As the countdown to their next interview began, Sarah and Tim grappled with newfound responsibilities. The weight of their influence loomed over them like a storm cloud, casting long shadows across the uncertain future that awaited them in this strange new world.

Sarah exited the dressing room, her heart pounding in anticipation. A woman with a gentle smile greeted her and motioned for her to follow. As they walked to the studio, the lights overhead flickered.

"Everything's ready for you," the woman said, her voice barely audible above the hum of the fluorescents.

In the studio, a careful arrangement of three chairs at a slight distance from each other created an open and inviting space. Positioned directly in front was another chair, elegantly reserved for Sarah.

Tim emerged from his dressing room, his nostrils filled with the aroma of food. He followed the scent to a snack room brimming with melon, cheeses, meats, and crackers. As he surveyed the spread before him, he felt conflicted. How could there be such abundance? When so many in Cascadia struggled for sustenance? His stomach twisted with guilt, but hunger won out. He quickly assembled a couple of sandwiches and retreated to a table with chairs.

"Are you ready to meet the panel?" Governor Skye Flower asked Sarah, pulling her from her thoughts.

"Ready as I'll ever be."

With a warm smile, the Governor introduced Ashley, a young teacher who couldn't have been over twenty-two. Sarah shook her hand, noting the firm grip and bright eyes. "We want Cascadia to be a mecca for higher learning,"

Next came Scott, a construction worker whose calloused hands were a testament to his tireless efforts at rebuilding the city.

Last, they presented Tanya as a member of the New Seattle police force, and her stern expression and confident posture marked her as a pillar of strength in this fledgling society.

"Thanks for being here," Sarah spoke to each of them, acutely aware of how vital they were to Cascadia's harmony. She couldn't help but wonder if it would take many more people like these to rebuild successfully.

As the clock ticked closer to the interview, Sarah's mind raced with questions and concerns. The future held so much uncertainty, but one thing was clear: she had become part of something bigger than herself.

With each bite of his second sandwich, Tim could taste the perfect combination of flavors - the crunch of the lettuce, the creaminess of the mayo, and the juiciness of the tomatoes. Despite the scarcity of food on the streets of Cascadia, the sight of cheddar cheese and cured meat was a welcome surprise. With each bite, a bitter taste lingered on his tongue, as if the weight of guilt had tainted the flavors, serving as a reminder of the countless sufferings endured by others.

The room was quiet, save for the distant murmurs of conversations and the hum of the fluorescent lights.

"Are you Tim?" A voice interrupted his thoughts, accompanied by the sudden touch of icy fingers on his shoulder.

He turned to see a woman with piercing eyes and a forced smile. She had pulled her hair back tightly, revealing a tense jawline.

"Uh, yeah," Tim nodded.

"I need a minute of your time," she began. "You can't trust everyone you meet here. Traitors are everywhere in Cascadia," she continued. "Watch your back and be careful with anyone you come across."

With that, she stood up and offered a tight-lipped smile. "Best of luck to you and Sarah," she said before walking away, her footsteps echoing through the silent room.

The insatiable hunger that once drove him had vanished and it was replaced by a gnawing feeling of suspicion and unease. Was she alluding to traitors lurking within Governor Sky Flower's inner circle? Were the people they trusted in this new land secretly working against them?

His mind raced. He had to speak with Sarah immediately. Without a second glance at the half-eaten sandwich, he threw it into the trash and stormed out of the room, his heart pounding in his chest.

CHAPTER 27

Rounding the corner, Tim's heart skipped a beat as he glimpsed the dimly lit studio, shadows dancing ominously within. The red light was on, casting a hue on the walls. He frowned, puzzled why no one had informed him that the interview was starting. He pushed open the door and entered the room. The atmosphere was electric.

There, at the center, was Sarah. Her eyes sparkled, her voice resonating throughout the space. Despite his efforts to remain detached, Tim knew that he was developing feelings for her, feelings that went beyond their professional relationship.

"Ashley," Sarah said, turning to the teacher, "how have you used your experience as a survivor to guide your students?"

"I believe it's our responsibility, especially those of us who were old enough to remember the earthquake, to educate and protect the younger generation as we rebuild."

Sarah asked, "Do you think being young allows you to connect better with the children?"

Ashley looked at her. "I don't think age or experience matters as much as who the younger generation will listen to and trust."

As Tim listened to the conversation, he couldn't help but think back to when he first met Sarah several months ago. A mutual friend had introduced them because Sarah was planning her documentary and didn't have a videographer for the project. She had invited him to her place to discuss the details, and he remembered being struck by her professionalism.

With her pulled-back hair, she looked more like a librarian than a documentarian. This initial impression, with her passion for telling stories, convinced Tim to jump on board with the project.

Sarah's gaze shifted to the foreperson of a construction crew. "Scott, how many homes have you and your team successfully rebuilt and built?"

"Today, on the third anniversary of the devastating earthquake, we have accomplished the monumental task of rebuilding 250 homes and constructing another 250."

A video played on the screen, showcasing Scott's construction crew celebrating their 500th completed home. "And we have no plans of slowing down. We believe we will reach one thousand in less than two years."

The production crew was clapping in the background, joining the celebration.

Sarah reached out to shake his hand. "That is truly incredible, Scott. Thank you and your crew for your hard work and dedication."

Sarah captivated Tim, commanding the room during her interview. He felt admiration, stirring up a whirlwind of emotions. Confessing his feelings threatened their working relationship but also endangered the life he had built with his fiancée.

The stage lights cast a glow on Sarah, illuminating her face as she continued the interview.

Tim's heart raced and his palms grew clammy as he felt an unsettling presence, unable to break free from the intense gaze that locked onto him. Memories flooded his mind, taking him back to the time he had shared the project with his fiancée, his heart sinking as he remembered the uncertainty that had filled her voice. He asked Sarah to dinner so they could all meet and make his fiancée feel better. And it worked like a charm.

But now, as he stood there watching Sarah expertly navigate the conversation, Tim wondered what his fiancée was thinking. Was she sitting at home, worried sick? The guilt washed over him like a relentless tide, threatening to pull him under. He shook his head slightly, forcing himself to refocus on the task at hand, capturing Sarah as she delved into the lives of these remarkable individuals.

Sarah turned to Officer Tanya. "Officer Tanya," she began, "how safe is New Seattle? We've heard stories in the U.S. about how lawless and dangerous this place is supposed to be."

Tanya's lips quivered in a chuckle. "Is that what they want you to believe? How long have you been here, Sarah?"

"Only a few days," Sarah admitted.

"And in those few days, did anyone attack you or make you feel threatened?" Tanya asked.

Sarah shook her head. "No, it's been quite peaceful."

"Exactly," Tanya confirmed. "The people living here want to be here. They want to rebuild their lives, not hurt others. The most significant issues we face are dealing with intoxicated bar patrons wandering the streets."

A small smile played on Sarah's lips, her laughter a welcome reprieve from the heavy atmosphere that seemed to hang over Tim's heart.

"And tell our viewers what makes your police department different from others in the United States?" Sarah prompted.

Tanya looked at her with pride. "All our officers must have a minimum bachelor's degree in either forensics or police science." The camera crew clapped as if this was a live show. "And second, all of our law enforcement officers must have extensive training in martial arts and become master negotiators."

"Very impressive," Sarah commented.

"And on top of that, all law enforcement must continue their education by taking required classes every year to improve their skills."

A production member approached them, his voice cutting through the atmosphere. "Cut," he declared. "This is more than enough."

From behind the cameras, the crew erupted into applause.

Governor Skye Flower emerged from the shadows and gracefully moved to the center of the stage. The clapping ceased, the room falling silent as if on cue, and all eyes turned to her.

"I would like to thank all of you," the Governor's voice filled the room. "Every one of you is fighting for the future of Cascadia. You will go into history as the saviors of a new land." She paused, her gaze sweeping across the faces before her. "There is food and refreshments in the break room. I am honored by your service." With that, she walked off the stage, her assistant trailing behind like a dutiful shadow.

Tim's heart pounded as he approached Sarah. He smiled, feeling the weight and significance of their work. Even if the United States banned him from reentering, he believed he had found a home in Cascadia.

"You were incredible!" Tim called out.

"Thank you," she said.

"There's something I need to talk to you about in private," he said.

"Should I be concerned?"

"Please," he urged. "Can we go somewhere more private?"

"Follow me," she instructed, her voice steady despite the uncertainty that had crept in.

As they walked away from the stage and into the hallway, Tim's mind raced with what he needed to tell her, the weight of his words. He struggled to keep his thoughts focused as they navigated the maze-like corridors.

His chest tightened, and he felt as though he'd been holding his breath all this time, waiting to share his troubling encounter with her. As soon as they entered her dressing room, he collapsed onto the couch.

"Tim, what is it?" Sarah asked.

"Something... strange happened," he began. "I was eating a sandwich in the break room when this stranger approached me. She was wearing a hoodie. I couldn't see her face. But she warned me."

"Go on," Sarah urged.

"She told me there are a lot of traitors in Cascadia, people who aren't truly loyal to the cause. And she warned us to watch our backs."

A chill ran down Sarah's spine. "Do you think we're in danger?" she asked.

"Maybe," Tim admitted. "We can't be sure, but we should be careful."

Before either of them could utter another word, a sharp, hollow knock pierced the silence, intensifying the heaviness in their hearts. "Sarah?" he called out, echoing through the empty hallway.

"What is it?" she asked, her voice filled with curiosity."

"Governor Flower is requesting your presence in her office," the voice echoed, its authoritative tone filling the room.

Sarah and Tim exchanged glances before they both stood up from the couch.

"We should go," Sarah proposed.

Tim trailed along, curious about what awaited them in the governor's office. Walking together, a tall woman emerged at the hall's end,
gesturing for them to come closer.

CHAPTER 28

A flickering fluorescent light in the Governor's office illuminated the room, causing shadows to dance across the sparsely decorated space. Nervousness consumed the Governor as her fingers rhythmically drummed on the surface of her large wooden desk, her eyes fixed on her assistant, Ally.

"I had a feeling this would happen," Governor Flower muttered, her voice filled with desperation, her hands trembling as she frantically searched for a solution. "It had crossed my mind as a possibility, but their swift action caught me off guard."

Ally gazed back at her with worry etched on her face. They had known each other since they were six and shared an unbreakable bond, closer than sisters. As they grew up, they remained inseparable, but while Skye Flower pursued politics and leadership, she even won class president in eighth grade, Ally stayed behind the scenes. She was introverted and content with supporting her best friend from the sidelines.

A look of fear that seemed to age her prematurely replaced Governor Flower's usually radiant smile. It had always been her greatest asset, but today she felt powerless as the weight of responsibility crushed down on her shoulders.

"Blue Skye," Ally's voice cut through the tense silence, using the familiar nickname only she could use. "We'll figure this out. We always do." Her words were calm but determined, trying to instill confidence in her shaken friend.

Governor Flowers' hands clenched into fists as she thought about the gravity of the situation. "Have we ever faced anything like this before?" She asked, her voice trembling. "Our people's lives are at stake and I'm responsible for their safety."

"You've been a protector your entire life," Ally reminded her, her eyes blazing with determination. "You have always risen to the challenge. This time will be no different."

Taking a moment to draw strength from Ally's unwavering support, Governor Flower closed her eyes and took a deep breath. When she opened them, a renewed sense of purpose.

"Thank you, Ally," she said. "Now let's figure out how to protect our people and keep Cascadia strong."

Ally nodded in agreement, pushing aside her fears as they focused on the daunting tasks ahead. Together, they would face whatever challenges came their way–they had done it before and would do it again with fierce resilience.

The dim light of the office cast ominous shadows on the walls as Sarah and Tim stepped inside, guided by Ally's silent gestures. Governor Sky Flower stood behind her desk, her usually radiant face clouded with worry. Gone was the smile that had once brought people together; in its place was a deep furrow in her brow.

"Please sit." Sky's voice bore the weight of the situation. As they settled into their seats, she extended her arm toward a side table and took hold of a bottle of vodka. "Would either of you like some?" she asked. "It's distilled locally, serving as a testament to our progress."

"Sure, why not?" Tim said.

Sarah shook her head, her lips pressed tightly together as if holding back an ocean of questions.

Sarah couldn't hold back her curiosity any longer as she asked Governor Flower, "Why have we been summoned here?"

"Sarah, Tim," Sky sighed, her eyes scanning their faces as if searching for the strength to deliver the news. "We received a news feed just minutes ago. The FBI has placed you, Sarah, on their most wanted list, offering a five-million-dollar reward for your capture."

Sarah's heart skipped a beat, her chest tightening as the words sunk in. She had always known their actions would have consequences, but this was beyond what she had imagined. Beside her, Tim shifted uncomfortably, awaiting his fate.

"Tim," Sky continued, her gaze now fixed on him, "you haven't escaped their attention either. The FBI has placed a million-dollar reward for your return to the United States."

Tim felt an icy shiver run down his spine as he exhaled sharply. He had hoped, perhaps naively, that he could avoid the government's attention—but it seemed his luck had run out.

"Is there anything we can do?" Tim asked, his voice quivering with desperation. "Any way to make this right?"

Governor Flower pursed her lips, weighing her options before speaking. As a heavy silence engulfed the room, Skye couldn't help but feel the weight of responsibility resting on her shoulders. She thought back to all the lives she had saved, and those she had helped save in times of crisis. She drew strength from those memories as she prepared to protect Sarah and Tim.

"I won't sugarcoat it," she admitted, her voice laced with sorrow. "This won't be easy. But we will face this challenge head-on, just like we always have with every other roadblock."

As the weight of their circumstances hung heavy in the room, Sarah and Tim looked at each other, their expressions a mix of fear and determination. They had come this far together, they would see it through to the end.

The air in the room felt heavy. Sarah's fingers clenched into fists, her nails biting into her palms as she fought to keep her voice steady. "Governor Flower, what are you going to do to protect us?" she pleaded, a desperate edge to her question.

"Allow me," Ally interjected, stepping forward, her eyes focused on Sarah and Tim. "I'm Ally, Governor Flower's assistant. Sky has arranged for her security team to escort you both during your time in Cascadia."

"Is that supposed to make us feel safe?" Sarah snapped, anger replacing fear. "We can never return home, and we'll be looking over our shoulders for the rest of our lives. What are you going to do about that?"

"I understand your concerns, and I promise we're doing everything to keep you both safe. Once the UN recognizes Cascadia and the free will of its citizens, you will be more secure."

"Years, Governor! It could take years before that happens! You know the United States doesn't give up easily." Her breath came out in shallow pants, her chest tightening at the thought of living in constant fear.

Skye nodded, her gaze unwavering as she met Sarah's eyes. "You're right–it won't be easy. But every step we take, like your documentary, brings us closer to our goal. It's ten steps forward for our fledgling country."

Sarah bit her lip, her resolve wavering as she searched Sky's face for reassurance. "I hope you're right," she said, the words barely audible.

"Hope isn't enough," Skye admitted, her eyes hardening with determination. "We need to fight for our future–and we will."

Within the dimly lit room, the small group of individuals grappled with the weight of the situation, their hearts heavy under the strain of an uncertain future. But within that darkness, a fire burned fueled by the shared resolve to protect one another and the people of Cascadia, no matter the cost.

Governor Sky Flower reached for the red phone, the urgency of her movements betraying her usual composure. Sarah and Tim exchanged nervous glances, acutely aware that their lives now hinged on the decisions made within these four walls.

"Bring them in," the governor instructed tersely into the receiver. As she replaced the handset, footsteps echoed through the hallway, approaching with purposeful strides.

Ally swung the office door open, revealing a formation of three men and one woman. Each bore the marks of a seasoned warrior, their faces etched with years of dedication to their craft. Governor Sky Flower introduced them as her trusted security team, her eyes fixed on Sarah and Tim.

The first man, Matt, bowed his head with a smile. "I'm happy to serve," he said. Another man, CJ, had a rough exterior but a friendly demeanor. "I'm here to protect," he stated.

"Lisa," she said.

It was the woman earlier who had been so demanding.

A towering man with a short afro and muscles that seemed ready to burst out of his skin approached Sarah and Tim.

"I'm Marvin," he announced. "I'll be your driver for the rest of the mission."

Tim raised an eyebrow. "We don't need a driver."

"Yesterday you didn't, but today you do. Trust that these professionals will keep you safe." She gestured toward Lisa and CJ, who would be in the lead vehicle, while Matt covered the rear.

Tim glanced at the intimidating security team, each armed with multiple firearms and ready for anything. He felt reassurance, knowing they had a powerful defense.

"Ready to hit the road?" Marvin's voice was serious as he spoke. "We've got a potentially dangerous journey ahead to Portland."

Sarah and Tim exchanged a determined look and nodded in agreement. Governor Sky Flower stepped forward, hugging them tightly. "Wishing you all the best on your quest for the truth," she said.

As Lisa held the door open, the group filed out of the office, carrying the weight of their mission on their shoulders. CJ turned to Sarah and Tim, his eyes searching for any sign of fear. "Do you feel safer with us by your side?"

"To be honest," Sarah stammered, "I can't figure out if having an army makes me feel safe or just reminds me of how dangerous it is."

As they settled into the Tahoe, Tim felt a moment of calm as the gentle hum of the electric motor filled the air. Sarah reached for his hand, feeling his fingers intertwine with hers.

"We're in this together," she whispered.

Chapter 29

The sun began its descent, casting a warm glow across the cracked and crumbling asphalt of the once-thriving I-5. Now renamed the Cascadia Interstate, it lay in ruins. Marvin carefully navigated the Tahoe through potholes and debris, each bump and crash reminding him of how far they had come since the disaster struck. The pang of sorrow he felt for the state of the world only intensified with every turn.

In the backseat, Tim was so engrossed in the old Sports Illustrated he had found that he didn't even notice the passing scenery. Amid the destruction, the glossy pages were a stark contrast, a poignant reminder of a bygone era. Sarah sat determinedly beside him, her pen gliding effortlessly across her notepad as she meticulously documented their journey. Her eyes burned with an unwavering determination to unearth and spread the tales of survival and strength from those who had endured the disaster. Every hastily written word was an unsteady testament to their trembling bravery, a desperate attempt to find solace amidst the shattering chaos.

"Tim," Sarah called out, but he seemed oblivious to her voice, lost in his world. She envied that ability to turn off reality. But there was no going back, not for any of them. Tapping him on the shoulder, she repeated his name louder. "Tim!"

He looked up, startled. "What's up?"

Sarah's voice broke the silence as they drove along the shattered remains of the Cascadia Interstate.

"Have you realized we haven't visited ground zero yet? We've been to so many places, but not there." She turned to Tim, her eyes full of curiosity and longing. "There must be so many stories on the coast. Imagine the lives of those who live near that naval blockade. It must be a whole new world for them."

Tim's expression turned somber, and he nodded thoughtfully. "You're right. How do we get there?"

But his words seemed to fall on deaf ears as they continued down the empty road.

The Tahoe rolled on, its engine humming as it pushed through piles of debris and abandoned cars.

Sarah felt a chill run down her spine. She couldn't imagine living in such isolation, being cut off from society, and being forced to fend for herself. And yet, she felt drawn to these stories of survival and hope, a mysterious puzzle waiting to be unraveled.

"Marvin," Tim called out suddenly, tapping their driver on the shoulder. "Do you know how we can get to the coast?"

Marvin's head perked up, scanning the road ahead with intensity. "Depends on where you want to go. Most places need a helicopter to get in."

"Three years later, and most routes are still impassable?" Tim's voice cracked, his stomach churning at the thought of being trapped in a confined space with minimal resources.

"Yep, but there is one route I know of: from Portland to Tillamook. Governor Flower made it a priority–said it was an economic lifeline for Cascadia, providing dairy and cattle."

Tim and Sarah exchanged glances, nodding.

"We're only fifty miles from Portland," Tim mused.

"True, but you know the only way to get from Seattle to Portland is by crossing the Columbia, right?" Marvin chuckled, sensing Tim's confusion. "You'll see soon enough. Just wait."

As the Tahoe continued its journey, Sarah felt the weight of their mission settling upon her shoulders. Each survivor they encountered, and each story they documented, painted a vivid picture of resilience, fear, and hope. The coast would undoubtedly reveal even more harrowing tales, and Sarah braced herself for the emotional impact ahead.

Tim, too, felt the gravity of their task. He stared out the window, watching the desolate terrain give way to the occasional green patch or surviving tree. They were venturing into a world of survivors forced to adapt and create new lives amidst the chaos. He wondered how they had managed, what secrets they held, and how their stories would change him.

As the sun disappeared, leaving only the silvery light of the stars, Sarah made a firm commitment to bring to light the stories of those who had endured.

A sliver of the moon hung low over the horizon, casting an eerie glow upon the battered landscape as the Tahoe rumbled along the cracked highway. The world held its breath, waiting for the delicate balance between light and darkness to be shattered.

"Hey, Marvin," Tim said, shifting in his seat to view the rugged landscape passing by. "Any ideas about where we'll spend the night?"

Marvin's fingers danced across the walkie-talkie, summoning a voice crackling with static from the other end. "We're taking the

Tillamook route. We're going to need a place to eat and stay overnight."

"Roger that," the disembodied voice responded. "I know just the spot. Follow our lead."

"Sounds good," Marvin acknowledged, his eyes locked onto the vehicle ahead of them as they continued driving down the bumpy road. "10-4."

The two lead vehicles inched forward, their tires crunching over rocks and debris as they navigated through the treacherous detours of the former I-5. As they approached Vancouver, the bleak desolation of the abandoned highway gave way to signs of life.

Sarah pressed her face against the window, taking in the sight of new buildings and homes that had sprung up amongst the ruins.

"Wow," she exclaimed, "the real estate market must be booming here. How does Cascadia even have an economy?" she asked, her brow furrowing as she gazed at the bustling town. "Isn't trading off-limits?"

Marvin sighed before responding, never taking his eyes off the road. "Well, we can't trade with the United States anymore, but we're still able to trade with Canada."

Tim's curiosity piqued, "How does the U.S. feel about that?"

Marvin chuckled darkly, the sound echoing through the cabin like a specter of the past. "Oh, you know they're not too thrilled about it. But hey, at least we have maple syrup and hockey sticks to keep us going."

As the convoy threaded its way through the city streets, the ghostly whispers of the wind seemed to taunt them with warnings of the unknown dangers that lay ahead. The tension in the air was palpable, and Sarah gripped the pen in her hand so tightly that it threatened to snap.

Placing a gentle hand on her shoulder, Tim murmured, "Easy there," his voice filled with concern. "We'll be alright."

"Thanks," she said, forcing a smile.

As they continued their journey into the heart of the darkness that had swallowed the world whole, Sarah knew she would not easily forget the stories waiting to be uncovered. And as the moon's eerie light played across the crumbling facades of the surrounding buildings, she couldn't shake the feeling that the shadows were watching, waiting for when they could claim their long-overdue victory.

The Tahoe rumbled toward the bridge that marked the gateway to South Cascadia. A chill crept down Sarah's spine.

"Border inspection station ahead," a sign warned, its letters faded and peeling. The few cars on the road slowed to a crawl, their occupants casting nervous glances at the ragged figure manning the station.

"Looks like we're up," Marvin muttered, steering the Tahoe toward the checkpoint. The guard, dressed in a tattered uniform that had seen better days, waved them through with a nod.

Sarah noticed a car pulled over. A man and woman stood beside it, clutching a young child as several uniformed officers searched their vehicle with a drug-sniffing dog.

"Marvin, why would they get stopped?" she asked.

He let out a slight laugh, shaking his head. "Rarely do you have families traveling these roads, especially with an empty roof rack."

"Empty roof rack?" Tim echoed.

"Exactly." Marvin nodded. "It's rare for anyone to travel this road without luggage. They must've looked suspicious."

Sarah leaned back in her seat, letting out an 'oh' as comprehension dawned. She felt sympathy for the family, caught up in the harsh realities of this new world.

The desolation of Portland soon gave way to charred remains of forested hills, a haunting reminder of the devastation wrought by the earthquake and the subsequent fires. "This was called Forest Park. It was such a beautiful backdrop."

Tim asked how anyone could have survived such an onslaught.

"Remarkably, some did," Marvin said. "And now, Governor Flower is trying to rebuild what's left."

As they traveled west, they saw a changed landscape, open fields with successful farms instead of barren land, showing how resilient people can be. A few trucks rumbled past them, laden with lumber, cattle, and other goods bound for distant markets. In this small corner of Cascadia, life had blossomed amidst the ruins.

"Welcome to our little utopia," Marvin grinned, his eyes twinkling with pride. "Governor Flower knew this route would be critical for commerce, and she was right."

Sarah's heart swelled with hope. The dark shadows of despair seemed to recede, banished by the promise of a brighter tomorrow. For now, at least, the future seemed a little less uncertain.

The Tahoe pulled into the gravel parking lot of the Dew Drop Inn. The log cabin-style building stood like a beacon amidst the surrounding darkness, its warm glow promising respite from the day's harrowing journey.

"A place to rest our weary bones," Marvin said, stretching his arms above his head. "This is probably the best restaurant in Cascadia. They almost always have supplies."

Sarah glanced at the trucks and service vehicles parked outside, noting their worn exteriors and makeshift repairs. Even the hardiest of these machines couldn't escape the scars left by the disaster.

"Must be the benefit of being on this main road," she mused aloud, her voice tinged with awe.

Marvin nodded in agreement. "Indeed. Governor Flower made certain of that."

As they approached the entrance, Sarah felt a newfound energy bubbling within her, fueled by the prospect of reaching Ground Zero and the coast soon. Sensing her excitement Tim, offered her a smile before pushing open the heavy wooden door.

"Hey there, weary travelers!" greeted a plump woman behind the counter, her apron covered in flour. "Looks like you could use some home-cooked goodness."

"We definitely could," Sarah said, taking in the delicious smells wafting from the kitchen. "Table for three, please?"

"Follow me," the woman said playfully, leading them to a snug booth where they could feel the warmth of the crackling fireplace.

"I must say, that is quite nice," Tim said.

"I feel like I'm sitting on history," Marvin jokes, testing the cushion's springiness.

"How about some drinks to start?" their hostess asked, whipping out her notepad.

"Water, please," Sarah said.

"We'll take three waters," Marvin added, rubbing his neck.

"You got it," the woman said with a grin before disappearing into the bustling kitchen.

As they waited for their drinks, Tim took in the eclectic mix of patrons around them - some deep in conversation, others lost in thought while nursing a glass of something strong.

"This place has character," he mused aloud.

"I love it," Sarah agreed, her voice quivering slightly, as she desperately sought connection with these strangers who had also braved their treacherous paths. Although they had their differences, there was an understanding that created a sense of connection between them.

"Here are your waters," their hostess announced, setting down a tray of chilled glasses. "Enjoy your evening."

"Thanks so much," they all said gratefully, feeling the cool liquid refresh their parched throats as they raised their glasses in a silent toast to new adventures ahead.

"Tomorrow, we'll make it to the coast," Sarah exclaimed, her voice tinged with determination and a touch of sarcasm. "And maybe we'll find some actual working toilets along the way."

Tim chuckled and nodded in agreement. "Yeah, or maybe a hot shower and authentic food that isn't canned beans."

Marvin joined in on the banter, grinning widely. "Ah, who needs fancy amenities? We've got each other and this cozy little inn. Plus, I heard they make killer apple pie here."

The trio traded stories and jokes as they devoured their meals and savored every bite of the delicious pie. As they drifted off to sleep that night, surrounded by the warmth and laughter of newfound companions, Sarah and Tim felt grateful for the small moments of joy amidst the chaos of their journey. And even Marvin couldn't deny that his apple pie was a definite highlight of their travels.

CHAPTER 30

The loud bang on the door jolts Sarah awake, her heart pounding in her ears.

Rubbing his eyes, Tim wakes up with a bewildered look. A shiver ran down his spine as he uttered, "Huh?" Their eyes darted around, searching for any signs of danger.

The door rattles again with another bang, causing Sarah to jump. "We have to see who it is." A muffled reply comes through the thick wooden door.

Battling against his heavy eyelids, Tim rubs his eyes and lets out a cough, attempting to banish his drowsiness before gruffly calling out, "Who's there?"

"It's Marvin. It's go time."

Sarah rushes to unlock the door, her veins pulsating. She comes face to face with Marvin's imposing figure blocking the entrance.

"Governor's orders," Marvin snaps. "Get dressed. You have fifteen minutes. Coffee is waiting downstairs."

Sarah slammed the door. Why the sudden urgency from the governor? She glanced at the clock's red numbers glowing in the darkroom. 5:15 am.

"Fifteen minutes to get ready at the crack of dawn," Tim grumbled, pulling on his jeans. "We're on a damn military schedule now."

Sarah grabbed some clothes and went into the bathroom. Her nerves jangled as she washed her face and hastily pulled her hair into a ponytail. Nothing had gone according to plan on this trip and now they were at the mercy of the governor and her men. She opened the door to find Tim waiting right outside.

"You okay?" he asked.

"I guess," Sarah sighed. "Not how I imagined things going, that's for sure."

The toilet flushed as Sarah spat out her toothpaste and turned to Tim. "How about you?"

Tim ran his fingers through his messy bedhead. "My hair is like a badger's nest."

Sarah chuckled from the doorway. "Have you looked in the mirror?"

Tim gave her a mock glare before walking into the bathroom. He began humming off-key as he brushed his teeth.

"I'm serious, though," Sarah said, leaning against the frame. "What would we do if we were stuck here in Cascadia forever?"

Tim stopped brushing and gave her a deadpan look. "Well, I've always wanted to become a bear whisperer. Maybe this is my chance."

Sarah rolled her eyes. "Great, I'll be stuck with a crazy bear man in the middle of nowhere."

Tim shrugged. "At least it's better than prison."

"True," Sarah nodded, "but we might have to hunt for our food. Do you think you can handle a spear?"

Tim grinned mischievously. "I was born for this. Plus, I make a mean squirrel stew." As Tim rinsed his toothbrush in the sink, Sarah's stomach growled.

"Looks like we're not the only ones thinking about food," Tim joked.

"I just hope breakfast is decent."

"Me too," Tim said.

"And who's paying for lunch?"

"I will, of course," Tim patted his belly. "I'll treat you to dessert if you find a spot."

They headed downstairs to find Marvin, Lisa, CJ, and Matt seated around a table, talking.

"Morning," Tim said as they approached.

"There's coffee on the table over there," Matt told them, pointing across the room. "Help yourselves."

Tim poured two mugs full. The rich aroma filled Sarah's senses.

"Oh God, I needed this," she murmured, sipping the hot coffee. The jolt of caffeine revived her fuzzy morning brain.

Tim took a long drink and sighed. "Best coffee I've had in ages."

Pale yellow light was filtering in through the windows. Sarah watched as the sky transformed from inky black to hazy gray blue.

The server sauntered over to their table, plunking two grubby menus in front of them. "Take your time," she mumbled, pouring more coffee into their chipped cups.

Tim scanned the breakfast options: eggs, sausage, pancakes, waffles, potatoes. The bacon had a line through it, with "Sold Out" written next to it. The daily special was homemade biscuits and gravy.

"I'll have the special," Tim declared.

"Just give me some eggs and sausage," Sarah stated.

As they waited for their food, they discussed their bucket lists.

"I've got five things I want to do before I die," Sarah said. "See the pyramids, go spelunking in a gigantic cave, visit the Galapagos Islands, scuba dive on a coral reef, and bungee jump off a bridge."

Tim nearly spit out his coffee at the last one. "Bungee jumping? Are you crazy?"

Sarah laughed. "Probably. But I want to face my fears."

"Have you ever gone caving before?" Tim asked with raised eyebrows.

"Just on a cheesy tourist tour," Sarah admitted. "But I want to get dirty, explore an untouched cave system."

As Tim nodded, his gaze drifted toward the agents' table. The room echoed with the boisterous laughter of Marvin, Lisa, CJ, and Matt.

"What do you think they find so amusing?"

"Who knows?" Sarah said with a shrug.

At that moment, their breakfast plates arrived, steaming hot and smelling delicious. But before Sarah could take a bite, Marvin sauntered over.

"You'll have to get that wrapped up to go," he said. "We're hitting the road."

Sarah's shot him a sharp glare. If they had not wasted so much time getting ready, they could have taken their time and truly savor their meals.

As she scooped the food into the to-go boxes, the aroma of the freshly cooked meal filled the air. As she contemplated the long drive to the coast, her growling stomach reminded her to eat before setting off.

Sarah and Tim gathered their takeout containers and followed the agents to the parking lot.

"Nothing like dining alfresco in a moving vehicle," Tim said wryly as they climbed into the backseat.

Sarah gave a short laugh. "Five-star cuisine it is not. But I guess we'd better get used to irregular meals. Who knows when we'll sit down to a real one again."

Her stomach growled in hunger as she glanced downwards at the container on her lap. The aroma of the scrambled eggs and sausage links was incredibly enticing, but eating them in the Tahoe would be far less enjoyable.

Tim had the same thought running through his mind. "I was looking forward to a meal at a table," he sighed. "But it seems like our bodyguards have other plans for us."

"I know, right?" Sarah shook her head. "Having them hover over us won't make it easy to get people to open up during interviews."

"You're not wrong," Tim agreed. "There's nothing like having cold and intimidating agents standing behind you to encourage transparency."

Sarah let out a dry chuckle. "Well, there's no point in dwelling on it now." She opened up her container and gestured to it. "Bon appétit!" she said before taking a forkful of eggs.

Tim smiled and followed suit. As they continued their journey to the coast, they ate their meals, wondering where their next destination would be. One thing was for sure: they had a long road ahead of them.

CHAPTER 31

The sun peeked over the horizon, casting a warm glow on the Tahoe as it cruised down the highway. The rhythmic hum of the electric motor blended with the gentle swoosh of the trees passing by, creating a soothing symphony that filled the car. Tim sat back in his seat, feeling the cool glass against his forehead as he gazed at the world speeding by. The landscape seemed to blur together in a hazy dream.

Tim's mind drifted to his only trip to the coast. He could almost feel the gritty sand between his toes and hear the laughter of his siblings as they chased seagulls on the beach.

Growing up in landlocked Kansas left little chance for seaside adventures, but Tim remembered that one family vacation with fondness. The day they arrived at Santa Monica, young Timmy couldn't contain his excitement–he bolted from the car sprinting straight into the frigid ocean, exuberantly splashing and frolicking until he was waist-deep in salty waves.

Although the drive may have been lengthy, the memories created during the journey made every moment worthwhile. To Tim, the beach held a significance that went beyond being just a location. The thought of that carefree little boy, who was so oblivious to the complexities of life and wholeheartedly embraced every moment, brought a smile to his face.

Sarah's face lit up, her eyes sparkling as she reminisced about her last day with Ethan, relishing the joy they shared.

"It was Labor Day. We had an amazing day. We rode the great wheel and went up the Space Needle." She sighed. "The following day, I woke up to the start of school. I went to the bathroom, and he called. I can remember it like yesterday. He was checking in with me before school. He seemed so happy. We were planning a trip to the coast that afternoon. It was the last time we spoke. Sometimes I wish we had been at the coast when it happened. We could have gone together." A tear slid down her cheek as she remembered their love.

Tim nodded, both of them lost in their memories. The thought of that beach now in ruins was both heart-wrenching and bittersweet.

As they dozed off, they held onto the dream of returning to the coast. As the Tahoe cruised toward the coast, the sun highlighted everything in its path. The smell of pine and Douglas firs wafted in through the open windows, giving off major wanderlust vibes.

The jolting sensation of the bumpy gravel track rudely snapped Sarah out of her daydream. The charred remains of the once vibrant forest loomed like eerie sentinels, casting long, haunting shadows. A thick gray blanket had smothered the sky, which had once been a clear blue.

Sarah felt confused. "Marvin?" she spoke up. "How much longer til the coast?"

A sinister laugh erupted from Marvin, accompanied by blasting heavy metal music reverberating through the car. A twisted grin spread across Marvin's face, causing every inch of Sarah's body to vibrate with unease. She fought against her restraints, her mind racing to make sense of their situation. Was this some sick joke? A twisted game? But deep down, this felt much worse.

As they hurtled down the road, each mile bringing them closer to an uncertain fate, images of terror fueled by the relentless beat of the music consumed Sarah's mind. The chaotic sound drowned her voice as she pleaded, "Where are you taking us?"

Tim's eyes snapped open, his breath catching in his throat, as he registered the unfamiliar surroundings and the deafening silence that enveloped him.

"We have to stick together," she mouthed above the blaring music, her heart racing.

Tim gave a definitive nod.

"We're in deep shit," Sarah said. "I don't know where they are taking us."

Tim's head was spinning. Was this really happening? Marvin's menacing smirk said it all. He was not just some random thug; he was a trained killer. Tim could feel the panic rising in his throat, choking him as he struggled to come up with a plan.

"We need a plan... Now!" Sarah said.

Tim's heart pounded in his chest as adrenaline surged through his veins, his mind racing to find an escape route. And then it hit him, they could bail out of the moving Tahoe before it was too late. It was risky, but staying stuck inside meant certain death.

"What? Are you insane?!" Sarah's eyes widened in shock at Tim's suggestion. She glanced at the rushing gravel road outside, her mind racing with terrifying possibilities. But what other choice did they have in the face of certain doom?

"Trust me," Tim assured her. He met her gaze with conviction as he thought about the fate that awaited them if they stayed inside. They needed to take a chance while they still had one.

Ready to make their move, Tim mouthed, "Are you ready?" and counted down in his head. Each second felt like an eternity, the tension building up inside him until it was almost unbearable.

Tim peered out the window and took in their surroundings. The treacherous slopes seemed to mock their chances of survival, but he refused to give up hope. He leaned closer to Sarah. "We need a plan for when we land."

Their eyes met. As they waited for the perfect moment to escape, time seemed to stretch out, each second feeling like an eternity.

"Where are you taking us?" she screamed, her voice drowned out by the relentless beat. Dread settled in Sarah's bones. This wasn't a trip to the beach.

She scanned the landscape. A creek was at the bottom of a nearby ravine. "There," she pointed, her voice trembling. "It's nearly suicide, but we have to try."

Marvin, oblivious to their exchanges, drummed his fingers on the steering wheel to the rhythm of the heavy metal music.

Tim glanced at Marvin, who seemed utterly absorbed in the music. "On three," he mouthed to Sarah. "One..." Their hands hovered near the door handles, poised to spring into action.

Sarah inhaled deeply, her heart thrumming against her ribcage. She thought about the story they would have if they survived. A story that seemed too extraordinary to be real, and yet here they were, living an action movie nightmare. In the briefest moment, she reassured herself that heroes don't die, and they were the heroes of this story.

"Two." He could feel the tension in his muscles, coiled like a spring ready to unleash. Despite the fear that gnawed at the edges of his thoughts, he felt an odd sense of confidence. He had always possessed the skill of talking people down, but the cold, calculating gleam in

Marvin's eyes sent shivers down Tim's spine; he knew he wasn't as strong as this relentless captor, but he would fight if he had to.

"THREE!" Sarah's voice rang out in unison with Tim's, their hands grasping for the door handles in a desperate escape attempt. Their eyes locked for a split second before they pulled the handles.

"Did you think you could escape that easily?" he taunted.

Tim searched for his pepper spray, but it was nowhere to be found. A wave of raw terror washed over him as he recognized their utter vulnerability. As he clenched his trembling hand into a fist, he could feel the adrenaline coursing through his veins. With all his strength, he launched his fist toward Marvin, the impact reverberating through the cabin. The punch landed square on Marvin's face causing his head to hit the driver's side window.

Marvin slammed on the brakes, causing Tim and Sarah to rock forward. Marvin gingerly probed his face, mulling over his next move. He was no stranger to confrontation, but those who dared cross him rarely lived to see another day. The question remained: what was he going to do with Tim?

He drew in a deep breath and swung open the Tahoe door, stepping out into the open air. A challenge always stirred something within him. His mind drifted back to an encounter with Johnny D just a few weeks prior. He had intercepted Johnny's suspiciously loaded vehicle; he'd apprehended countless looters over the past year, most of whom wisely chose not to provoke someone of Marvin's imposing stature.

But Johnny was different, foolhardy or desperate enough to confront Marvin head-on. As Johnny charged at him, he chuckled at the audacity of it all. The regret painted across Johnny's face when his attempt to mace Marvin failed was almost comical. Marvin hoisted him off the ground and threw him down with brute force.

Johnny lay motionless as Marvin coolly drew his gun, uttering, "Looting is punishable by death." He pulled the trigger without flinching. By now, dealing death blows had become second nature to him.

Tim and Sarah exchanged a wordless look of understanding. The remaining Tahoes formed an impenetrable barrier around them, intensifying the standoff ahead.

With each heavy footfall on the gravel, Marvin exuded intimidation that sent shivers down their spines. Tim clung desperately to the door handle.

"Please," he whimpered, his voice filled with desperation, but his plea fell on deaf ears. With a forceful yank, Marvin swung the door open and seized Tim by his collar, instantly transporting him back to the torment of childhood bullies, and making him feel small and powerless all over again.

Marvin's lip curled into a sneer.

"Seriously bro, that was just dumb," he jeered, his eyes flashing with malice. He casually pulled a gun from his vest, waving it around like a prop in a cheesy action movie. "You were kinda cool, Timmy boy," Marvin drawled as he pressed the muzzle against his temple. "But you know what? I've offed like a dozen people this year."

Tim's heart raced as he felt the cold steel against his skin. Fear bore down on him, making his entire body shake uncontrollably.

Matt, CJ, and Lisa climbed out of their Tahoes, their gazes riveted on the unfolding spectacle before them. Marvin turned to CJ, his eyes gleaming with a predatory anticipation. "What's the price on his head?" he inquired.

"A cool million," CJ responded.

Marvin's smirk stretched into a malicious grin. "Do we still get our share if he's six feet under?" he taunted, turning toward Sarah.

"Please," Sarah pleaded. "Don't hurt him."

Marvin casually flicked his wrist, his gaze fixated on Tim, who stood quivering. "You've made your decision," he stated.

With practiced ease, he held up his revolver, pulling back the hammer. Then, with a swift and brutal motion, he struck Tim across the head. The force of the blow sent Tim sprawling to the ground like a discarded puppet.

A wave of raw anger washed over Sarah's fear as she rushed toward Tim, her heart pounding against her chest in sheer terror. "You're a monster!" She hurled the words at Marvin like stones.

His only response was a low chuckle that echoed eerily around them as he started rummaging through the back of their SUV. When he re-emerged, he held several items, and there was an unsettling gleam of satisfaction in his eyes.

"Don't be brave," Marvin sneered at Sarah. "We have a pleasant surprise waiting for you."

Marvin revealed a roll of duct tape. CJ assisted by putting Tim's hands together. Marvin began duct-taping his wrists together, wrapping the tape around them over and over until it was extremely tight.

Sarah's eyes widened as Lisa grabbed her arm and dragged her to Marvin's SUV. Marvin and CJ lifted Tim's limp body into the back. As Lisa taped her hands together, she asked. "Why are you doing this?"

Lisa's words cut through the air like a knife. "You know the answer."

Marvin ran his hand over the leather seats of the SUV. "Just think of it as an exciting adventure."

Tim groaned as he regained consciousness, unable to move or rub his aching head. The sound of the SUV door closing felt like a final nail in his coffin, sealing him into his hell. The stifling air inside made it hard to breathe, each second feeling like an eternity as he sat there, slick with sweat and filled with fear.

"Feeling claustrophobic?" Marvin taunted from the driver's seat, his insincerity dripping from every word. "Just wait until you see your little surprise." Sarah and Tim exchanged terrified glances, bracing themselves for whatever nightmare was waiting at their destination.

"We will find a way," Sarah whispered.

Tim's mind raced, searching for any escape routes from their captors. Beside him, Sarah wept silently.

CHAPTER 32

They rolled up to a house that was in complete disrepair. Windows were smashed in, and the door was hanging off its hinges like it was too tired to do its job. The place was a mess of rot and ruin that echoed the chaos inside them. Sarah could feel her heart doing the drum solo from hell against her ribs as she peeped at the time on the dash: 10:37 am.

The Tahoe's engine hummed to a stop, the silence slicing through the group with an unnerving chill. The house loomed ominously, its shattered windows and unhinged door resembling a tomb, spewing its morbid tales into the crisp morning breeze.

Sarah glanced at the center console, her eyes landing on the digital clock that still read 10:37. It felt like time had frozen in this moment of tension. She could feel her heart racing. In a hushed whisper, she reassured Tim, "Once we're inside, we'll have light to work with. Just be cautious and watch your steps." The SUVs behind them seemed to stand guard, their occupants peering anxiously at the rundown house up ahead. Tim nodded, fully grasping the gravity of Sarah's words.

Marvin barked, "Shut it,!" His voice was menacing. He flung open his door and stepped into the glaring daylight. CJ gravitated toward him and they conversed in hushed murmurs, casting furtive glances back at Tim and Sarah, who remained ensconced in their vehicle.

A wave of unease washed over Tim, so intense that he sank deeper into the plush fabric of his seat.

"Can you make out what they're saying?" His voice was barely audible above the hush that hung in the air.

"Nothing. If we can't hear them... they probably can't hear us."

Despite every instinct screaming at him to stay hidden, Tim risked a quick look outside. His eyes met CJ's, a distant look laced with an unsettling hint of cunning. Summoning all the courage he could muster, Tim tried to rein in his racing thoughts. "We need to get out of here. Even if they don't hurt us, they'll just turn us over to the authorities."

"How do we shake free from four seasoned assassins?" Sarah asked.

Tim squeezed his eyes shut. "Busting out now won't cut it," he admitted, his gaze sweeping over the dilapidated house before them. Plywood covered the windows like haphazardly applied plasters, and the once vibrant paint had faded and crumbled away. The silent rooms seemed to reverberate with the screams of those swallowed by the earthquake's fury.

"Three years on," Sarah uttered, "and thousands of these shells still stand. Just barely." As they assessed their scarce alternatives, they felt time slipping through their fingers like sand. The surrounding atmosphere became dense and suffocating with looming catastrophe. In this abandoned home strewn with fragments of shattered lives, they'd have to outwit their captors for a desperate sprint toward liberation.

CJ and Marvin approached the SUV.

"Move," Marvin barked, wrenching open Sarah's door so violently she recoiled in shock. With her hands bound, she carefully slid off the seat, landing on the gravel below with calculated precision despite the grim situation.

"Tim," she thought, her heart contorting. If she were alone, maybe she could stage a bold escape. But visions of CJ and Marvin inflicting pain or death on Tim if she attempted anything tormented her.

"Start walking," CJ commanded, his handgun aimed at her like a lethal punctuation mark at the end of a chilling sentence. Marvin trained his weapon on Tim, ensuring their terror kept them obedient.

"Play it cool." Lisa cautioned, her arms folded defensively across her chest. Sarah could feel the chill of Lisa's grasp on her arm as she guided them through what was once a cozy family home, now reduced to a skeletal shell. The air was thick with the scent of decay, making each breath an effort. Shards from the shattered ceiling and fragments of the roof were scattered in what used to be a kitchen.

"This way," Lisa commanded, her voice laced with disdain as she led Sarah into a dark room. The windows had been boarded up, cutting off any trace of natural light. With a push, Sarah landed on a grimy mattress that protested under her weight. "Welcome home; you're in for the long haul."

Sarah's eyes struggled to make out the surroundings in the darkness. She could barely discern the faded band posters clinging to the peeling wallpaper and an old dresser on its last legs in one corner. This room was once someone's home, a haven from the outside world. Now, it was just a sad shell of what it used to be, a constant reminder of the harsh reality they were facing. For Sarah, there was no escaping the truth anymore.

"What's their end game?" Sarah voiced her thoughts. "To wear us down until we're as empty and lifeless?" She sent a silent plea skyward, begging for some cosmic interference. Their fate dangled in the cruel grasp of their captors.

Tim's heart pounded at the echo of footsteps closing in.

"Your turn," Marvin spat out, his eyes gleaming with sadistic pleasure as he wrenched open the door of the Tahoe. Tim steeled himself, ready to confront whatever twisted games they had lined up.

Marvin seized Tim's arm, yanking him from the vehicle and tossing him onto the ground like yesterday's trash. Tim tried to rise, but his body rebelled under the crushing weight of fear and fatigue.

"On your feet," Marvin snarled, landing a savage kick to Tim's ribs. "Enough!" Marvin snapped, hauling Tim upright by his shirt collar. Tim forced himself to stand tall, aware that resistance would only fuel their sadistic enjoyment.

"Move it," Marvin ordered, shoving him with such force that he nearly toppled over.

Marvin led him into a room even more claustrophobic than Sarah's makeshift cell; an overpowering stench of decay assaulted Tim's senses. The dim light revealed a dilapidated crib and a rotting rocking chair. Dread washed over him as Marvin shoved him inside.

"Get in there. Now!" Marvin directed, pushing Tim onto the grimy floor. "I'm in a good mood today." He pulled a switchblade from his pocket, holding it close to Tim's face. "Just remember, next time you get any ideas about escaping, I'll use this knife to give you a gentle reminder." Fury blazed in Tim's eyes, but he knew defiance would only invite more pain and suffering.

"Thought so," Marvin smirked. He dragged the blade across Tim's face slowly, close enough to make him wince, before slicing through the tape binding his legs. "This is probably as good as it gets for you," he said. "Once you reach the States, they'll toss you into some Supermax for terrorists." With that, Marvin slammed the door behind him, plunging Tim into an abyss of darkness.

Tim sat in the dark, his mind racing with fear and confusion. The surrounding silence was suffocating, making it hard to think. He strained his eyes, trying to make out any shape or form in the pitch-blackness of his prison. His body trembled from the cold and fear that consumed him. He desperately wanted to make sense of their dire situation but was overwhelmed by conflicting emotions. Fear fought against hope, and he felt trapped between them.

The memory of that grim, filth-encrusted corridor haunted him. They ushered him past two doors before throwing him into this hell-hole. Sarah was somewhere behind those doors, her anxiety undoubtedly mirroring his. Tim's jaw tightened, a bulwark against the terror gnawing at the edges of his resolve.

In her inky-black cell, Sarah's heart hammered into a chaotic rhythm of fear for Tim. Every scuffle of boots made her hyper-alert, conjuring horrifying images of him being tormented by their captors. She yearned for any sign he was okay and let out a piercing scream.

"WHAT?!" Lisa's shrill voice echoed through the door, causing Sarah to recoil instinctively. The door flew open and Lisa's hawk-like eyes scrutinized Sarah with unsettling intensity.

"A massive rat just darted by," Sarah stammered out.

"Pathetic," Lisa sneered before slamming the door. Alone in the suffocating darkness, frustration and worry chewed relentlessly at Sarah's mind like starved predators.

Tim's body tensed with fear as he struggled to stand up, feeling a searing ache in his ribs and head, his breath trapped in his throat. It was Sarah! She was still alive! Fueled by an unwavering determination and an intense longing to reach her, he pushed himself forward with all his might.

"Think, Tim. Think," he muttered, racking his brain for a way out. But with every groan of the old floorboards and every sound from their twisted captors, hope seemed to plunge deeper into an endless void.

CHAPTER 33

The meager light seeped through the gaps of the hastily board-ed-up window, sketching eerie patterns on the faded and peeling wallpaper. Sarah squinted, her eyes darting around the room for any means of escape. Her heart pounded, sending icy tendrils slithering through her veins. She clenched her fists with a deep, shaky breath, mustering every ounce of courage before launching a punch at the wooden barricade. The sharp sting that shot through her knuckles was immediate, but it was nothing compared to the chilling dread gnawing at her insides.

"Damn it," she muttered under her breath, realizing that breaking through the window wasn't an option. Her eyes darted around the room, landing on the small twin mattress. She grabbed it and flipped it over, only to find nothing.

"Okay, think, Sarah," she said, her hands wringing together. She walked over to the dresser, heavy and immovable. She couldn't help but notice how someone had hammered it to the floor. Her breath caught in her throat, the walls closing on her.

As Sarah rummaged through the dresser, she fought to keep her focus amidst the chaos of their captured life. Her inner voice nagged at her to stay on task, but her curiosity got the best of her as she sifted through the random assortment of items: gum wrappers, bright lipsticks, and a collection of photos. One caught her eye. It was a faded group shot of a smiling teenage girl with her family in front of their now-demolished home. The sight brought a pang of fear and longing, reminding Sarah of the reality that surrounded them.

But then she found it. Buried beneath layers of clothing was a screwdriver. Sarah's heart raced as she realized this could be the tool that would save them. For a moment, she entertained the thought of using it against their captors, but quickly dismissed the idea. Survival was their only goal.

Meanwhile, Tim struggled to his feet in the darkness of his room. His mind raced as he desperately tried to reach Sarah in the adjacent room. And then it hit him like a bolt of lightning - Morse code. It was something they had studied together for fun, never imagining it would become their lifeline.

Tim positioned himself near the wall closest to the barricaded window and began tapping out an SOS signal in Morse code. "... --- ..." he repeated repeatedly, pausing between each sequence to listen for any response. But all that greeted him was an eerie silence. He called out into the darkness, "Sarah... can you hear me?"

Sarah was navigating her space. Determination surged within her as she gripped the screwdriver. The cold metal felt solid against her palm as she traced its grooves. Continuing her exploration, she moved toward an old dresser standing awkwardly. As she peered behind it, her heart skipped a beat at what she saw—an inconspicuous door without a handle. It seemed forgotten by time and dusted with age.

She climbed onto the dresser, carefully avoiding looking down at the yawning gap below. She placed both feet on its surface and pushed against the door with all her strength. It gave way slightly under pressure. "Just move," she grunted aloud.

Suddenly, a dull thumping noise reached her ears. Could there be animals stuck inside? But then the noise started again, and it clicked. "Tim?" she called into the darkness, her mind racing to decode the pattern of knocks.

Tim leaned against the wall, his hope teetering on the precipice of despair. He was on the verge of surrender when a rhythmic series of thumps reverberated in the blackened void. Relief coursed through him like a lifeline, tugging his lips into a weary smile. Sarah was alive.

"Get it together," he muttered to himself. He readied himself to communicate again, despite his rudimentary grasp of Morse code. Drawing a shaky breath, he rapped out h-e-l-l-o against the wall and waited with bated breath.

The silence stretched out agonizingly before Sarah's response pierced through it. Straining to discern her message, Tim decoded: Safe. An unspoken pact passed between them in the darkness; he echoed her message back.

"Safe," Sarah said into the oppressive quiet, her grip tightening around the screwdriver's handle. This was their moment of truth. She strained against the door, feeling it yield slightly under her desperate efforts. Bit by bit, she waged war against its stubborn resistance, fueled by visions of freedom and reunion with Tim.

As they wrestled with their confinement, Sarah and Tim's hopes became entwined like strands of a lifeline thrown into an abyss. The odds loomed ominously over them, but they clung fiercely to their shared resolve.

The feeble glimmer of light painted shadows on the walls around Sarah as she perched atop the dresser. She squinted at the thin shaft of light seeping through a crack above where a board barricaded their only escape route–a door without a handle.

"What will it take?" she murmured. She had always thrived under pressure, and this time would be no different. With renewed vigor, she descended from the dresser and wrapped her fingers around the screwdriver. The cold metal seemed to pulse with promise, infusing her with determination.

"All or nothing," forcing the flathead screwdriver beneath a stubborn nail. Each one resisted, clinging onto the battered dresser with a tenacity that mirrored her own. Sweat streamed down her face, stinging her eyes, but it was a mere inconvenience in the grand scheme. Survival was on the line.

Tim fumbled his way through the suffocating darkness of the room. His fingers brushed over what could only be a door - yet there was no knob to turn, no latch to lift. Fear gnawed at his gut, but he shoved it aside; they had too much riding on hope to allow it to falter now.

As Sarah strained against the obstinate nails, fragments of memory danced before her mind's eye: Tim teaching her Morse code under starlit nights. She could almost hear his patient voice detailing each dot and dash - an innocent lesson now transformed into a potential lifesaver. The recollection fueled her determination and with one last heave; she wrestled free the last nail.

"Done," she said, wiping away beads of sweat from her forehead with an exhausted hand. "Now we need an escape route."

Chapter 34

Sarah stared at the barricaded door that stood between her and freedom. She glanced at the dresser, knowing that moving it would be a noisy ordeal on the wooden floor.

"Help!" Sarah cried out. The silence that followed was suffocating, and she could feel her hope beginning to wane. With renewed urgency, she called out again, louder this time. "Help me!"

The door creaked open just enough for Lisa's cold eyes to peer through. "What do you want?" she demanded.

"I need to use the bathroom," Sarah said.

Lisa rolled her eyes and shrugged her shoulders. "Fine, but make it quick."

Sarah hopped over the threshold, her mind a whirlwind of thoughts that invariably led back to Tim trapped in a room down the hall, their shared dreams of becoming frontline journalists now buried under the rubble of their predicament. She hoped, with every ounce of her strength, that he, too, was scheming up an escape plan. A wry smile tugged at her lips as she imagined him devising elaborate plans involving secret passages.

Tim trembled on the frigid floorboards, his eyes wide with terror as he grappled with a question that consumed his every thought, like a menacing predator lurking in the shadows. Will he be able to survive this life? Being a fearless journalist meant protecting not just himself, but others too. Despite being tall and strong, he felt inadequate in front of their captors. He pictured himself becoming a martial arts pro, taking out all his opponents like a badass movie star. But those daydreams seemed crazy and unrealistic, considering how things were. His eyes grew heavy under the burden of self-doubt and terror, succumbing to an uneasy sleep filled with dreams of daring rescues and narrow escapes.

Sarah stepped out of the shadowy bedroom, Lisa's icy stare tracking her every move. With a grin playing on her lips, Lisa pointed down the hall with her flashlight and said, "Good luck; no water, so you'll have to hold your nose." As Sarah navigated through the musty corridor toward Tim's room, panic surged within her like white-water rapids. This won't be easy, she acknowledged silently as she steeled herself for what lay ahead.

"Right there," Lisa barked, gesturing toward a grubby door. With her hands still bound, Sarah looked at Lisa with a helpless expression. "I can't lower my pants."

Lisa rolled her eyes and heaved a sigh, stepping forward to pull down Sarah's pants and underwear. She made a show of turning her head away as if the task was beneath her. The feeling of vulnerability was suffocating, but Sarah gritted her teeth, focusing on the impending escape that hung like a sword over their heads.

Entering the filthy bathroom, she gagged, barely able to hold back the bile rising in her throat as she caught sight of the clogged, waste-filled toilet. There was no way in hell she would sit in that vile seat. Instead, she shuffled over to the shower and crouched to relieve herself, the cold tiles biting into her skin.

"Move it!" Lisa barked, pounding on the door. The sudden noise made Sarah jump. With every second that ticked by, their captors were growing more impatient. Desperation crept into her trembling hands as she frantically searched the bathroom cabinets for anything useful – a weapon, a tool, anything to give them an advantage.

Her search proved fruitless. The medicine cabinet held a lone bottle of heartburn medication. But she couldn't let despair take hold.

Sarah knew that every move she made was another step toward saving Tim and herself from this nightmare. Time was running out, but she refused to let fear paralyze her. With a deep breath, she steeled her resolve and prepared for their escape.

The bathroom door slowly creaked open, revealing Lisa's impatient scowl as she stood there. "Finally," she sneered, her voice laced with a venomous edge that sent shivers down my spine.

A weak chuckle escaped from Sarah's lips. "I really had to go,"

"Whatever." Lisa bent down, gripping the waistband of Sarah's pants and underwear, and pulled them up roughly. The contact made Sarah's skin crawl, and for a moment, she envisioned herself striking Lisa across the face, but she knew better than to give in to that impulse. They couldn't afford any more setbacks.

Entering the hallway, Sarah mustered up the courage to confront Lisa.

"What are you planning to do with us?" she demanded. Lisa remained silent. Undeterred, Sarah pressed on. "Are you going to sell us? Is that it?"

Something dark flickered in Lisa's eyes as she smirked, then shoved Sarah hard down the hall. Stumbling, Sarah looked back at her captor, confusion twisting her features. "What did I do?" she managed before Lisa cut her off.

"Get in your room," Lisa spat.

In the meantime, Tim lay sprawled out on the cold, unforgiving floor of his makeshift cell, feeling the pull of sleep threatening to drag him under like an undertow. Fatigue clung to his every muscle, yet the distant murmur of voices roused him from his stupor. Was that Sarah's voice? He strained his ears, trying to decipher her words. Her tone was resolute, almost defiant. Their shared experiences during this trip had been profound, and if they survived this nightmare, their bond would be irrevocably altered.

"Tim," he muttered, "you're not in Kansas anymore." His feeble attempt at humor echoed hollowly in the oppressive darkness enveloping him. The silence pervading the room amplified the gravity of their predicament. Yet it was Sarah's voice that pierced through this somber quietude.

An idea sparked within Sarah like flint striking steel. She began removing each drawer from the dresser; each extraction, rendering it lighter and easier to maneuver.

"This is it," she murmured under her breath as she gripped the skeletal frame of the dresser. Her fingers quivered as she cautiously pushed it away from their only exit–success!

Sarah Bridges held her breath, the screwdriver gripped tightly in her hand. She wedged its sharp tip into the seam of the door, using the heel of her other hand as a crude hammer. Each thump echoed ominously in the small space, a countdown to either salvation or disaster. "Just a little more," she said. Her mind wandered to Tim. They would break free from this wretched place together.

Time stretched like an endless road as she worked on the stubborn door. With one last forceful push, it gave way and swung open with an eerie groan. A blast of air rushed in.

"Stay steady, Sarah," she muttered.

With the barrier removed, she knew acutely that their window of opportunity was shrinking rapidly. Every second was precious and nightfall was fast approaching. Under its cloak of darkness, she intended to strike and hopefully secure their freedom.

CHAPTER 35

The last rays of the sun snuck through the cracks in the board-ed-up windows, casting a dance of shadows on the hallway floor. Sarah's heart thumped as she stood by the door, her mind whirling with thoughts of their daring escape and the high-stakes game they were about to play.

"Alright," she breathed out, bracing herself for their next move in this real-life game of Escape Room. "Here goes nothing."

Sarah moved toward the exit door. Her fingers brushed against the wall, her ears tuned for any hint of their captors' awareness. When silence met her knock, she repeated it, louder this time. After several nerve-wracking moments, she allowed herself a fleeting sigh of relief and retreated into the shadowy recesses of the closet. She closed the door behind her with a grace that belied her anxiety.

"Steady," she said to herself. "You can do this." Her fingertips traced over what felt like paper-thin plaster masquerading as a wall. This was the moment, breaching this feeble barrier and engaging in a dangerous game with Tim without alerting their captors. The stakes were high;

if they didn't take this risk now, they might end up as permanent prisoners or worse, incarcerated by Uncle Sam himself.

Grasping the screwdriver, Sarah drove it into the wall, puncturing a small hole. The sound reverberated, causing her to cringe. But when no sounds of alarm echoed from other parts of the house, she pressed on.

As she worked, she noticed the irregularity of the floor beneath her feet, prompting her to look down. Her heart plummeted as she spotted the handle to the crawl space, a new, terrifying obstacle in their path to freedom. The thought of venturing into the dark, unknown space below filled her with dread, but she steeled herself against the fear. This was their only chance.

"Freedom," she said. "We can do this." Sarah pulled open the crawl space door. The cobwebs hung like tattered curtains. One leg disappeared into the crawl space, followed by the other; Sarah braced herself for the unknown and dropped nearly four feet.

"Here goes nothing," she murmured under her breath, clutching the screwdriver tightly as if it were her lifeline. Crouching low, she navigated the confined space, the damp earth pressing against her knees and hands. Her senses sharpened, ears straining for any sound that might betray her presence.

"Please, be okay," she thought. Inching closer to her imagined destination, the distinct sound of someone snoring greeted her. Tim! A sob escaped her lips as she whispered a heartfelt gratitude, her voice cracking with the weight of grief she had carried.

The snoring continued unabated. Undeterred, Sarah knocked again. The floorboards groaned, revealing their weakness. She pocketed the screwdriver and, with a deep breath, pressed both hands against the floor. She could feel the board lifting slightly.

"Nearly there," she whispered to herself, swallowing the lump of terror that threatened to strangle her. Taking one more measured breath, she crouched lower, coiling her muscles before releasing them in a surge. The floorboard surrendered with a muted crack, its sound barely audible against the thunderous pounding of her heart.

Sarah dislodged two additional boards with her screwdriver. The gap was now sufficient for her to gaze through, uncovering Tim sprawled on the floor above.

"Stay sharp," she admonished herself. "We're on the brink of freedom."

"Tim," Sarah implored. "Wake up!"

Tim shifted his position. She clenched the screwdriver tightly in both hands. With a swift flick of her wrists, she propelled the tool toward his legs. The sudden sting was enough to jolt him into consciousness.

"Wha–" Tim stammered. "How did you get down there?"

"Later," she interjected. "We need to go. Now."

With a nod, Tim claimed the screwdriver and threw himself into the task. He took the screwdriver to his bound legs and removed the duct tape. Together, they attacked the stubborn floorboards with determination. Each plank they pried free seemed to bolster their resolve, their muscles thrumming with adrenaline-fueled strength. They created a makeshift portal wide enough for him to slip through.

Tim sat on the floor and lowered his legs through the narrow opening. As he slid, his body jolted, followed by a muffled scream.

"What happened?" Sarah's voice trembled with concern.

"Caught my back on a rusty nail," he grunted. His shirt was soaking up blood, staining it an alarming shade of red that spread slowly like a sinister watercolor painting. Sarah swallowed hard but maintained eye contact with Tim. "We'll patch it up later. For now, we have to get out."

They walked toward the exit. The lock mocked them with its obstinate resistance. Unfazed, Tim took several steps back before launching himself at the door to break it open; his shoulder, absorbing the impact that reverberated around them.

"Let me use this," He wedged the screwdriver into the rusty lock and twisted with all his might until there was a satisfying click and the door swung open reluctantly.

The forest outside was dense and foreboding under the cloak of nightfall. "Where do we go?" Tim asked.

"Follow me," Sarah instructed. "I think I know how to get to the creek."

They sprinted, their heartbeats drumming in their ears as they put as much distance between them and their captors. Tim's feet betrayed him. He lost his balance and tumbled down a slope, narrowly missing a menacing jagged rock. Sarah followed with more caution, her breaths coming out in ragged gasps that echoed eerily around them.

Marvin's sinister voice echoed through the darkness, sharp and piercing like a knife. "Timmy and Sarah," he taunted, "Ready or not, here we come." The distant sounds of honking cars only added to the sense of impending doom.

Tim swiftly used the jagged edge of the screwdriver to cut through Sarah's bound hands. She returned the favor, freeing him from his restraints. They clung to each other for a moment, finding solace in each other.

"No matter what," Tim breathed into her ear, "I'm here by your side."

They plunged deeper into the forest.

CHAPTER 36

The moon hung low, casting shadows on the ravine below as Sarah and Tim peered into its depths. They could barely make out the winding road that had brought them here, but it was there, a faint memory of their journey.

Tim's voice broke the silence.

"Let's go upstream! They will assume we went down because that's where we came from."

"Let's do it," Sarah responded.

They began their trek along the shallow creek, their footsteps splashing through the water, enveloped by the stillness of the night. The only sounds were their labored breathing and the occasional rocks as they jumped from one ledge to another. Sarah thought that it was too quiet, an unnatural hush that seemed to hang in the air, waiting to strike.

"Every inch is a battle," Tim grunted, their bodies straining against the incline of the creek bed. The looming boulders were both a shield and an obstacle, obscuring their sight and halting their advance. "We need to hunker down until dawn," he proposed.

"Those bastards are on our heels. They won't back off." She gestured to where a sharp ascent lay beneath dense undergrowth. "Our path lies there."

But they couldn't afford the luxury of contemplation, as they channeled every shred of their vitality into the desperate endeavor to widen the gap between them and their pursuers. The relentless landscape seemed to conspire against them, its gnarled roots and uneven terrain hindering their progress with each agonizing stride.

"Keep pushing," Tim murmured, his words barely audible over his gasping breaths. "We'll carve out our way."

Fear pounded in Sarah's chest, her mind teetering on the edge of despair. Was this truly their escape route or just another path leading nowhere? They plunged deeper into the abyss.

As Sarah moved through the dense foliage, a bead of sweat rolled down her forehead, shimmering in the light. Refusing to be daunted, she clenched her jaw and stared at the steep incline before them.

"Move," Sarah hissed. Tim grimaced, pain gnawing at his side, yet he nodded in silent affirmation, steeling himself for the uphill battle ahead. "We must reach higher ground."

With each step they took skyward, Sarah's breaths grew ragged and shallow, punctuating the hushed whispers of the undergrowth beneath them. The surrounding shadows twisted and cavorted like malevolent phantoms, their eerie dance a constant reminder of the looming specter of detection.

"Hold on," Tim breathed in a weak rasp, his face slick with sweat. "I need to rest."

Sarah bit back an impatient retort, cursing each precious second squandered. They halted their trek on a precarious ledge jutting defiantly from the mountainside; their bodies shuddered with fatigue as they sought respite in this transient sanctuary amidst their relentless flight.

"Let me check your back," Sarah suggested, her fingers quivering as she cleared away the grime and blood. Tim complied, exposing a severe laceration across his back. "We have to find someone. This is getting infected."

Panic threatened to engulf Sarah. Her eyes darted around, scanning for any hint of human life. But all that met her gaze was an endless expanse of greenery in every direction. Where were they? How far from help?

"Just keep moving," Tim encouraged. "We can't stop now."

They resumed their trek, battling through thorny bushes that clawed at their clothes and skin, leaving a trail of red in their wake. With each step forward, the world was closing in on them.

"There," Tim gasped, showing a rocky protrusion jutting out like a ship's bow from the hillside. "I think we'll be safe there."

"I hope you're right," Sarah responded.

They staggered toward the rocky refuge and collapsed onto the ground, fashioning makeshift beds from pine needles. As they settled into their sparse shelter, nightfall enveloped them completely.

"We need to rest," Sarah murmured while her eyes scanned the darkness for threats.

With the arrival of night, a deep silence settled over their surroundings, as if the world held its breath. Tim grappled with gravity, his muscles straining to hoist him upright. "Sarah," he uttered, "I'll stand guard for the first few hours, then we'll swap."

"Thank you," Sarah responded. She clung to him as if his presence alone could fend off the creeping dread gnawing at the edges of their courage.

"You know," Tim murmured into her ear, pulling her closer to feel the warmth of his breath against her skin, "I couldn't have wished for a better partner on this wild rollercoaster we're on."

A chuckle escaped from Sarah's lips. "I'm sorry. I never pictured us battling these odds together."

Their gazes locked in the dim glow filtering through the darkness; for a fleeting moment, everything else ceased to exist. They kissed passionately, seeking solace from the harsh reality that surrounded them.

"Time to rest," he urged. "I'll hold the fort."

Sarah collapsed onto her makeshift bed and let her eyelids fall shut; a hushed thank you drifted toward Tim just as slumber swallowed her whole. The haunting silence engulfed them again, as Sarah's voice dissipated into thin air, leaving Tim alone with his thoughts. Time seemed to stretch into infinity as he stood guard against unseen dangers. Their tomorrow remained as erratic as ever, yet steeled their determination. Dawn was only hours away.

CHAPTER 37

T he sun's first rays stretched across the sky, casting a glow on the rocky terrain where Tim lay half-asleep.

The air was crisp with a morning chill, but Sarah didn't feel cold as she opened her eyes. Careful not to disrupt the serene stillness, she rose and quietly approached Tim. As she tapped him lightly on the shoulder, he jolted awake, and his eyes widened in surprise before recognizing her.

"Morning," Sarah grumbled, her voice muffled by the crumpled sleeve of her shirt she was using as a makeshift pillow.

"Huh?" Tim mumbled, his eyes still closed against the morning light. "Oh... yeah, morning."

Sarah squinted at him, her eye narrowing as she took in his messy hair and the faint drool on his cheek.

"Platinum," Tim declared, pausing for effect.

Sarah turned to him. "Platinum?" she repeated, watching as he rubbed the back of his neck.

"Yeah," Tim confessed with a shy grin. "That's my mom's little saying for when the day starts with no disasters."

Sarah laughed. The sound seemed out of place amidst the surrounding destruction.

Tim shifted uncomfortably before adding, "Considering I'm still breathing... I'd say it's mega-platinum."

She shook her head in amusement. "Mega platinum, huh?"

The sky became a vibrant canvas of orange and pink, illuminating their surroundings with increasing clarity. Tim's gaze swept across the landscape, landing on the decrepit house that had been their prison. "There it is!" He announced.

"Quiet," Sarah cautioned. "We don't know where they've gone."

Tim nodded. He looked back at the house. Sarah observed his tense posture, her instincts warning her of the dangerous plan brewing in his mind. Despite the challenges, he remained resolute in his determination.

"If we try to hoof it, we're as good as dead," he stated. "But we could take one of their Tahoes... they are practically tanks."

"And how do you propose we snatch a vehicle from under their noses?" she retorted.

"I'll figure something out," he assured her. His hand instinctively moved toward the injury on his back.

"First things first," she commanded, pointing toward the creek that snaked below them through the valley floor. "We need to clean your wound."

Tim's eyes traced the treacherous slope to the water's edge. He shook his head in defiance. "There's no time," he insisted.

Sarah realized she had no alternative but to let him take the lead. Her gaze followed him, a knot of apprehension twisting in her stomach as she pondered whether this pristine dawn would spiral into a nightmarish conclusion.

"Promise me," Sarah implored.

"I'll be back before you know it," he assured her. He extricated himself from the warmth of their shared embrace and turned toward their aim.

As he navigated the rocky terrain, gravel crunched underfoot, shifting and threatening to send him tumbling down the treacherous incline. One glance at the sheer drop-off was enough to confirm that any misstep could prove lethal.

He slunk to the ground, every muscle coiled with tension. Every crunch of leaves and snap of twigs sent shivers down his spine, amplifying the eerie silence.

"Stay sharp," he said to himself.

As he slowly moved closer to the house, he saw two parked Tahoes. The third was nowhere to be found. A door slamming jolted him back to reality. Two figures emerged from the house, their weapons glinting in the sunlight. Tim threw himself flat on the ground, willing to blend into the earth in a last-ditch effort to avoid detection.

The goons checked their weapons before climbing into one of the Tahoes. Panic threatened to choke him. His only saving grace was that his tan cargo shorts and green shirt blended with the landscape. The Tahoe pulled away, heading up the road in Sarah's direction.

Tim surveyed the slope leading to the house. It seemed impossibly steep, but it was their only chance. "Please, let this work," he thought.

The wind whipped across his face as he hurried along the cliff edge. With every step, the rocky terrain beneath his feet threatened to give way.

As he peered over the ridge, he spotted Sarah crouched behind a bush. Tim mimicked the call of a bird, drawing her gaze toward him. He pressed a finger to his lips.

"How the hell do we navigate this?" Sarah questioned.

Tim gingerly inched over the cliff's edge. His pulse hammered as he succumbed to the tug of gravity, plunging down the ten-foot descent to the cushioned earth below.

A subdued echo filled the air as his shoes collided with the loamy soil beneath him, and he twisted his neck upwards to find Sarah's eyes locked on him from her elevated perch.

Slowly and carefully, she moved across the rough terrain until she stood on the edge of Tim's waiting embrace. "Trust me," Tim reassured her. With a leap of trust, Sarah allowed herself to glide down the slope. Surrendering to the rush of adrenaline, she found comfort in the secure embrace of Tim's arms, a smile spreading across her face.

As they navigated with cautious steps, the sound of running water grew louder until they reached the creek. They were now only yards away from the Tahoe that could be their salvation.

"Let me clean your wound," Sarah said, her voice filled with concern as she noticed the bloodied gash on Tim's back. He nodded silently, wincing as she found a stick to open it further.

"Are you sure about this?" he asked.

"Trust me," she echoed his previous plea. "Bite on this," she instructed, offering him a rugged piece of wood. Tim clenched his teeth around the stick, his jaw muscles straining with the effort.

With meticulous accuracy, she manipulated a stick to pry open the wound. The pain elicited a low groan from Tim's gritted teeth. A surge of crimson seeped from the gash, saturating the earth beneath them before gradually ceasing its flow. The inflamed flesh bordering the wound was a glaring beacon of their precarious situation.

"Tim, we need help," Sarah implored. She splashed droplets of crisp spring water onto his injury, attempting to cleanse it despite their scant supplies and less-than-ideal conditions.

The sun cast shadows across the clearing, turning the house into a monstrous specter. With Tim's wound cleaned, Sarah insisted he keep his shirt off until it had sealed itself shut. She knew deep down that every moment they lingered in this place was another chance for their world to shatter.

"Listen," Tim whispered, his words barely audible over the deafening silence shattered by the sudden burst of gunfire. His eyes widened. "They're close - but not too close."

"Why would they be firing off rounds?" Sarah questioned.

"Likely trying to flush us out."

Sarah willed herself to shake it off, refusing to let terror rule her actions. United in their resolve, they scaled the ravine and dared a glance over its lip. The gravel road stretched out in both directions, devoid of life and eerily silent.

Tim's eyes darted around their surroundings. "We have to move quickly. The electric motors are silent killers."

Sarah surveyed the dark thicket behind their house. "It's too risky. We can't do it."

"We have no choice. We'll sprint across and lose ourselves in the woods."

Sarah's hand trembled as she reached for him. "Please, Tim. It's too dangerous."

He placed a trembling hand on her shoulder, desperately attempting to mask the terror that lurked behind his gaze. "Trust me. This is training for when we go into a war zone."

She could only murmur a protest before they crouched down, waiting for the perfect moment to make their run. When Tim said "go," they ran with all their might, their hearts pounding in their chests as they fled like desperate animals.

The scent of Douglas firs was now intertwined with the stench of fear. It wafted through the air, a bitter reminder of the thin line between hope and despair. As they ventured further into the unknown, Sarah's fingers dug deeper into Tim's arm - an unspoken plea for reassurance in this world turned upside down.

Danger lurked like a predator stalking its prey, never relenting, always present. Each step they took was a dance with death - one misstep or moment of hesitation could spell their end. Their survival hinged on their ability to keep moving in this relentless pursuit against time and terror.

CHAPTER 38

Amid scorched trees, Tim and Sarah stumbled upon a small oasis of vibrant greenery. It seemed to mock the desolate wasteland that surrounded them, a defiant display of life amidst death.

Their eyes were drawn to a massive stump, a haunting reminder of what once was. Tim gestured toward it, breaking the eerie silence that hung like a shroud around them.

"Let's take shelter there," he suggested.

Fear gnawed at Sarah's heart as Tim set off toward the structure, leaving her alone in that unforgiving world.

She clung to his departing figure, desperately wishing she could join him. But survival instincts kicked in and she knew she needed to stay put.

"Catch you on the flip side," Tim's voice echoed in her mind before disappearing.

Sarah thought that they should stick together, but she reminded herself that they were in this together and had to make tough decisions for their survival.

Gazing at the house, Sarah struggled to believe the nightmare she was living. Kidnapped and thrust into becoming a hero for a nation in ruins. Her face broadcasted to millions, she wondered how they would ever make it out of this alive.

She never realized the impact her words could have on this remote, struggling community. The weight of her newfound responsibility settled on her shoulders, and she realized the profound effect it was having on Tim and her own life. She had to be strong for him, for all of them. As she crouched in the hushed grove, waiting for his return, she sent a silent prayer: 'Let us survive this. Let us find a way out of this darkness. And please, let Tim come back unharmed.'

Tim approached the house. He knew he had to be extra careful; the goon squad could lurk anywhere. As he circled the perimeter, he took a deep breath, steadying himself. "Okay, Tim. You can do this," he muttered. "You're strong enough." He thought of Sarah, hidden away in the grove of trees, and how she looked at him before he left her side. He couldn't let anything happen to her. With one final steadying breath, he reached for the door handle. It was now or never.

"Tim... please be safe," Sarah said, watching him enter the house. Her emotions were a whirlwind, fear, worry, but also love. She couldn't help it; after losing her fiancé, she never thought she'd feel so deeply for someone again. Yet here she was, heart pounding for a man engaged to someone else. "Stop it," she murmured. "Focus on getting out of here alive first. Then we'll deal with... whatever this is."

As Tim stepped inside, the silence sent shivers down his spine. Shadows danced across the walls like tormented souls.

"Stay focused. Find something useful and get out," he told himself, pushing down the spike of fear that threatened to take hold. He moved cautiously through the darkened rooms.

"God, I hope he's okay," Sarah breathed, unable to tear her eyes away from the house. The guilt of her feelings for Tim gnawed at her, but she couldn't deny the truth anymore—she was falling in love with him. It wasn't just the adrenaline; it was how he looked at her like she was the only person who mattered. She shook her head, trying to clear her thoughts. "Let's get to safety first," she reminded herself.

Back inside the house, Tim had found nothing so far. Each empty room felt like a punch to his gut, the crushing disappointment fueling his desperation. He knew time was running out and Sarah was waiting for him. He needed to find something, anything that could help them escape.

Sunlight pierced through the open ceiling, casting elongated shadows on the peeling wallpaper. The once-ordinary house haunted Tim. He could almost taste the air.

"Come on, there has to be something here," Tim muttered. As he entered the kitchen, his fingers fumbled through drawers in search of anything that might aid their escape. All he found was a decomposing rat caught in a rusty trap, a grim reminder of what awaited them if they failed. "Dammit," he hissed, frustration bubbling up within him.

A plastic table, amidst the dilapidated living area, emphasized the desolation and loss that permeated the space. A duffle bag lay nearby that he picked up.

"Jackpot." A satellite phone, a walkie-talkie, pepper spray, and several handguns greeted him upon unzipping the bag. His hands trembled slightly as he held a gun. Why would they need so many? Were they preparing for a standoff?

Sarah couldn't shake the nagging thoughts about the people on the list she received from the Kansas State researcher. She had been so focused on getting the interviews that she hadn't questioned their legitimacy. But now, with so much at stake, she couldn't help but wonder who these people truly were. Were they spies working against Cascadia?

"Please," she prayed, "let us make it out alive."

Tim's fingers tensed around the duffle bag, its weight both a blessing and a burden. Every second that ticked away felt like an eternity, but he couldn't waste any more time. He needed those keys, the keys to their freedom.

Pain radiated from his back, a reminder of the torment he had endured in this godforsaken house. Steadying himself against the wall, he forced the agony to the back of his mind. "Come on, think," he muttered, his breath misting in the chilly air. The answer was so obvious it was almost laughable. The keys must be there. Tim's heart raced as he moved through the dimly lit hallway, every step bringing them closer to escape.

Sarah's nerves were fraying like a worn rope, ready to snap at any moment. What was taking Tim so long? Her imagination conjured up horrifying scenarios. "Get a grip," she said.

The sound of gravel crunching under tires sent a shiver down her spine. Panic clawed at her as she spotted the approaching Tahoe. Time was running out; they were closing in. She stared at the front door, willing Tim to appear.

"Move, Tim. For God's sake, move," she implored.

The front door towered before Tim. A bag filled to the brim draped over his shoulder, anchoring him with a sense of resolve. "Keep it together, Tim," he murmured, drawing inspiration from countless adrenaline-fueled films that flashed in his mind like vivid memories. "A firearm is your greatest leverage." His nerves hardened into steel at the thought of the daunting challenge ahead; there was no room for faltering or missteps. He sucked in a lungful of air, fortifying himself against the unknown terrors lurking beyond the front door.

The coldness of the metal handle seeped into his hand as he firmly pulled the door open.

The moment the door swung wide, tires crunching on gravel assaulted his ears. They were here. Panic bubbled in his chest, threatening to overwhelm him. He had to think fast.

"Where can I hide?" he thought, eyes darting around as he assessed his options. Suddenly, the answer came to him—the crawl space beneath the floorboards. It was perfect.

Tim raced back down the hallway to the room that had once been his prison cell. The pain in his back protested with each step, but he pushed through it, driven by adrenaline and desperation. He pried up another floorboard, quickly disappearing into the darkness below.

As he crouched down in the confined space beneath the house, he tried to locate where he believed the table with their captors' belongings had been. Maybe he could turn this nightmare around.

"Come on, Tim," he said, trying to tap into the confidence he knew deep inside him. "You can do this. You're the hero now."

The air crackled with a dangerous energy. Sarah watched in horror as the Tahoe skidded to a halt, its twin right beside it, gravel crunching beneath their tires like an ominous warning. Two figures emerged, their faces twisted in cruel sneers. A guttural curse escaped one of them before they marched toward the house.

"Look at this," one of them barked, pointing at something on the ground. They both assumed battle-ready stances as they breached the entrance of the home.

Tim held his breath and braced himself for a fight for survival. The thud of boots echoed ominously above him as the men entered. It was now or never—his chance to become the hero he'd always dreamed of being.

"Stay safe," Sarah said hoarsely, her eyes darting between the intruders and the spot where Tim had disappeared into the darkness. Her hands clenched into fists of frustration and desperation. "God, protect him," she pleaded.

Crouched and ready to strike, Tim ignored the searing pain in his side as he waited for the right moment to move. "Focus," he urged himself. "You can do this." The sounds from above grew louder with each passing second.

Helpless to protect Tim, Sarah closed her eyes and prayed with all her might. All Tim could do now was fight for his survival. "Please," she said before opening her eyes, her gaze fixed on the front door, hoping and praying for a miracle to save them both.

CHAPTER 39

Beneath the creaking floorboards, Tim tried to steady his breath. Dust swirled around him, catching at his throat and stinging his eyes as footsteps approached from above. He could hear the irritation in one man's voice when he spoke up.

"I can't believe this. Are those fuckers watching us?" The floor shifted above Tim's head, sending a shower of dirt and debris down onto his face.

"They took the fucking bag!" CJ exclaimed.

"Must be close," Marvin muttered.

CJ scoffed. "I guess you didn't scare them enough."

"Fuck you," Marvin said. "I should have killed him. Next time I see him, he'll wish I was only using a gun."

Tim felt a shiver run down his spine at the threat. He opened the bag, feeling the cold steel of the gun. These guys are dangerous, he thought, gripping the weapon tightly.

Sarah hid behind the trees. She wondered where the other two men were.

"Where is he? He should have made a run for it," she said to herself. The temptation to go to the under-house access gnawed at her, but she knew it could be a trap. Overwhelmed, tears filled her eyes as she tried to give herself a pep talk. "He's fine. He's just waiting them out."

As Sarah crouched in the shadows, desperately trying to convince herself that everything would be alright, Tim remained hidden, clutching the gun. They were both acutely aware of their danger, and the stakes grew higher with each passing second. Time slipped through their fingers, and they could only pray they'd survive.

A bead of sweat trickled down Tim's forehead as he tried to suppress his breath. The musty smell of the damp earth beneath the floorboards filled his nostrils, suffocating him. He lay there, paralyzed by fear, the weight of the gun in his hand both comforting and terrifying.

"Lisa, you copy?" CJ's voice crackled through the CB radio.

"Go ahead." Lisa's reply came through the static.

"How far are you from base?" CJ asked.

"Two miles north," she responded.

"Get up here now!" CJ's voice thundered. "They took our bag."

"Oh my fuck," Lisa uttered in frustration. "CJ, you fucking said it was safe!" she shouted.

CJ chuckled. "You could give them a hundred guns and they still wouldn't hit us."

"Be there in five," Lisa snapped back.

"We're going to scare them out of the forest," CJ explained. "They couldn't be more than a hundred yards away."

Sarah leaned against a tree. The eerie quiet unnerved her, making her wish to be a fly on the wall inside the house, seeing what was happening.

As the last Tahoe approached, the crunch of gravel jolted her out of her thoughts. Her breath caught in her throat. Tim didn't stand a chance. She couldn't comprehend why they wanted to torture them. These people, who had seemed decent, were now relentless predators hunting their prey.

As Sarah's mind spiraled, she couldn't help but think it was all too good to be true. Whether it was these four or someone else, the American government had placed such a high bounty on their heads that would ensure they would be hunted for the rest of their lives.

The silence weighed on Tim. Marvin's voice broke through the stillness.

"Hello, Gov," he began. "Six million is life-changing. My family is struggling daily. We want what's right."

Tim strained to hear more. Marvin paused again, tension building like a storm on the horizon. "I don't agree," Marvin continued. "Your story means little once America has them."

A whisper from CJ. "Tell her ten million."

"Ten million and your heroes are free," Marvin said. He paused, letting the words hang in the air. "You can't afford to lose them, Skye. Once America broadcasts Sarah's pretty face as a captured terrorist, Cascadia will be no more."

The governor's reply came. "I can only offer you three million and land."

"What the fuck!" CJ nearly yelled.

Marvin hissed, "Quiet, man! I don't want the Gov hearing you."

"Forty-eight hours," Marvin said. "Think about our demands. How much is Cascadia worth?"

Silence reclaimed its stranglehold on the room before Marvin erupted, a volcano of anger. "God damn it!" he roared. "She ain't budging!"

"Well, we have at least six million coming soon," CJ said, trying to console Marvin.

"We ain't getting nothing unless we find them."

The sound of a door opening reached Tim's ears, he lost his breath. A female voice rang out. "What's up, Marvin?"

"Still don't have them," Marvin admitted.

"Let's hunt some rats," Lisa said.

Tim crawled toward the exit with the duffle bag. A raccoon appeared and hissed at him, but he maneuvered around it. The ground scraped against his hands and knees. All that mattered was reaching Sarah. As he emerged from the crawl space, adrenaline coursed like wildfire.

Sarah dared to glance from the rough bark of her temporary shield, her gaze absorbing the world beyond their improvised sanctuary. "Oh, thank God," she breathed out. "You're safe."

"We have to move!" Tim yelled. "They know we're close. They are relentless."

They surveyed the surroundings until their gaze settled on a hill that jutted into the sky with such audacity that it appeared to defy nature. "We aim for there." Time said.

"You must be joking," Sarah shot back.

A figure detached itself from the house, surveying its surroundings. Tim unzipped the duffle bag and revealed its cargo to Sarah.

Her eyes widened. "Holy hell Tim! How'd you get their stash? Do you know how to handle one?" She asked.

"I had some practice a few years back," Tim confirmed. "Let's move."

They launched into a frantic sprint, the thunderous pounding of their breaths beating in their ears.

CHAPTER 40

Sarah and Tim found themselves at the base of an incline, a vertical challenge that seemed to mock their lack of climbing ability. But they had no choice. Their pursuers were relentless, and their only shot at survival was to scale this slope. Sarah looked over her shoulder and spotted the four ominous figures huddled together.

"Alright," Tim broke the silence, fishing a gun from their duffle bag. He checked the safety before slipping it into the pockets of his cargo shorts, which also housed a canister of pepper spray. He caught Sarah's apprehensive gaze. "We've got this."

Sarah attempted to mirror his smile, but her eyes couldn't hide her worry. She couldn't ignore the crimson stain spreading around Tim's wound; it made her stomach churn. Yet his unyielding spirit ignited a spark of hope in her heart.

"Let's get moving," Tim proposed, taking point as they began their grueling climb.

Meanwhile, Marvin orchestrated his plan.

"CJ, hit up that road. Lisa, you take the lower ground. Matt, make tracks to that ravine and check out that creek bed. They could be hiding behind some boulder."

"Should we shoot them if we find them?" Lisa asked. She had been a sharpshooter with the U.S. Army until the quake turned her into a medic. She hadn't lost her shooting abilities and was ready for action.

Marvin scoffed. "No, not at all. America won't give us a bounty unless they're alive. But..." he trailed off, "they said nothing about bruises or broken bones."

"How do we stop them if they have guns?" Lisa questioned.

"Watch and learn." Marvin pulled open a duffle bag, revealing its contents. Inside were several canisters that he presented to the group.

Sarah and Tim pushed up the jagged cliff, their skin glistening with sweat despite the cool breeze. The sound of foliage or cracking branches sent adrenaline surging through them. Every upward stride felt like an endless journey. The impending danger of their pursuers urged them onward, forcing them to battle against both physical exhaustion and mental fatigue. Their palms were slick with sweat as they maneuvered through the terrain, clutching desperately at ferns and prickly shrubs for balance. Every fiber in their bodies cried out for respite, but adrenaline spurred them on relentlessly.

"Keep going, we're almost there," Tim whispered through gritted teeth, his face contorted in pain from his deep red wound. He glanced back at Sarah, who was pale and trembling, her eyes darting nervously between the ground beneath her and the ominous figures below.

As the crew readied themselves, Marvin explained how to use flash-bangs.

"These things will knock anyone off their feet within twenty feet," he bragged, passing two stun grenades to each of his partners in crime. "Now let's do this."

CJ and Matt responded with a fist bump, their bodies buzzing with anticipation. They split up, all four dispersing in different directions, amped for what lay ahead.

Sarah tapped Tim's shoulder, her breath coming in shallow gasps. "One of them is closing in," she said.

Tim's gaze snapped toward the figure inching closer to their hillside refuge. "Hold your ground," he commanded.

A chilling thought crept into their minds: would this waking horror ever cease? The day was spiraling further from any semblance of a fairy-tale ending. They were the prey in a deadly game, pursued by hunters who derived perverse pleasure from their fear. The prospect of escape seemed as elusive as a mirage.

"Can we outpace them?" Sarah asked.

"We must," Tim responded. "We can't afford to be caught." Their gazes intertwined, and with an unspoken agreement echoing between them, they pressed forward. Clinging to the fragile thread of hope that they might somehow evade their relentless tormentors.

Silence hung in the air, shattered only by the distant caw of a crow. Lisa's boots crunched on the gravel road as she walked, the ravine to her left and the lifeless forest to her right. Her eyes scanned the landscape, searching for any sign of her targets. She clenched her teeth, knowing that capturing them would be the grand prize they all sought.

"Come out, come out, wherever you are," CJ taunted, his voice echoing through the desolate landscape. He raised his gun to the sky and fired three shots, hoping to flush them out. Flocks of startled birds erupted from the trees, their frantic wings beating against the wind. But there was no sign of their prey.

With each step, Matt's boots sunk into the damp earth of the ravine, scanning for any hint of his prey. A low rumble echoed, a sound that couldn't be mistaken for a mere woodland creature. This was something far more formidable. Adrenaline surged through him as he raised his gaze to meet the form of an enormous bear looming on the right side of the ravine. Its obsidian eyes held a chilling focus that sent shivers down his spine. Marvin had said there'd be no worries in this neck of the woods, but bears? That little detail had been left out.

"Aw, hell," Matt grumbled under his breath, fumbling for his firearm. But before he could steady his shaking hands, the behemoth charged with terrifying speed. Its muscular frame rippled with raw power as it slashed through the air. Matt raised his arms in a feeble gesture of defense, yet the overwhelming strength of the assault knocked him down.

His scream ripped through the silence as he found himself pinned beneath its crushing weight. With one final swipe from its monstrous paw, Matt's world faded and he fell limp on the forest floor.

The bear seemed to smirk in satisfaction at its handiwork before it ambled to the creek for a drink and then lumbered back toward its lair.

Matt's blood-curdling cry reverberated throughout the valley. Marvin sprang into action as he sprinted toward Matt's scream had originated from. Had Sarah and Tim jumped him? The silence swallowing up Matt's last echoes only amplified their dread.

"Move!" Marvin bellowed out.

Huddled together on the steep hill, Sarah and Tim heard the horrific scream. They exchanged wide-eyed looks, trying to make sense of the situation. Was it a trap? A desperate ploy to lure them out?

"Could be a trap," Sarah said.

"I don't think so," Tim responded, watching as one of their pursuers raced away from the base of the hill toward the scream. He chuckled grimly. "Looks like they're getting a taste of their own medicine."

"Guess so," Sarah agreed. Time was running out, and they needed to make a move.

"We have to get to the Tahoe. It's our only chance."

"They're too close," Sarah protested. "As soon as we show ourselves, they'll have us."

"We have to," Tim insisted. "We can't keep climbing these cliffs, hoping for safety."

With a resigned nod, Sarah agreed. "Okay, Tim."

They descended the steep hill, driven by the knowledge that their lives hung in the balance.

CJ, Marvin, and Lisa pressed closer. The rustling of leaves underfoot and the distant chorus of birdsong faded into insignificance against the stark backdrop of this gruesome scene.

"Jesus," Lisa croaked out. "I knew they'd resist... but this?"

Marvin gazed at Matt's grotesque injuries. "Seems like they're not playing." His eyes hardened. "We pull out the big guns now–aim for their legs only." He paused, his mind racing through their rapidly shrinking list of options.

"CJ and I will spread out. They can't have gotten too far." Turning to Lisa, "You need to get one of the Tahoes and get him to a hospital." The words hung heavily, underscoring the dire nature of their predicament.

"Nothing's fast around here," Lisa shot back, her frustration boiling. "We're over an hour away from everything!"

"Shut up, Lisa!" CJ snapped. "Get the damn Tahoe!"

With a defeated nod, Lisa turned on her heel and headed back toward the vehicles.

Meanwhile, Tim and Sarah reached level ground. As they cautiously made their way around the far side of the house, they spotted the Tahoes parked alongside each other.

"Okay," he said. "I'm grabbing the one closest to the house and back it up to you. We leave as slowly as possible so we don't draw attention. On the count of three, I go."

Taking a deep breath, Tim counted down. "Three." He dashed to the Tahoe, yanking open the driver's side door. Sliding into the seat, a sense of unease crept over him. "It can't be this easy," he murmured.

His heart skipped a beat as he looked out the window and saw Lisa approaching, her determined stride sending shivers down his spine. Oh my God, he mouthed, panic rising within him. With trembling hands, Tim pushed the car start button and watched as the dashboard lit up. He shifted it into reverse, slowly backing toward Lisa while praying their plan would succeed.

Lisa walked toward the Tahoe, her shoulders slumping. She cursed under her breath, unable to fathom how two amateurs - no, not even amateurs, just people who'd probably never even thrown a punch in their lives - were outsmarting seasoned professionals like herself and her team. The situation felt surreal, like the universe was playing some cruel joke on her. "Damn it, Sarah and Timmy boy," she muttered.

With eight grueling years under her belt as a Navy vet, Lisa had seen her fair share of chaos. But when the earth danced beneath her boots, she fell back on what the military had drilled into her. Swiftly rallying a ragtag team of neighborhood rescuers, they clawed survivors from the wreckage. She had saved countless souls, but the recognition she deserved was few and far between. Yet for Lisa, it wasn't about the shiny medals or commendations.

"Never thought I'd be schooled by some randoms," she muttered. Crime filled those days, making it feel like walking through a treacherous minefield. No matter what, Lisa stood firm in her resolve to bring down the bad guys. "Chasing bloody unicorns," Lisa mumbled, as the Tahoe appeared.

Memories of past victories only amplified her feeling of falling short. How could someone who'd scaled such heights stumble when it mattered most? Victory was within arm's reach, but now, more than ever, this was no game.

"Get your head in the game," she psyched herself up. "You've ridden out bigger shit storms than this."

"Outta that damn car! Now!" She yelled out with raw urgency. Her gun pointed straight at Tim, whose eyes shot defiance right back at hers.

"Hurry," Lisa growled as she watched Tim throw the Tahoe into reverse. They were so close to nabbing their marks and claiming the reward that would be a game-changer for her family. "Listen up!" She roared. "You're cornered. Give it up now!"

Tim responded, thrusting his hand out the window and flipping Lisa off with brazen disregard.

CHAPTER 41

"Get in!" Tim called to Sarah, who took advantage of Lisa's momentary distraction to jump into the back seat of the Tahoe. "Lay on the floor!"

Sarah quickly complied, pressing herself against the cold metal surface.

Lisa's face contorted with rage. She raised her gun and began shooting at the Tahoe. Each bullet slammed into the windshield, the sound echoing through the vehicle like the pounding of drums. Tim instinctively ducked, every muscle tense. But the impenetrable glass held, resisting Lisa's attempts to kill him.

Tim's mind raced, fear intertwining with the fragments of strategy. Cautiously, he pressed his foot down on the accelerator, inching the Tahoe toward Lisa. She unloaded her clip, bullets ricocheting off the armored plating with a metallic clang.

"Is it going to hold?" Tim questioned in his head, the worry gnawing at his resolve. But there was no time to dwell on it. He floored the accelerator just as CJ and Marvin appeared on the scene. The Tahoe leaped forward like a predator, causing Lisa to jump away.

"Damn it!" Tim muttered under his breath as he swerved to avoid a tree by mere inches. Marvin and CJ opened fire, their bullets joining the cacophony of sounds assaulting Tim and Sarah's ears.

"Please," Sarah said. "Let us get out of this alive."

Tim's focused on the road ahead, his instincts guiding him through the chaos. The Tahoe's engine roared like a furious beast, straining to carry them away from the danger that pursued them relentlessly.

"Come on," Tim thought, willing the vehicle to carry them to safety. "Just a little further."

The world outside the Tahoe seemed to slow down as they raced toward an uncertain future, their fate resting in the hands of a single man. But at that moment, Tim knew he would do everything in his power to protect Sarah and escape the clutches of the ruthless gang that hunted them. And in the face of such adversity, there was nothing more terrifying––or exhilarating–than the hope that burned within him.

The piercing sound of gunfire filled the forest, suffocating any other noise, as Sarah lay low behind the front seats of the Tahoe. Her hands pressed tightly against her ears, she could feel the vibration of each bullet impacting the vehicle, rattling her very core. Fear clawed at her chest, making it difficult to breathe as she silently prayed for escape from this nightmare.

"Sarah, hold on!" The Tahoe veered off the main road and began climbing a hill. Gravel crunched beneath the tires, and the barrage of gunshots faded.

"Okay, you can get up now," Tim said. "We're safe... for now."

Sarah took a deep breath and cautiously emerged from her hiding spot, slipping into the passenger seat. She surveyed the scene, noticing the minor damage. The front windshield had some scratches, but it appeared to have remained intact.

"Look at this road," Tim muttered, scanning the landscape. "I think we're the first ones on it in years." The gravel road was unkempt, its surface uneven and marred by potholes, a remnant of the quake that had hit the region. As they continued their ascent, Sarah noticed the blackened, charred trees give way to healthier specimens, untouched by the great fires that ravaged the land.

"Do you think we lost them?" Sarah asked, her voice wavering with uncertainty.

"Maybe, but we can't let our guard down."

As they drove further along the deserted path, a weighty silence settled between them, punctuated only by the occasional crunch of gravel beneath the tires. The air was heavy with unspoken fears and questions, each more pressing than the last.

"Tim," Sarah said. "What do you think they'll do if they catch us?"

His knuckles went white on the steering wheel as he considered the question. "I don't know, Sarah," he admitted. "But I won't let them take us without a fight."

Their fate seemed to hang in the balance, like the dark clouds that loomed overhead. With every turn of the wheel and crunch of gravel beneath them, they moved farther away from the danger that hunted them, yet closer to the unknown darkness ahead.

Marvin stood tall, his unwavering gaze commanding Lisa and CJ's attention. "Lisa," Marvin barked, his voice hard as steel. "You're taking Matt to the hospital now."

Her lips drew into a tight line. "I have a score to settle with those two. You think I'm just going to let them go?"

"Enough!" Marvin snapped and silenced her protest. "We'll handle them. But first, we need to make sure Matt gets help."

CJ shifted nervously from foot to foot. "Why aren't we chasing them, anyway? They got away!"

Marvin chuckled, shaking his head at CJ. "That road they took? It leads to a dead end—a five-hundred-foot overlook. They've got nowhere to run."

"Really?" CJ asked, incredulous.

"Damn right. Lisa, you're taking Matt to the hospital. Once he's in your car, you head out. CJ, you're with me. We block the road in the narrow canyon about a half mile from here. They won't have a choice but to stop."

Marvin yanked open his duffle bag, revealing a cache of weapons—including a single, deadly grenade. CJ's eyes widened in shock. "You're not seriously going to use that, are you?"

"Of course I am," Marvin affirmed, a wicked grin on his lips. "Once they're trapped, I'll toss this little beauty behind the Tahoe."

"But what if that kills them?"

"Trust me," Marvin said. "It'll only stun them."

"Alright, then," CJ agreed. "Let's get on with it."

The air hung heavy as Lisa, Marvin, and CJ drove up the hill toward Matt, his shallow breaths sounding like a death rattle. The surrounding forest held its breath, as if sensing the impending danger.

"Alright, let's make this quick," Marvin barked as they pulled up beside Matt. CJ and Marvin worked in tandem, lifting Matt's limp body into the back seat of the Tahoe. "Go, Lisa! Not a second to spare!"

Lisa's hands trembled on the steering wheel as she sped down the road. The highway loomed ahead, just fifteen minutes away, but it felt like an eternity. She racked her brain for a plausible explanation to give the hospital staff. Any hint of suspicion could bring the Cascadia government down on their heads, and she couldn't afford that.

Meanwhile, Tim navigated the worsening gravel road, the Tahoe lurching over larger holes that made it impossible to go faster than ten miles per hour. A few wide cracks crisscrossed the path, forcing him to stop and assess the situation. He stepped out of the vehicle, ears straining for any sounds of pursuit, but all he heard were birdsong and the rustle of leaves.

"Sarah, look at this," he called, eyeing the six-inch-wide crack. She opened the door, her voice tense. "Tim, we need to go. Now."

"I don't hear anyone coming," he reassured her. "Maybe they know this road is impassable."

Sarah joined him by the crack, peering into the seemingly bottomless void. Tim tested the ground on the other side with a stomp, then nodded determinedly. "I think it's okay to pass. If we can get past this, maybe we can get away."

"Let's not get overconfident," Sarah warned, her eyes darting around the silent forest. They climbed back into the Tahoe and carefully inched over the crack, Tim's knuckles white on the steering wheel. As they cleared the obstacle, he raised a triumphant fist.

As they continued their desperate escape, both knew that danger lurked out of sight, waiting to strike when they least expected it.

The sudden absence of trees loomed before them like a gaping void, swallowing the path ahead and leaving Tim with a sinking feeling in the pit of his stomach. He slowed the Tahoe to a crawl, dread clawing at his chest as he turned to Sarah. "What is that?"

Sarah's eyes widened. "It's the end of the road," she said.

"Oh, my God!" Tim yelled. "They knew all along we were coming to this. They're just going to wait us out." The despair in his words hung heavy, choking him as he slammed on the brakes about ten feet short of the cliff. He threw open the door and stormed out, cursing loudly.

Sarah hurried out of the Tahoe, her heart aching for Tim as she tried to offer comfort. She noticed the flush creeping up his face, concern etched in her features. "Let me see your back," she urged.

Tim agreed, turning to allow her inspection. The redness around his wound had intensified, a clear sign of infection. Sarah shook her head, fear tightening her throat. "We need to give up and ask for mercy, Tim. You have an infection, and it's spreading. If we don't get you to a hospital soon, it will get much worse."

"There's a duffle bag in the back seat. Get it."

She hesitated, shaking her head. "I don't plan on getting into a gunfight. We need mercy from them. They don't want to kill us because we're probably only worth this much to be turned over to America alive."

Tim interrupted. "We have a satellite phone. We can call for help."

Doubt clouded her expression as she wondered who they could even call. It wasn't as if twenty cops were ready to come up that hill. But with no other options, she trusted Tim and fetched the duffle bag, their lifeline dangling by a thread in a world that seemed intent on tearing them apart.

The weight of the duffle bag pressed against Sarah's legs as she heaved it onto the ground. The contents clinked and clacked like an ominous symphony, reminding her of the danger that lurked within. She unzipped the bag, revealing its deadly cargo.

"This better have juice," Sarah muttered, her hand closing around the satellite phone nestled among a cache of firearms. She jabbed the power button and the Satcom emblem blinked into existence on the screen, casting an unearthly light across her features. The phone hummed to life, its digital purr slicing through the silence as time seemed to stretch on forever.

"Check the contacts," Tim urged, his tone taut with expectation.

Sarah scanned the contact list until one name snagged her attention: Gov.

"This could be it," she stated, glancing up at Tim. "Either we're dialing up the Governor or someone in their camp."

"Do it," Tim said, his gaze riveted on the screen. Sarah hesitated a fraction of a second before pressing down, "connecting" flashed across the display, followed by an electronic ringtone.

"It's ringing," she announced.

Trees groaned, their shadows dancing like specters under the light. The wind howled through their makeshift clearing, carrying an ominous chill. As each ring echoed in her ears, Sarah felt hope slipping away.

"Please," she begged. "Pick up already!" Time seemed to halt.

"Damn," Tim growled, his jaw set tight with frustration.

As they teetered on the edge of despair, Sarah wondered if giving in to their pursuers might be their only shot at survival. But even that choice had its own set of grim repercussions.

"Please," she said one final time, her plea barely rising above the relentless ringing. "Just answer."

CHAPTER 42

The echo of the phone's ring gradually waned into nothingness, leaving an eerie silence. Sarah and Tim locked eyes. The quiet was suffocating.

"Sarah," Tim's voice pierced the stillness, his words heavy with dread. "What if she's involved?"

"The Governor?" Sarah asked.

"Yes, Skye Flower. What if this some twisted game by Cascadia to extort money?"

The question loomed over them, and the potential implications were terrifying. This was no ordinary day at work—it was a high-stakes gamble in which they could lose everything.

Sarah shook her head, the weight of his words pressing down on her. "It's not possible. She couldn't be. No way," she said, but her thoughts betrayed her conviction. Images of Governor Skye Flower, surrounded by shadowy figures. After everything they had seen, anything was possible.

As the seemingly endless minutes ticked away, they wracked their brains, scouring their memory banks for any phone numbers of contacts they had in Cascadia, their thoughts racing like wildfire. A sudden spark of memory flickered within Sarah.

"Oh my God," she breathed. "I think I remember Angela's number."

Sarah diligently studied her contact list, committing each name and number to memory. Yet now, that crucial information seemed to be lodged somewhere deep within the recesses of her mind, buried beneath layers of fear and exhaustion. She tried to prod her memory.

"Try this," she said to Tim. "509-476..."

The phone buzzed, making Tim jump out of his skin. His eyes darted to the caller ID. "The Governor," he muttered under his breath.

Sarah's fingers were shaking, and the phone threatened to fall from her grip.

"I got this," she said, taking the phone from Tim. The sun was an unforgiving spotlight, morphing the morning chill into a warmer breeze. Her thumb jabbed at the green icon on the screen, and the speakerphone kicked in.

"CJ? You mulling over our offer?" Governor Flower's voice echoed through the tiny speakers.

"It's me, Sarah Bridges," she shot back. "We need help."

The line went silent before Governor Flower asked. "Are you okay?"

"Hell no." Sarah's voice cracked. "Tim's messed up bad... he has a nasty infection. We gotta get him to a hospital."

"Are you in a safe place?" Skye asked.

"We are, but not for much longer," Sarah said.

"Alright, I need you to turn on your GPS tracker. Go to settings and turn on tracking."

"On it," Sarah responded, fingers flying over the screen. "You should see our location."

"Gotcha." The governor paused before continuing. "You're not far from our last known spot... My pilot estimates we can be there in an hour."

A knot twisted in Sarah's gut. "Governor... isn't anyone closer?"

"Sure, there are," came the response after a pause filled with static and hushed voices at their end. "But I trust them about as much as I trust a venomous snake not to bite me." Another pause followed. "I'll be coming with my pilot and my bodyguards."

Tim's voice wavered. "How can we trust your team?"

Skye responded. "The trust we place in those who have sworn to protect us is crucial for our democracy in Cascadia. Without it, our democracy could be buried six feet under. Hit me up if anything changes. Stay low until we get there."

The phone disconnected to silence.

"We can't wait," Tim rasped out. "They will be here any minute now."

"Maybe we can see where Marvin is." Sarah scrolled through the menu. "We got them," she confirmed.

"Then that means they can also see our location," Tim said.

"Right," Sarah nodded. "They're probably watching us."

As Sarah had feared, Marvin and CJ were scouring their device, tracking their targets.

"CJ, you never listen!" Marvin growled. "That is a problem if you're working with me."

"Fuck you, Marvin," CJ spat back. He gave a sarcastic bow, the edge of his anger slicing through the air between them. "You're nothing out here. Just a glorified bounty hunter."

Sarah felt the grip of fear as she stared out, listening to the distant howl of the wind. She knew they were watching and waiting for them to make a move. And yet, what could they do? With Tim injured and their lives in danger, they had to trust the Governor and hope that she would come through.

"Tim, we'll get through this. We have to." Sarah whispered.

Marvin's stare bore into CJ. "You think you're God's gift, huh?" he spat, crowding into CJ's space until their faces were inches apart. Marvin's breath was a hot gust of stale coffee and something sharper, unpleasantly sour. "Back the hell off," Marvin warned.

CJ staggered back, his boots skidding on the gravel beneath them. "Matt's on death's door. Our firepower is in their grubby hands. We're down one Tahoe and they've got Satcom to boot. I'm taking point."

"In your dreams!" Marvin barked, drawing his weapon and sending CJ sprawling onto the rough ground with a swift shove. He planted his boot onto CJ's chest. "Listen up," he commanded, "you play ball or you're out." His gun hovered over CJ's temple; an unspoken ultimatum hanging heavily between them. Swiftly disarming CJ of his handgun and tucking it away in his waistband, he growled, "You comprehend?"

CJ's eyes blazed with defiance, but he managed a nod of understanding.

Marvin pressed harder into his chest. "Do you COMPREHEND?"

"I get it," CJ choked out. "Now get your damn boot off me."

Marvin eased off and hauled CJ upright by the arm. "If you'd just keep your ears open, you'd know they ain't budging an inch," he grumbled dismissively before scanning their surroundings.

"They're stuck like rats in a trap." After a moment he continued: "We'll wait 'em out." Marvin's gaze settled on a pile of large rocks nearby. "We need to set up a roadblock. Start hauling those rocks onto the road. I'll gather some branches."

Despite the tension, they worked in unison to construct the makeshift barricade. Marvin felt a prickling sense of unease as he kept one eye on CJ, wary of his partner's hostility. He'd never imagined that CJ, his right-hand man for over half a decade, would turn on him like this. But here they were–stranded in no-man's-land, waiting out greenhorns.

Once they had wedged the last branch into place, both men retreated to their respective corners. A sense of foreboding spread like a smothering shroud over their temporary campsite; the quiet before the inevitable storm.

CHAPTER 43

The sun was casting brilliant shades of blue over the landscape. Despite the picturesque scene, Sarah couldn't shake off the feeling of foreboding that seemed to hang in the air. She and Tim were on the run, searching for a new hiding spot to escape their pursuers. The Tahoe had been their refuge, but now it felt more like a trap.

"Sarah," Tim breathed. "We can't stay here any longer. We need to find a better place to hide."

Sarah's eyes darted around, desperately seeking a solution. Then she spotted a rocky cliff face in the distance. "There," she pointed. "There could be a cave we can hide in."

Tim's eyes lit up. "That's perfect, but how do we get up there?" He searched for any unmarked path that could lead them to safety. A faint animal trail caught his attention, winding through the craggy terrain. "I see a route," he said. "It won't be any hairier than the past two."

Sarah's breath hitched in her throat. "What about your wound?" she asked.

"I don't have a choice. We need to move." Tim started toward the trail.

They made their way up the rugged hill, following the faint animal path, a snarl echoed. "What's that?"

"Keep moving." Tim pulled out the bear spray and unlocked the safety. "I'm ready for whatever that is."

The snarl grew louder. "Where is it?" Tim asked.

"I don't know."

Out of nowhere, a colossal bear slammed onto the ground behind them, its monstrous frame surpassing 400 pounds. Tim's heart plummeted as he realized they were face to face with a grizzly. But here? Not one nature manual mentioned anything about grizzlies.

Sarah's breath caught in her throat, her mind going blank as she stared into the eyes of the predator. Frozen in terror, they could only watch as the beast lumbered closer, its powerful muscles rippling beneath its thick fur. With every step, their fate seemed to draw nearer.

Tim refused to cower. He placed himself between Sarah and the ferocious beast. "Run and don't look back!" He commanded. Sarah hesitated before sprinting away, her feet pounding against the forest floor.

The bear let out a menacing growl. In one swift motion, it swiped at him with its massive claws, sending him flying. As he crashed to the ground, his bear spray fell from his grasp and rolled several feet away.

Tim scrambled toward the canister just as the bear lunged at him again, its roars shaking the surrounding earth. As he grabbed hold of the spray and turned to face his attacker, a primal roar tore from his throat, challenging the beast before him.

"Come on, work!" Tim muttered as he tried to activate the bear spray, only to realize the safety was still on. Panic clawed at his insides, but he pulled the safety off just as the enraged animal lunged forward. Closing his eyes, he released a cloud of the irritant upwards. The bear cried as it retreated a few steps, allowing him to sit up and aim the spray directly at its face. The beast cried out in pain and confusion, turning tail and lumbering back down the trail from which it had come.

"Tim!" Sarah's voice cracked as she returned, her eyes fixated on his bloodied arm. "Oh my God!"

The sight of his mangled flesh threatened to rob Tim of consciousness, but he fought to stay focused. Sarah removed her shirt, clad only in her bra, she wrapped the fabric tightly around his wound.

"I'm so sorry. So sorry for all of this," Sarah said. "It's been an endless nightmare."

"Hey, it's okay," Tim reassured her. "You had no clue that even half of this would have happened."

Sarah nodded, her gaze lingering on Tim's bandaged arm as blood began seeping through the makeshift dressing. "What do we do now?" she asked, her voice barely audible.

"Same thing we planned. We continue toward the overlook. The Governor should be here soon."

Sarah checked her phone. It had been nearly an hour since their call. Their breaths mingled with the howl of wind as they prepared for the imminent confrontation.

"Think they're still headed this way?" CJ questioned.

Marvin, rooted outside, grimaced and took out his frustration on the gravel underfoot, sending a scatter of stones ricocheting off the vehicle.

"Let's hit it, Marv," CJ pressed.

Marvin strode to the driver's side with a menacing look and snapped, "Slide over. I'm taking the wheel."

"But this is my ride," CJ objected.

"Your ride? This beast was Cascadia's. It ain't your wheels, so shift your ass over!" Marvin barked. With a resigned sigh, CJ complied and slid into the passenger seat as Marvin commandeered the driver's spot.

"We'll roll slow," Marvin dictated. "No clue what nasty surprises they've left for us."

"Yeah, right," CJ retorted under his breath, rolling his eyes dramatically. "I could just hoof it."

Marvin responded to his attempt at humor with nothing but a snarl. "Zip it," he warned.

"You got it, chief," CJ shot back.

High above them, Sarah clutched her phone, checking for missed calls. More than an hour had passed since their call with Governor Flower. Anxiety gnawed at them.

"Oh God… They're coming our way," she said before dialing Skye.

Skye answered after one ring. "We're fifteen minutes out."

"They'll be here in a heartbeat," Sarah said.

The gasp on the other end betrayed Skye's fears. "Are you tucked away?"

"Yes, on an outcrop with a bird's-eye view of the Tahoe."

"Hold tight. Don't give them any targets," Skye instructed. "I've got two sharpshooters. We'll do whatever it takes to get you out of there."

"Please hurry," Sarah begged before the line went dead, leaving her and Tim alone on their perch. "Guess it's just us now," she locked eyes with Tim. His face was ashen and he nodded slowly.

CHAPTER 44

Wind slithered through the remains of the once lush forest, its bitter touch raising goose bumps on Sarah's exposed skin as she stood sentinel near the harsh cliff edge. She scoured the scarred landscape like a hawk.

"Still nothin'?" Tim's voice grated from within their makeshift cave refuge.

"Nada," Sarah retorted. "They're up to something." She shot a side-long glance at Tim, who mustered a ghost of a smirk despite his ordeal.

Marvin and CJ edged closer to the abyss that yawned before them, a chasm that seemed to plunge into the very bowels of the earth. The high beams of their Tahoe, parked behind them, cut through the darkness. Marvin felt a dread curling in his gut–an insidious thought that Sarah and Tim might have set up some fatal trap for them. His jaw clenched, teeth gritting together in a silent snarl.

"This is twisted," CJ murmured as they ventured further into uncharted territory.

"Keep your cool," Marvin warned him. "Go on. Check if it's safe to cross."

"If you say so, boss man," CJ retorted with a grumble, stepping away from their vehicle. "I'm not Marvin's goddamn minion." His boots crunched over gravel and dried leaves.

Marvin watched him closely, fingers itching to grab their stash of weapons tucked away in the Tahoe. If shit hit the fan, he had to be ready. His mind was a tumultuous storm, anticipation and anxiety grappling for control.

CJ scrutinized the crevice before shouting at Marvin, "It's half a foot wide at least! Gotta be fifty feet deep. Probably wider in some spots!" But deep down there was an uneasy sensation nagging at him, a suspicion that this could all be part of some devious plot concocted by their crafty enemies.

"Give it a good thump! Let's see if it can hold our weight," Marvin shouted.

CJ stomped with all his might on the fractured ground, feeling the weight of impending danger. The earth held firm under his boots. He scanned their surroundings, a sense of foreboding creeping over him as if they were being watched by unseen predators lurking in the shadows.

"Stomp harder! We need to know if the Tahoe can cross," Marvin barked.

"Fine," CJ grumbled before unleashing a powerful stomp that shook the ground. It felt stable enough. But as he stepped over, the earth crumbled beneath as darkness swallowed him.

"Marvin!" CJ's voice echoed as he fell into an endless abyss. A sickening thud abruptly silenced his screams as he hit solid ground.

"Son of a bitch!" Marvin cursed, rushing to the edge of the crevice. He peered down into the void where CJ lay motionless. A wave of grief washed over him, replaced by a seething anger that threatened to consume him. "Goddamn it!" Marvin spat out, wiping away tears from his eyes. His mind raced to come up with a new plan. With no way to drive over it, he returned to the Tahoe and retrieved their duffle bag of weapons.

"Lisa! You copy?" he barked into his walkie-talkie repeatedly until receiving a response.

"Just left the hospital," Lisa sighed on the other end of the line. "Matt's in awful shape... punctured lung... broken ribs... internal b leeding..."

"Damn!" Marvin roared in frustration, pounding his fist against the side of their vehicle so hard it reverberated through its metal frame. "How soon can you get here?"

"If I push it? Forty minutes."

"Do it," Marvin growled back at her. "See you in forty."

As he clicked off the walkie-talkie, Marvin's eyes narrowed, his anger churning like a brewing storm within him. He knew that Sarah and Tim were nearby, waiting for their rescue. With each step, his boots crunched against the sharp gravel. His thoughts drifted to the prize at the end of this treacherous mission - six million dollars split between him, Lisa, and Matt. "Just a little further," he said to himself with determination. Victory was within his grasp, and he could practically taste it.

On a rocky ledge, Sarah kept a watchful eye on their surroundings. The enemy had stopped moving, but she suspected that it was a trap. She turned to check on Tim, who was sleeping soundly despite his injuries. For a moment, she allowed herself to relax.

She spotted a lone figure approaching on the road below.

She tapped Tim's shoulder, and he jolted awake. "I'm ready! I'm ready!" he said. "What's happening?"

"Someone is coming. I don't know if it's a trap."

"Stay alert," Tim hissed, his weapon ready in his hands. "We can't let our guard down."

The two held their breath. Tim and Sarah waited with bated breath for their next move. In the eerie stillness, they could almost hear the steady beat of their hearts pounding out a rhythm of dread.

"We've got this," Sarah said.

Marvin stealthily retreated into the shadows, hoping to elude any potential detection. Aware of the gamble associated with this mission, the irresistible allure of the reward compelled him to proceed. A fortune of six million dollars would provide security for him, Matt, and Lisa and all of their families. "Today's the day," Marvin muttered under his breath, his fingers deftly arming the gun in his ankle holster. With another pistol strapped to his waist, loaded with rubber bullets to avoid lethal damage, he felt a surge of confidence. The two stun grenades clipped to his jacket gleamed menacingly in the dappled light. All it would take was one well-placed grenade to draw Tim and Sarah out of hiding. Then the game would truly begin.

Tim and Sarah scanned the area for their enemy. Despite their determination, doubt lingered in their minds.

"Where did he go?" Tim asked, his eyes darting back and forth as he peered over the edge. The man had vanished.

"Maybe he's trying to take us by surprise," Sarah suggested, her gaze sweeping the landscape below. "We should move from the ledge so he can't see us."

The wind picked up, sending a shiver down Marvin's spine as he approached the Tahoe, his gaze fixed on the rocky ledge where they were hiding.

"It's time to make some noise," Marvin muttered, reaching for a stone from the creek bed. He flung it toward the vehicle, but his aim was off, and the rock fell short with a dull thud. "Damn it." He grabbed another stone and tried again.

This time, the stone struck the roof of the Tahoe, echoing through the canyon like the crack of a gunshot. Marvin's heart raced-this had to work. He needed to draw them out, to make them understand they were cornered, and he was coming for them.

Marvin drew his ankle gun, flicking off the safety and scanning his surroundings for the perfect vantage point. His sharp eyes landed on a rugged rock outcropping just above the ledge. Taking careful aim, he unleashed a barrage of shots, the sound of gunfire piercing through the air.

Above, Tim and Sarah tensed, ready to spring into action as they listened to the chaos below.

"I can't see him," Tim said, glancing over the edge every few seconds while gripping his weapon tightly. The sudden thump from down by the Tahoe made them both jump.

"What was that?" Sarah's voice quivered.

"No idea. He's probably trying to lure us out. Get into the cave."

As Sarah retreated to the safety of the cave, Tim stayed near the ledge, his eyes darting back and forth as he searched for their attacker. The sound of gunfire echoed throughout the canyon, bullets narrowly missing them and striking the outcropping with alarming proximity.

"Holy shit," Tim murmured, his voice shaking. "He knows where we are."

"Stay calm," Sarah urged. The unmistakable thrum of helicopter blades grew louder. "Thank God," Sarah breathed. As the helicopter came into view, she wasted no time in calling the governor to warn her about the shooter lurking below.

A cacophony of gunfire shattered the tense silence, echoing off the canyon walls as Marvin peered out from his hiding spot, eyes narrowed. He had them cornered. The dust and small rocks kicked up from the outcropping confirmed their exact location and a sinister smile spread across his face.

"Got you now," he muttered, heart pounding in anticipation. His mind raced with thoughts of vengeance as he scanned the hillside for a trail leading toward Tim and Sarah. An animal trail caught his eye, winding its way up to the ledge where his prey hid.

A distant chopping noise filled the air as the blades of a helicopter sliced through the atmosphere. The helicopter drowned out all other sounds, as Marvin's mind raced with desperation, searching for a way to escape. Clutching the grenade, he knew this was his last chance.

Governor Skye Flower, her eyes glued to the landscape below.

"Two minutes!" called the pilot, and the chopper swung into a northbound approach.

Skye turned to her crew. "Are you ready?"

Two snipers assumed their positions by the open doors, and the pilot focused on the task. Closing on their target, the pilot pointed below. "Target spotted."

"Two rescues on the ledge," one sniper reported, his eyes locked on Tim and Sarah. The Governor nodded. "First target is the shooter."

The helicopter's heat sensors honed in on the shooter with deadly accuracy, as the sniper waited with bated breath. Skye's voice crackled over the CB. "Marvin, drop your weapons now!"

Marvin refused to back down, his finger trembling on the trigger as he took a shot at the chopper. The blades whirred furiously as the pilot swerved to dodge the bullet, determined to take out their target at any cost. Skye's eyes blazed with an intense fury, her voice sharp as she hurled her words like daggers, slicing through the tense silence.

"You are clear to eliminate the target."

A deadly warning reverberated throughout the canyon, its weight suffocating in its intensity. "This is your last chance," Skye snarled into the CB, her thumb hovering over the button that would unleash destruction upon their enemy. "Surrender now or face death."

Uncertainty hung in the air as the standoff reached a critical point, becoming increasingly suffocating. As Marvin weighed his dwindling options, each second felt like an eternity, every decision potentially leading to disaster. The deafening roar of the helicopter blades was the only sound, drowning out all other noise as it circled above like a relentless predator.

Marvin's mind raced as he weighed his options. With one gun strapped to his ankle and another loaded with rubber bullets in his hand, he stepped into the open.

"Drop your weapons!" the voice boomed through the megaphone with chilling authority. In a split-second decision, he hesitated before slowly sinking to one knee, his heart racing as he tried to buy some time.

His hand found the icy hardness of the concealed firearm. "You could've stopped this," he hissed, leveling his weapon at the chopper. He gripped the gun, his palms slick with sweat, before pulling the trigger. But instead of taking out his adversary, Marvin crumpled over.

In the helicopter, Governor Flower spewed a torrent of expletives. This mission had taken an unforeseen detour, and Marvin's lifeless form sprawled below.

"Keep your eyes peeled," cautioned one sharpshooter as they surveyed their surroundings with laser-sharp focus, clutching tenaciously onto the copter rail.

Tim and Sarah watched Marvin's exchange with Governor Skye Flower. As gunfire shattered the silence into shards of sound, they recoiled simultaneously. Tim risked a glance over the precipice at Marvin's fallen form–a pool of blood had formed around his body.

"I think we're clear," he said softly.

With the helicopter above them, the rescue gear slowly descended onto their rocky perch. With a sense of urgency, the medic assessed Tim's condition, his voice tinged with desperation.

"Hang tight dude, we're getting you out of here," he said, as he maneuvered Tim onto the stretcher.

Tim fought to keep his eyelids from closing. With precision, the rescue team lifted the stretcher into the helicopter and then assisted Sarah.

Governor Flower locked her gaze onto theirs. "I'm so sorry," she murmured. "I truly am."

CHAPTER 45

The white walls of the ICU couldn't contain the weight of the world that pressed down on Sarah and Governor Skye Flower as they sat on a bench outside Tim's room. The hum of mechanical life support systems echoed through the corridor and antiseptic lingered in the air.

"I'm Doctor Taylor," a woman in pristine white garb approached them. "Are either of you related to Tim Rezner?"

Sarah said, "Almost." She immediately regretted not lying on the intake form.

Doctor Taylor tightened her lips. "I'm not allowed to share information with anyone besides his family."

Governor Skye interjected. "Doctor, I understand your protocols, but this is more important."

The doctor asked, "And who are you?"

"Governor Skye Flower of Cascadia."

Doctor Taylor straightened up. "I'm sorry, Governor. I wasn't aware."

Governor Flower waved a hand. "Don't worry about it."

"Well then," Doctor Taylor began. "Tim suffered serious wounds on his right arm and back. The infection on his back was spreading. We cleaned it. The wounds in his arms required stitches. And he suffered a minor concussion. He probably wouldn't have survived another day."

"Mr. Rezner will have medication to take, and his recovery will probably take a few weeks," Doctor Taylor continued.

"Can I see him?" Sarah asked.

The doctor nodded, and Governor Skye Flower said she would wait outside the room while Sarah went in.

As Sarah pushed open the door, the steady hum of machinery filled the dimly lit ICU, punctuated by Tim's snoring. Sarah hesitated in the doorway, her heart swelling with relief as she took in the sight before her. The rhythmic rise and fall of his chest brought an unexpected smile to her lips.

She approached his bed slowly. The scent of disinfectant couldn't completely mask the faint smell of blood, reminding her of their ordeal just hours earlier. Shadows stretched across his face from the slats of the blinds; they had been through hell and back together, and yet here he was, still breathing, still fighting.

Sarah's eyes were wide with tears as a few droplets splashed onto Tim's face. His disheveled hair and sleepy expression made her want him even more. She reached out. "You're such a mess."

"Hey now," Tim grumbled.

Sarah leaned closer, "I couldn't have done any of this without you."

Tim let out a genuine chuckle. "You mean nearly getting us killed?"

Sarah couldn't contain her laughter. "Okay, fine, maybe not that part." She brushed away the remnants of her tears and looked at him fondly. "But we'll have one hell of a story to tell."

"A crazy, unscripted action movie with a side of pain," Tim mused, his voice still rough from sleep.

Sarah furrowed her brow. "I wish it was just an action movie though..."

Before she could finish her thought, Tim pulled her in for a hug. "Don't worry about that now. We made it through, didn't we?"

"We did," echoed Sarah. "And I missed you so much. You must have nine lives or something."

Tim grinned at her. "Only if I can spend them with you." Sarah's heart swelled as their lips met.

Outside, Governor Skye Flower's gaze lingered on the floor, her thoughts spiraling as she processed the events. The air was heavy with betrayal and the responsibility of holding a new nation together.

"Governor," a voice broke through the silence as one of her agents approached. "I have news for you."

"Proceed," Skye said, steeling herself for whatever information lay ahead.

"Agents apprehended Matt C. They located him in a hospital in Tillamook with injuries, but he should be fine to face justice. Do you think they will face execution?"

Skye's expression hardened. "Our constitution does not mention the use of capital punishment," she said. "Instead, they can rot in prison."

The agent smiled and nodded, relieved by her answer. "Yes, Governor." With a respectful salute, he turned and left the governor to her thoughts.

Inside the room, Tim's muffled cry of pain cut through the quiet, followed by his reassuring words he was okay. Sarah leaned in, their lips meeting in a passionate kiss that spoke of loss, survival, and newfound love. As they parted, the specter of Tim's fiancée hung heavily between them.

"What about your fiancée?" Sarah asked. "What happens now?"

"I have to end it. There is no way I will ever be welcome back to the United States as a free citizen. And it will not be safe for her to even try coming here. She could end up in prison." Tim said.

"I'm so sorry. I never once thought our futures in the U.S. could be jeopardized."

"We have survived the most horrific experiences together." He cleared his throat and continued, "I love you, Sarah Bridges, and I want to spend the rest of my days by your side, whether it's a few years or decades. You are the only one I want to be with."

Tears welled up in Sarah's eyes. "I love you too, Tim Rezner." They sealed their love once more with a kiss amidst the chaos of their lives.

The hospital's sterile scent filled the room. The door creaked open, and Governor Flower strode in with a weariness etched onto her face like deep scars. Her once cheerful expression was now replaced by a steely determination and exhaustion, evidence of the immense burden she carried as the leader of a nation.

"May I enter?" she asked, her voice strained.

Sarah and Tim exchanged a glance before nodding. "Please, do come in!"

A wave of sorrow washed over the governor as she took in Tim's broken form and Sarah's tear-stained cheeks, a physical manifestation of their shared pain and suffering. But amidst the darkness, she couldn't help but feel overwhelming admiration for their unwavering resilience in the face of unimaginable hardship. A radiant smile spread across her face as she gazed at them with pride and joy, her heart swelling with emotion. "Tim, you are a genuine hero of Cascadia."

"If you want to work by my side, you are welcome to join," she offered.

Tim smiled weakly, appreciating the offer but knowing where his true passion lay. "Thank you, Governor, but the camera is my passion."

Governor Skye nodded in agreement. "Well, it was worth a try," she said. Her eyes revealed a glimmer of hope as she reached into her pocket and produced a sleek SAT phone. "I'm sure both of you have some calls you'd like to make."

Tim took the phone from her outstretched hand, feeling its weight and importance in his palm. The governor added she would wait outside if they needed her before leaving.

The door closed and a sense of finality hung in the air. As they pondered their uncertain future, the weight of their situation bore down on them, heavy and suffocating. The oppressive silence hung in the air, making their every breath seem deafeningly loud as they strained to break the quiet with words.

"Sarah," Tim began, his voice barely audible above the hum of medical machinery. "I need to make a call."

Her eyes met his, and she nodded. "Do you want me to leave?"

"No," swallowing hard against the lump in his throat. "I'd rather have you here for this call."

Tim's hand trembled, the digits on the Sat Phone blurring as he punched in a number he knew by heart. The shrill ring echoed ominously in the confined space, its resonance sinking into his very bones with an oppressive sense of finality.

"Hello? Who is this?" Monique's voice cut through the static-laden silence.

"It's me," he croaked.

"Tim!" Monique cried out, her relief so tangible it seemed to breach the crackly connection. "God... are you alright?"

"Mo," he stammered, choking back a sob that threatened to break loose. "Feels like we've been apart for decades. I'm... I'm laid up in a hospital."

"Holy shit, Tim... What happened?"

"We got snatched... They tried to ship us off to America as if we were terrorists," he forced out.

"I can't imag..." Monique's words trailed off.

"And there was this gunfight... and a bear..." His attempt at levity fell flat amidst their shared trauma.

"Is Sarah okay?" Monique asked.

"She's holding up better than I am. Didn't have to donate any skin."

Monique's voice caught in her throat as she whispered, "Tim, I've missed you so damn much. The news has been spewing shit about you being terrorists, but we all know it's just smoke and mirrors."

"Are you doing alright? How are you holding up?"

"I miss you." Her confession came out brokenly. "I miss everything about you."

A lump lodged itself stubbornly in Tim's throat. "M... You mean everything to me. But I can't come back."

A sob escaped from Mo. "I knew this was coming. I didn't want to face it. But hearing your voice... It's a lifeline. We held a vigil for you and Sarah."

"How did it go?" Tim asked.

"Pretty damn powerful... There were more than enough folks pissed off about what America did to you guys. It's not right, all because of some interview. In a country that boasts free speech." Her voice trailed off into silence.

The line went silent before Tim gathered the courage to speak again. "Mo, I love you. I always will."

Mo's sobs grew louder. "My parents and I went to a lawyer when we heard the news, but we are powerless. The only option is for you to turn yourself in."

Tim winced at the thought of living out his life in prison, separated from the woman he loved. They were powerless against the government's wrath.

"It hurts," Mo choked out between tears. "I never thought it would be like this. Please, Tim... Just let me know you're okay. I'll always love you."

"I will, Mo," Tim promised, his tears falling freely now. "I love you." And with that, the call ended, leaving a lingering ache in both of their hearts.

"I'm sorry, Tim," Sarah murmured. "You love her so much. Neither of you deserves this."

"Monique doesn't deserve this," Tim choked out, his gaze distant, lost in memories of a life that now seemed so far away.

"Neither do you," Sarah added, her voice tinged with sadness as she reflected on the man who had grown to be so much more than just her partner.

"Thank you for being here," he said.

"Always." In that moment, they knew that whatever trials lay ahead, they would face them together.

A faint knock on the door pierced the melancholy silence that had settled over the room like a shroud. Sarah glanced at Tim, who gave a weary nod of assent.

"Yes, Governor, you may come in," she called out.

As Governor Flower entered the room, her trademark smile shone brightly. She approached Tim's bedside, the sound of her footsteps echoing in the sterile hospital room. "How are you, Tim?"

Tim managed a weak chuckle, his eyes reflecting the pain he tried to mask. "I could be better. Thank you so much for saving us. We probably would have never made it out alive."

"I will ensure your safety by assigning two agents as your body-guards," the governor whispered, her voice carrying the undertone of their vulnerability.

"Wow," Sarah breathed. "This is incredible. You might win your independence after all."

Skye spoke with excitement in her voice. "Indeed," she said, her eyes shining with determination. "Soon, we will have Cascadia as our land."

"How long will we need protection?" Tim asked.

"Until they remove the bounty from your head," Skye said gravely, her words filled with finality. Tim let out a sigh, his shoulders slumped in defeat.

"I had a feeling that would happen," he murmured. "Can we trust these guards?"

"We thoroughly questioned and tested them with lie detectors. These agents are trustworthy," Skye reassured him confidently. "Please forgive me, I must attend to some urgent matters." She straightened up and prepared to leave, giving Sarah a warm embrace. "Words cannot adequately convey the depth of gratitude I feel toward both of you."

Despite his injuries, Tim gave Skye a gentle hug as well.

"You can keep the phone," she told them. "It's fair that you have a means of communication."

"Thank you," Tim and Sarah said in unison, as Governor Flower bid them farewell and exited the room. With a click of the door closing behind her, a new chapter began, one that would change everything they knew forever.

CHAPTER 46

A standing-room crowd had gathered in the newly restored Keller Auditorium of Portland. Sarah sat poised on stage, Tim at her side. President Skye Flower, a towering figure on stage, commanded attention with her powerful voice that resonated throughout the auditorium. The audience hung onto each word she uttered, finding solace in her confident delivery.

As President Flower began her speech, her voice reverberated through the room, commanding everyone's attention. "Adversity and hardships tested our community, but we emerged as a united and fortified community, standing stronger than ever."

A hand shot up from the crowd. Skye acknowledged him with a nod and encouraged him to voice his thoughts.

"Could you shed some light on Cascadia's current relationship with the United States?" he asked.

"A question that weighs heavily on many hearts," Skye responded thoughtfully, after gathering her thoughts. "Our ties with the United States are nuanced and complex. But Cascadia stands tall. We are self-reliant and independent. We will not let past errors dictate our future." A wave of approval washed over the audience, involuntarily nodding in agreement.

As President Flower concluded her empowering speech, thunderous applause filled the auditorium, resonating like an unstoppable tidal wave. The sweet fragrance of flowers enveloped the air, their vibrant colors raining down on the stage like confetti, a jubilant celebration of her inspiring words. Radiating with happiness, she gracefully descended from the podium, her smile contagious as she enthusiastically shook hands with people who joyfully handed over their old Oregon license plates, their excitement palpable in the air.

When she reached Sarah and Tim, Skye took their hands into hers and leaned in close enough for only them to hear what she had to say next. "You've got this."

Sarah could barely find her voice to respond, but managed a shaky, "Thank you for everything." Her heart swelled with newfound courage and resolve.

As the president walked offstage, a woman approached the podium, her voice amplified by the speakers in the square.

"Our next guest has an incredible story. After narrowly escaping terrorists, he faced a serious infection and even a bear attack. But he didn't give up and fought to survive. Please join me in giving a warm welcome to Mr. Tim Rezner!" The crowd erupted into applause and cheers, their excitement nearly roaring.

Sarah watched as Tim rose to his feet, his eyes shining. Despite his composed demeanor, she could sense the adrenaline coursing through him. This gathering was more than just a group of survivors, they were warriors who had emerged victorious after facing unimaginable tragedy.

They had come a long way and were ready to celebrate in their beloved nation. Tim looked at the sea of joyful faces before him. He could practically taste the excitement.

"Let's give it up for everyone here today!" Tim exclaimed, his voice booming over the lively crowd. "I want to thank Portland for making this happen, and Cascadia for being the ultimate land of freedom!"

The audience erupted in a thunderous roar, leaping to their feet, their cheers drowning out the music. Their voices soared through the auditorium, vibrant and full of life, filling Tim's soul with an exhilarating sense of euphoria. He stood to the side of the podium, waiting for the applause to ebb away like the tide.

"Six years ago on this very day," Tim continued, his voice steady and unwavering, "the most destructive earthquake in human history hit Cascadia. The 9.5 quake started at 9:23 in the morning, and the shaking didn't stop until 9:29." His words painted a chilling picture, and he saw the memories flicker across the faces of those who had lived through it. "The tsunami destroyed much of the West Coast, affecting Japan, Alaska, Hawaii, and other coastlines."

A heavy silence fell over the audience, their faces etched with sorrow as they relived the heart-wrenching memories. Tim swallowed hard before pressing on.

"After the first quake, over one hundred aftershocks hit, many above 8.0, leaving little left to destroy. Massive wildfires ravaged several million acres of forest. As these events occurred, resources became so limited that people died of starvation. The massive earthquake and wildfires displaced over six million people from Eureka, California, to Vancouver, British Columbia. Over 800 thousand people lost their lives."

The silence that followed was deafening. Grief hung in the air, a palpable force that threatened to crush them all beneath its weight.

Tim clenched his fists, anger simmering beneath his calm exterior. "Little did the U.S. government realize or care that people were starving and there were not even half the shelters that were needed for the displaced," he said, his voice laced with bitterness.

A few random cheers erupted from the crowd, and someone yelled, "Fuck the United States!"

Tim let the crowd quiet again before speaking. "What came out of this was the birth of a new country: Cascadia." The crowd erupted once more, most on their feet, their voices rising like a phoenix from the ashes. Tim raised his hand in gratitude, acknowledging their resilience and strength.

Tears welled up in Tim's eyes as he looked at the resilient faces around him, their applause fading into a bittersweet melody of hope and sorrow, a poignant tribute to the strength forged in the depths of tragedy. United, they would persist in carving a fresh trajectory for this tenacious nation, molded by the flames of destruction and strengthened by the indomitable resolve of its citizens.

The stage lights cast a warm glow on Tim's face as he looked out at the sea of people before him, their faces reflecting the same yearning for a brighter future that simmered within his heart.

"In September 2030, Sarah and I started our documentary," he continued. He remembered the day they left their humble Kansas homes, wide-eyed and full of dreams, never imagining that their journey would lead them to play such a crucial role in saving a fledgling nation.

"Once we arrived in Cascadia, President Flower changed all our plans," Tim said, a hint of amusement creeping into his tone. "We didn't know what to expect when she asked us to interview her. And we didn't expect to be taken hostage by government agents." The words hung in the air, the memories of the people they had met during those dark days that truly moved him. Battle-weary survivors, each with stories of unimaginable strength and perseverance, became the beating heart of their mission.

Tim declared passionately, his eyes glistening with determination, "Cascadia has birthed a land where people brim with joy, work hard to create spaces, and build differently." Tim bowed twice, feeling humbled and invigorated by the love and support that surrounded him.

When the ovation ceased, Tim knew it was time to share the spotlight with someone who had become his rock through it all.

"I would like to introduce an incredible person," he said, his voice thick with emotion. "Without her resilience and bravery, I would be dead now. Sarah Bridges has continued to educate the outside about life on the inside. Sarah, please come up!"

The applause was thunderous. As Sarah approached Tim, she embraced him tightly, feeling his warmth against her body. "You are amazing."

He felt his cheeks flush as he retreated to his chair, unable to contain his smile.

"Seattle was more than my home. It was my life," Sarah began. "Like many of you, I lost family and friends. Today, we build a new life, a New Seattle." The crowd listened with rapt attention as she spoke. "Cascadia's salvation is its people, people who have survived through so much in so few years. As Tim and I continue our journeys through Cascadia, we meet more and more amazing people. People who have endured horrible living conditions. It has only made Cascadia stronger." Her gaze swept over the audience. "I am happy to call myself a Cascadian." As the noise died down, Sarah smiled. "I have a special surprise."

The stage transformed as children and adults holding candles streamed down the aisles, their faces alight with determination and pride. The auditorium buzzed with anticipation, a palpable energy that coursed through every heart in the room.

"Today," Sarah announced, her voice resounding with conviction, "is the birth of our national anthem." A collective gasp swept through the audience, followed by an "oooh" sound. The audience's eyes focused on the large screens mounted on either side of the stage, anticipating the appearance of lyrics that would soon guide their voices in unison.

As the stage curtains parted, revealing a symphony orchestra poised and ready to play, Sarah's eyes sparkled with unshed tears. She took a deep breath, steadying herself. "Now, if everyone is ready," she said. A smattering of applause rippled through the crowd.

Sarah walked over to the chorus, feeling the weight of responsibility settle upon her. Tim joined her, his presence a comforting anchor amidst the sea of faces. The conductor raised his baton and brought it down with a decisive motion, signaling the beginning of a new era for Cascadia.

"Through the dark times, we stuck it through," they sang, their voices tentative at first, but growing stronger with each word. Sarah felt a shiver run down her spine as the melody enveloped her, the harmonies weaving together.

"Through the dark times, we persevered," the chorus continued, and the audience joined, their voices lending strength to the declaration. As they sang, Sarah's mind wandered to the countless stories of bravery and resilience she had encountered in Cascadia. Each of them, and so many others, looked downcast, their eyes brimming with unshed tears, a reminder of the sacrifices made for Cascadia.

"Through the dark times," echoed through the auditorium as Sarah's thoughts wandered to those they had lost along the way, their sacrifices never to be forgotten. The melody swelled, lifting their voices in unison, embracing the promise of a brighter future for all.

The rallying cry of "WE are Cascadia! WE are Cascadians!" resounded through the air, each voice blending seamlessly in a powerful chorus. The words rang out like a clarion call, echoing off the walls and soaring into the hearts of all who heard it. As the last notes faded away, the audience rose to their feet, their thunderous applause shaking the very foundations of the room. It was as if a tidal wave of support washed over them, cleansing away the darkness of the past and leaving only light of a new beginning.

But this was not the end of their story. It was just the beginning. A new world was being born—one forged by courage, resilience, and an unshakable belief in the strength of the human spirit. The Cascadians stood tall and united on this momentous day, knowing nothing could break their bond. They had weathered the storm together, and now they would rebuild together. Their determination and unwavering spirit would pave the way for all of Cascadia.